Beyond Billicombe

Sherry Chiger

To Andy, Chloe, and Augie

Special thanks to the Fred Munnelly Writer's Retreat.

PROLOGUE

"Jax! Hey, it's me."

"Hey, Zee. What's up?"

"Nothing much. I'm stuck in traffic, and since I haven't heard from you in a while, I figured I'd call."

"It must be, what, five in the morning there?"

"Six. All this time, and you still can't get the time zone thing right."

"You know maths wasn't my strong suit."

"True."

"So where're you going at six in the morning, then?"

"Early call. We're shooting on the beach this morning, and the permit's only good till eleven or something."

"They making you wear a bikini?"

"Yeah. I've been living on apples and celery for a week. I'm telling you, once this scene is wrapped I'm heading to the craft table and gorging myself on M&Ms. But what have you been up to?"

"Oh... nothing much. Was doing a bit of painting and that, but that's dried up, so I'm looking for work."

"Any luck?"

"If there was, I wouldn't still be looking, would I?"

"True. Sorry. That was stupid."

"No. I'm sorry I snapped."

"So, I was thinking: How about if I come to visit?"

"Visit here?"

"I could come down to Billicombe, or you could meet me in London, or we could go someplace different altogether. Want to go to Paris?"

"Paris?"

"Just a suggestion. I don't care where, really. It's just I haven't seen you in almost a year and I really miss you."

"I miss you too."

"You could at least try to sound like you mean it."

"I do."

"I know. So what do you say?"

"Well, I can't really afford to go anywhere right now..."

"My treat."

"Don't you think I've taken enough dosh from you?"

"This would be a gift. And it's as much a gift for me as for you. I really want to see you. And I could use a vacation."

"Listen to Miss America. 'Vacation.'"

"Okay, I could use a holiday as well."

"Everything okay?"

"Oh yeah. It's just that I haven't been anywhere non-work-related since I came over to see you last December."

"Yeah, and that was a right little holiday, wasn't it?"

"It was for me. Jax, I miss you. I miss hanging out with you. I miss all the stupid shit we do together. I even miss your stupid dog imitations."

"Hey, they're not stupid. It took years of practice to master that portrayal of Lassie."

"So I can come? Don't make me beg like a pesky little sister: Mum, Jax won't play with me."

"Okay."

"Really?"

"You tell me when and where, and I'll be there."

"I'm thinking the week of Thanksgiving. We have a break from filming then."

"Let me know the date and what airport to meet you, and we'll do it."

"Really? Oh my God, I'm so excited. I cannot wait to see you! If we meet in London we can go to the Tower. Remember when we went when we were little, and you told me that sometimes visitors were followed out of there by the headless ghost of Anne Boleyn, and I kept looking over my shoulder the rest of the day, and Mum thought I had some sort of twitch in my neck?"

"Yeah."

"I can't wait! Oh, yay, the traffic jam is finally breaking up. Christ, it'll just be nice not to have to drive for a week."

"Thanks, Zee."

"For what?"

"You know... everything."

"Hey, you'd do the same for me."

"You'd never get yourself into the shit I have."

"Well, what's done is done. Okay? Listen, I've got to go, we're really moving now. I'll call you once I've got my ticket. I love you, Jax."

"Love you, Zee."

That was the last time she spoke to her brother.

CHAPTER 1

Suzanne saw it as part of her job to know how each emotion translated into the tweaking of each facial muscle and positioning of each facial feature. She knew, for instance, that if she bit on the left side of her lower lip with her two front teeth and opened her eyes wide enough for her lashes to nearly reach her eyebrows that she looked mischievous yet winsome; if she kept her mouth in the same position but lowered her lids so that they felt heavy, she looked mournful.

She might not have felt mischievous yet winsome as she widened her eyes, but once she'd aligned her face properly, more often than not the emotion proceeded to fall into place. And if it didn't—if, say, it was the eighteenth time she'd been asked to look mischievous yet winsome, because during the first take a boom mike had fallen into the shot, and in the fifth take she'd stumbled over a line, and in the eleventh take the other actor in the scene had forgotten one of his lines, and during the seventeenth take the assistant director had sneezed—if she couldn't dredge up the matching emotion, she was a good enough actor to fake it.

So Suzanne knew, as she stood at the top of Barrow Lane, that right now, sucking slightly on her cheeks, she looked jaded with just a spark of vulnerability breaking through. Not that there was anyone to see it.

She'd turned down Barrow from the High Street, which for a Sunday night in April was busier than she'd expected. Billicombe was a resort town, and although its popularity had peaked during Queen Victoria's lifetime, summer remained its stock in trade. In one of his letters, Jax had included two sketches on a sheet of lined paper of the High Street. One, labeled "summer," showed the sidewalks crammed with figures: families pushing strollers about to tip over, bags heaped atop the swathed legs of babies barely visible beneath their swaddling; kids eating towering cones of candy floss and swinging sand buckets; girls in the highest of heels and the shortest of skirts;

and scattered among them all, a complete football team, intent on playing as if the jam-packed scene were an empty pitch. Like most of Jax's sketches, it was dense with ink; you had to really study the picture, square inch by square inch, to take it all in. The sketch below, labeled "not summer," showed the same street, the pavement bare save for a lone tumbleweed, the sort you'd see in a cartoon of a Western ghost town.

But tonight, even at a bit past eleven, the High Street wasn't quiet. This was the first evening since Suzanne had arrived in town three days ago that it hadn't pissed down rain, so maybe that had something to do with it. She'd shared the High Street with clusters of girls her own age clomping two and three abreast from one pub to the next, ankles wobbling above their fuck-me pumps and bare legs mottled purple and red from the damp chill; groups of lads calling out to one another across the road, darting around the rubbish bins and the Victorian-style wrought-iron lamp posts that studded the brick sidewalks; several couples leaning into one another; a handful of older, stooped men zigzagging and careening from side to side like bumper cars; a drunk of indiscriminate age shouting at everyone and no one. She tried to translate the scene into one of Jax's sketches, all black lines against white paper, instead of shadowy tones with the occasional flare of color picked out by a streetlight.

She wasn't ready for such freneticism. Which was why, earlier that evening, she'd stopped in at the supermarket and bought a small bottle of vodka. While she didn't want to get drunk surrounded by strangers, she did want to get drunk. It wasn't something she did very often. The last time had been months ago, at her agency's Christmas party, and even then she hadn't been so out of it that she'd done anything stupid, like get sick on the way to the ladies' room like one of the junior agents, or repeat the same stories over and over, or shout when she thought she was speaking in a normal voice. She hadn't really been drunk, now that she thought about it; tipsy, just relaxed enough that she was almost able to enjoy herself.

She held the vodka in a brown paper bag in her left hand and a cigarette in her right. The High Street babbled just a few yards behind her, and the Bristol Channel undulated far down below, past the bottom of the lane, across the two-way street they called the Promenade, and beyond the scrap of rocky beach. The sea rolled toward the rocks as if by rote, not bothering to muster enough energy to create whitecaps. The water and the sky were nearly the same shade of inky blue; the sky wasn't so much darker as more intense.

And whereas the sea was stippled and rippled with sinuous shadows, the sky was flat in contrast.

She was going to skitter down the lane, cross the Promenade, march down to the beach, sip her vodka, and wait for the sunrise. She'd probably doze a bit, but she had faith enough in her inner clock to wake her in time.

Barrow Lane, like all the other roads leading down to the Promenade from the High Street, was sharply raked, perhaps an even forty-five degrees. Billicombe had been built among hills. *Combe*, Jax had written in one of his dozen or so letters, meant "valley" in Welsh or Old English. When viewed looking up from the Promenade, the High Street did indeed seem high, but streets beyond it rose higher still. So many of the houses and B and B's and inns could boast of having views of the channel not because the seaside was so expansive but because most of the structures were built along the hillsides. Beyond the houses and B and B's and inns were still more hills, undeveloped except for the odd smallholding or horse stables or caravan grounds.

She took a final drag from her cigarette, chucked it onto the pavement, and ran down the lane. The steepness of the lane propelled her faster than the pumping of her leg muscles, so that after a few seconds she felt as if she were no longer controlling her downward projection. When she reached the Promenade she couldn't brake until she was several feet beyond the curb and into the street itself.

She was surprised by the emptiness of the Promenade. To the left a hotel was set back from the pavement, a tour bus parked in the circular driveway in front of the lobby. To the right, on the other side of Barrow Lane, stood a darkened church. A bass line throbbed from perhaps a block away, no doubt from the Bastille, the only pub on the Promenade. The High Street was lousy with pubs, outnumbering even the charity shops, but the Promenade was home only to the Bastille, several hotels catering to pensioners, and the church.

A constant pounding of waves against the rocks accompanied the bass line. Above them swooped the caws of the gulls. The moon was just a crescent; the stars were on standby; long shadows cut the pavement diagonally.

She felt more alone than she did even in her trailer back at the caravan park. She told herself that she liked it.

So when a man called out to her, "Excuse me," she jumped as she whirled around.

He was walking out from the bus shelter in front of the hotel. How had she not noticed the shelter, or him?

"Excuse me," he said. "Do I know you?"

She looked up at him, squinting. "No." He was tall, taller than Jax. She didn't quite reach his chin.

"Oh." He sounded disappointed. "Are you sure?"

"Yes. I'm not from here."

"Oh." He cleared his throat. "It's just that, well, you looked vaguely familiar, and I was hoping you could tell me where I live."

Her heart beat faster. Another drunk, though his speech wasn't slurred. Hugging her bottle to her chest, she said, "Sorry, can't help you."

Instead of turning away he continued to stare down at her. His eyes were in shadow, so that he almost appeared to be wearing a mask over them, like the Lone Ranger. He wasn't swaying, and he didn't smell of booze. Maybe he was a junkie instead, coming down from his nod. In which case maybe he *could* help her.

"How can you not know where you live?" she asked.

Although she couldn't make out his eyes, she could see his lips clearly. He exhaled, puffing them out. "I'm not drunk," he said.

"I didn't think you were. I figured you for a smackhead instead." Good Lord, what kind of dialogue was this? She almost laughed.

He sighed. "I was in a car accident awhile back, and it left me with some memory problems."

Right. "Don't you have any ID on you with your address?"

"Not my current address."

She wished he'd bend forward so that she could get a better look at the upper part of his face. "Sorry."

Nodding, he turned and headed back to the bus shelter. "Ta."

Suzanne watched as he pulled out some tobacco and papers from the back pocket of his jeans. Bracing himself against the Plexiglas, he rolled himself a smoke, then felt the pockets of his oversize jacket for a lighter.

She fished her own lighter out from the pocket of her gilet and walked over to hand it to him. Enough yellowing light spilled out from the lobby of the hotel that she could see all of his face now. Other than his nose, the bottom half of which jutted off to the slightly right, most likely from a break that hadn't been set properly, his features were unremarkable. And his eyes looked clear. Not glassy. Focused. Maybe he wasn't high after all.

He lit up and handed her back the lighter: "Cheers." She lit a cigarette of her own, still casing his face. He knew what she was doing; she could tell by how he was struggling to wipe his expression blank.

If his memory was shot like he'd said, he wouldn't be of much use. But still... "I was going to sleep down on the beach tonight. I've got some vodka to keep me warm. You're welcome to join me."

Now he was examining her. She looked down and left, lifting the corners of her mouth upward slightly. Her inscrutable expression.

"All right," he said after a brief pause. He leaned away from the side of the shelter and shoved his hands into his jacket pockets, waiting for her to lead the way.

She zipped up her gilet as they crossed the Promenade. Having lived in the L.A. area all these years, Suzanne had expected to be perpetually freezing back here in England. Everyone insisted your blood thinned. Jax had said he hadn't properly warmed up from the time he landed at Heathrow, the September before last, until the following May. Suzanne didn't mind the cold, though. Besides, it wasn't as cold as she remembered London being when she was a kid, or when she'd visited Jax two Decembers ago. The dampness, that was tougher to adjust to. It seeped into your marrow and refused to budge. Even when she was sweating under the blankets in the trailer at night, she still shivered from the damp.

The man followed her toward the paved area the locals called the Pavilion. A metal railing cordoned off where the Pavilion stopped eight or so feet above the rocky beach, directing you to the steep cement stairs that led down to the beach itself. He continued to follow her down the steps and sat beside her on the second-to-last stair.

She unscrewed the bottle as quickly as she could, her fingers already stiff from the raw sea mist. The slapping of the waves against the pointed rocks that stood sentry maybe ten yards beyond would have been loud enough to drown out the shrieks of the gulls, had the gulls not been goaded by the slaps to shriek louder still.

She took several long gulps, straining not to grimace as the vodka burned her throat. She handed him the bottle, but didn't let go when he reached for it. "I don't suppose you have some sort of cup or something with you," she said.

He lifted his brows. "I'm not in the habit of carrying one, no."

"It's just that..." She paused. "It's just that I don't know where your mouth's been."

He laughed. "I don't know where your mouth's been either," he said.

She'd laugh along, she decided. "Fair enough." She released the bottle. He took several healthy swigs, then passed it back. She wiped the rim with her sleeve, then caught herself doing so and laughed again, this time for real. As if a quick wipe would prevent anything. "Cheers."

She was leaning against him, her shoulder jutting into the upper portion of his right arm. A black spaniel loped down the steps to the beach, panting and waving his tail as if it were a football-club banner. An elderly man followed, groping the iron railing as he made his way down, glaring with flared nostrils at Richard and the girl for blocking part of the stair.

Richard shifted forward, to free his arm from her weight. As soon as he did so, he shivered. The warmth of her body had been shielding him from the cold, which now launched a full assault on his limbs.

The girl jolted upright, blinking hard as she gazed out to the sea. "Oh, I missed the sunrise," she said, as disappointed as a child who'd tried but failed to stay awake long enough to see Father Christmas slip the gifts under the tree. He tried to stare at her without her noticing. She looked younger than her voice had led him to expect, still a teenager. The voice was odd, an alto limned with fine gravel, and the accent was odd too: like an American trying to sound English, or a Brit trying to sound American, harsh r's fighting it out with rounded vowels.

"It wasn't much to miss. There was a lot of fog. And mist."

"Oh." She still sounded disappointed. "Why didn't you wake me?"

"I didn't realize I was supposed to," he said sharply. He added in a conciliatory tone, "If it had been anything to see, I would have."

"Oh."

She was avoiding looking at him. He recognized the rigid posture, the strained profile, from Pam those first weeks after he'd been discharged from hospital. Those last weeks before she'd moved out. He stood up, shaking his legs awake.

She squinted up at him. "Where are you going?"

"Home. I remember where it is now." That's what had woken him, as the night was evaporating from the sky. An image of his flat and the knowledge that it was 67 Fortescue, ground floor. "I was just waiting for you to wake up."

She stopped in the middle of pulling a cigarette out of her pack. "You didn't have to."

"I wasn't going to leave you here on your own," he said.

She smiled, almost shyly, revealing just a hint of her top front teeth. "That's really sweet."

Now he turned away.

"So, is your flat near here? I'm only asking because I'm wondering if I could use your toilet." She stood up as another dog, a Jack Russell in a hand-knitted red-and-navy sweater, skipped down the steps, then stood at the bottom and turned around, entire rump waggling, to wait for the chunky, freckled woman who followed.

"It's maybe three minutes from here."

"Cool," she said, as if by telling her how near it was he was also granting her permission to come along.

They skirted around more dogs and their owners as they headed up the Promenade. "I've never seen so many Jack Russells before," the girl said, smiling down at one who had stopped to sniff her shoes before being yanked by his impatient owner at the other end of the lead.

"They were originally bred here," Richard said.

"In Billicombe?" She looked around, at the precisely landscaped garden to the right, just beyond the waist-high stone wall, and at the Bastille to the left, across the street, where a man with gray-and-brown snakes of hair crouched, scouring the ground for salvageable cigarette ends.

"No, but in Devon." They passed the Bastille, and he nodded to indicate that they should cross the road.

Beside the Bastille was a mini terrace of three two-story homes. Then there was Fortescue Road. They crossed it and began the uphill march.

When Richard had first moved here, with Pam, he could barely make the hike from the Promenade up to the High Street without stopping for breath, and once he reached the top he'd be gasping and his shins burning. He'd just built up his lung capacity and muscle tone so that he could take the walk at a normal pace, while carrying on a conversation to boot, when he'd had the accident. Now he couldn't make it from bottom to top without stopping, though that was due at least as much to the stabbing pains of his back and left thigh as to his difficulty in coaxing enough air into his lungs.

He halted just shy of halfway up the road. Rows of three-story brick buildings, some still single homes but most converted into flats, lined both sides of the street, the front doors set back from the pavements by walkways four strides long. Well, four of his strides. He looked back at the girl. Probably six or maybe even seven of her strides. She was a little thing. The thick frizz of milk-chocolate waves that fell into her eyes and across her cheeks made her look even littler. Scrawny. He wondered if she was a runaway. He wasn't going to ask.

He led her up the walkway to number 67, unlocked the front door, then headed down the narrow, unlit hall past one door, stopping at the next. The door to his flat stuck sometimes; he had to lean into it with his shoulder as he twisted the key to open it. He stepped aside to let the girl in first.

"Jesus," she said.

He'd forgotten how messy the flat was. Well, not forgotten so much as been unaware. Seeing it now, though, over the girl's shoulder, as she must see it... He sidled past her and scooped up armfuls of papers and books and Styrofoam takeaway containers from the floor, dumping them onto the couch. The room stank of stale cigarettes and flat beer and sour milk.

The girl—had she told him her name? what was it?—turned her head slowly from one side to the other, taking it all in. She wrinkled her nose as if to block out the smell. "Jesus. How do you live like this?"

She must be American, to be so rude, especially as he hadn't invited her; she'd invited herself. "The loo's back there." He pointed to a narrow hallway at the end of the lounge. She picked her way with exaggerated care, mincing around a mud-covered trainer, a yellow-gray sock, an empty box of cigarette filters.

As soon as she was gone he frantically sifted through the bundles he'd heaped upon the sofa, culling out the obvious rubbish to cart into the kitchen and chuck. He was still doing that when she returned.

"How does this sound?" she said as she made her way toward him. "I help you clean this place up. Then you come back with me to mine, I take a shower, and you take me to lunch."

He'd been planning to fall into bed as soon as she left. His temples were beginning to thump, from the vodka no doubt.

"Why?"

She smiled, close-lipped this time. She might have been pretty, though it was difficult to tell, what with her hair hiding her eyes. "You were nice enough to wait for me to wake up, so I owe you one. And you can't live like this."

He started to say something about needing a kip, but from the way she stood, with her legs apart and her hands on her hips, and from the set of her pointy jaw, he knew it was futile. "Can I at least roll myself a fag first?"

Cleaning the lounge had turned up nothing of the slightest use to Suzanne. She hadn't really expected it to. Contrary to what her mother liked to say, she was well aware of the difference between real life and Los Angeles, even if the writers of most of the scripts she read weren't. So she hadn't expected to find, oh, Jax's passport peeping out between the pages of a discarded magazine or his favorite T-shirt, the one with Tintin holding Milou, wrapped around a week-old sandwich.

She did find out a lot about this Richard character, though. His name, for starters—though his first name she learned by asking him, not by riffling through his detritus. "If I'm going to be risking my health handling your trash," she said, "the least you can do is tell me your name."

"So we never introduced ourselves?" He looked up from the green rubbish bag he was sifting papers into. "Good. I thought I'd just forgotten your name. I'm Richard. And you?"

She'd hesitated, but only for a second. "Suzanne." If he asked for a surname, then she'd make one up.

So she knew his name was Richard Sommers (the surname she saw on several envelopes), that he was into computers and maybe even worked as a programmer or something similar, judging by the types of magazine lying about. He was heterosexual (a back issue of *FHM* with the photos of Jennifer Ellison more crumpled than the rest of the pages). He smoked a lot. His drink of choice was Stella, though he wasn't all that fussy. He listened to James and read science-fiction novels. At one point he'd been on crutches (a pair had been buried under an ironing board that itself had been hidden beneath a pair of retro floral curtains). He lived alone. And he was a complete and utter slob.

Suzanne had always liked cleaning. She appreciated the instant gratification. Back home she had a cleaner come every Thursday, but every Wednesday night she found herself dusting and vacuuming and emptying the fridge of yogurts that were past their due date and produce that was going soft. She always figured, if worst came to worst, she could support herself as a Merry Maid. "You wouldn't last two minutes," her mother snapped back once, during an argument in which Suzanne stated as much. "You think you'd be coming into clean, tidy homes like ours? You have no idea how most people live."

After clearing Richard's living room, and vacuuming the carpet and upholstery (which necessitated replacing the vacuum bags twice), and picking caked-on Lord-knows-what from the coffee table, and dismantling the light bulbs from his floor lamp so that she could wipe away the dead flies that had sacrificed themselves around them, she was almost ready to concede that perhaps her mother had a point.

But now the room was presentable. You could put your hand on top of the small round table that stood between the couch and the armchair without leaving a palm print amid the dust. You could actually sit on the couch. The tang of vinegar had replaced the sludge of smoke. She stood in the center of the room—you could now stand in the center of the room—and turned a full 360 degrees, surveying their work.

"That'll do for today," she said, arms folded across her chest.

"You don't want to start on the bedroom, then?" Richard watched her from the sofa.

She hesitated. "I'm joking," he added quickly. She smiled in relief and brushed her palms against one another.

"Right," she said. "Why don't I wait here while you take a shower, and then we'll go to my place."

Richard rubbed the back of his head. His hair was several shades lighter than hers was now, a patchwork of tufts. "You're a bossy little thing, aren't you?"

"I prefer to think of myself as decisive."

He laughed, a short bark. "And I prefer to think of myself as rich, but that doesn't make it so." Nonetheless he unfolded himself from the sofa and headed to the doorway leading off the lounge. His spine curved slightly toward the right, and he was favoring his left leg. "Are you all right?" she asked.

He turned around, his brows drawn together in confusion. "What do you mean?"

She shook her head. "Nothing."

"Can you call us a cab?" Suzanne asked when Richard reemerged, a rumpled navy polo shirt hanging loose about his torso, his wet hair finger-combed, a few pieces standing upward at the crown.

"Where are we going?" He paused, looking around for his mobile.

Suzanne lifted it from the mantel and handed it to him.

"Caldicott Cross Caravan Park." She liked saying the name, all those hard *c*'s.

He gazed at the phone. She fished a business card from A-One Taxi out of her back pocket and gave it to him. He recited the destination into the phone but then moved it away from his mouth. "Shit. I don't suppose you remember my address, do you?" She told him, and he repeated it into the phone, shaking his head and grimacing.

"What kind of brain injury do you have?" she asked once he'd ended his call.

"Are you American?"

"Half. But I've lived there since I was ten. Why?"

"Because only an American would ask something like that to someone she barely knows." He shook his head again, this time in the manner of a pensioner deploring the lack of manners among kids today.

She decided to deploy a cheeky grin. "I sorted through half your worldly goods, so I think I know you well enough by now."

He was studying her, but she couldn't make out his expression. "How old are you?" he asked.

"Twenty-one."

"Really?" He clearly didn't believe her.

"I look—" she'd almost said "play"—"younger, what with being short and all." He crossed his arms, still unconvinced. "I can show you ID."

He laughed, the same abrupt bark as earlier. "I'll let you slide."

"So sometimes your memory is perfectly fine," the girl—Suzanne, that was her name—was saying, "and sometimes it's your short-term memory that goes, and sometimes you have gaps in your long-term memory. Is that it?"

"Yes, doctor." That was as good a summary as any, so far as it went. But the injury went so much further. It was really a matter of losing time, which wasn't the same as losing track of time.

"I was so engrossed in what I was doing, I lost track of the time": Richard was sure he'd said that on more than one occasion. But this, losing time altogether, was something else.

He could be sat in his armchair—an armchair he didn't recall ever buying—remote for the telly at hand, about to roll a fag, the sickly scraps of sun through the kitchen window barely making their way into the lounge, the

crowing of the seagulls louder than his own thoughts. And then, he was still in the armchair, but the only light was from the telly, and the ashtray on the table beside him was overflowing, and he was out of tobacco. He didn't recognize any of the actors waving their hands and shouting on the screen. There was a cold cup of tea beside the ashtray, but he didn't remember making it. He didn't remember anything that had happened since he was about to roll a fag back when it was still daylight and he had a quarter-full pouch of tobacco. He was still sat in the chair and the seagulls were still cawing outside, but everything else had changed, and he couldn't remember any of it changing.

That, my friend, was losing time.

Sometimes he didn't lose time so much as misplace it. Like the morning when he was brushing his teeth with a new brand of toothpaste. He didn't like the taste of it, so minty the buds of his tongue stood up in alarm. He thought, I'd better write down what brand this is so I don't buy it again. And then he was in the Asda with Pam, which meant he was back in London, because there was no Asda here in Billicombe. He was carrying the shopping basket, and Pam was debating whether to get a tube of tomato paste or a jar. She finally chose the jar, and she dropped it in the basket with such force that the basket's plastic-padded handle almost slipped from his grip. "What are you so angry about?" Richard asked. And then he was answering the doorbell, trembling and panting as if he had just run from the Asda to his flat. An impossible run, of course, but then how had he got here, to this flat that wasn't his London flat, to let in some woman with severely straight gray-and-white hair who wasn't Pam. He almost said to the woman at the door, "Who are you? Where's Pam?" But he should know who she was, he was certain of that much. He should know who she was, because he hadn't just been in London. He'd instead been caught between time frames, past and present, and he had learned not to say anything in the moments it took for him to catch up from wherever time had taken him and where it dropped him off.

The occasions when Richard didn't know what time of day it was, or what day it was, or how he came to be standing in front of the cooker holding a pot that had oval markings burnt onto the bottom, like chalk outlines around a corpse, as egg dripped from the ceiling, on those occasions he could recall the past just fine. That same woman with the straight lank hair—his carer from the NHS; was Gillian her name?—she came on another such occasion, when he was opening the kitchen window full tilt to release the smoke from the cheese toastie he'd forgotten in the oven. He let her in, and she immediately sussed what had happened, and proceeded to fire questions at him: Do you recall your name? Where you live?

He fired the answers right back at her. "And yes, I know how I got here too. I was in a bloody car accident, twenty-first of October, broke my left femur and collarbone, had emergency surgery on my spine, and suffered a head injury. Yes, I know all that, but what I fucking don't know is how long I had the goddam oven on!" He apologized almost immediately for shouting, but Gillian—or was it Joanna?—just waved it off. "It's all right," she said, in the tone of voice a nursery teacher might adopt when addressing a toddler in a tantrum. "I understand how frustrating all of this can be."

Richard didn't know what was more frustrating: losing time but at least knowing who he was and what his backstory was, or being in the moment but having lost everything up until then. He'd come out of the Somerfield's on the High Street recently, having stocked up on noodles, tea bags, whatever lager was on sale, and tobacco. As he tossed his shopping list in the metal rubbish bin outside the store, a barrel-chested bloke lumbering toward him called out, "Richard, me old son!" Richard looked around to see who the man was addressing, but the only others nearby were two elderly women walking one wheat-colored curly-haired dog between them.

"Richard, mate!" The bloke brushed his knuckles against Richard's arm. "Good to see you out and about! How you feeling, then?" So he, himself, must be Richard. It wasn't just that he had forgotten his name; he'd also forgotten that he had a name, that it wasn't enough to just be; he had to be something that could be defined and outlined and labeled for identification and use by others.

And with a sucker punch he realized that he didn't know his surname, or where he lived, or where he was meant to be taking the carrier bag that rested on the pavement between his legs. That moment, even at that moment, was crystalline: the dull ache of his left thigh, the cooing of a nearby wood pigeon, a faint whiff of dog shit, the stray silver sparks amid the barrel-chested bloke's otherwise rusty close-cropped beard, the two deep horizontal lines forming between the bloke's brows, the panicky seizing of his own chest that made each breath a struggle as he drowned in how lost he was. He could have told the bloke exactly what he had in the carrier bag and exactly how much he'd paid for it; he could have described the contents of the trash bag that three gulls had been ripping open just down the street as he'd walked to the Somerfield's, but he couldn't have told the bloke, or himself, his own bloody name.

Now, as they sat at a table in the snack bar of the caravan park on the outskirts of Billicombe, Richard was telling Suzanne all of this. He didn't know why. Maybe it was because he knew she was just passing through. She'd said she was renting a chalet, though she'd called it a trailer, at the caravan park for a few weeks. She was taking a break, "having a bit of a vacation," as she put it.

"A vacation from what?" he'd asked, but she hadn't answered. In fact she'd asked him more questions instead.

And he'd answered them all. Maybe he missed having someone to talk to. Or maybe it was because she looked so damn familiar. When she'd come out into the main room of her chalet after showering and getting dressed, she was towel-drying her hair, and for the first time he could clearly see her eyes. They were so large they looked almost perfectly round, the sort of eyes a kid draws on a fairy princess who is supposed to be very beautiful. Her lashes were still clumped together and dark with water, and her brows, much paler than her hair, were two perfect but not overly precise arcs. He was sure he'd seen those eyes before, but of course he couldn't summon up where or when. Noticing him staring at her, she'd bent forward and shook her head, like a dog caught in a surprise downpour. When she straightened up her hair hung in irregular spirals over her face.

"Isn't it tough living on your own when you keep losing track of things and forgetting where you live?" she was saying now. Their table was beside a window that looked out onto the neighboring horse farm. A lone horse meandered through the field, bending its head to sample bits of grass before moving on to another spot, and another.

He decided to turn the tables. "Where in America do you live?"

She looked down at the uneaten crusts of her cheese toastie. "Southern California."

"Near Los Angeles?"

"Not far."

"And what brought you way out here? We don't get many Americans visiting."

"Would you remember if you did?" She peered up at him through her fringe, grinning.

He laughed but didn't change the subject. "So what brings you here?"

She lit a cigarette, eyes on her plate. "Like I said, I grew up in London till I was ten, and I remember coming here once when I was a kid. We had a great time, my brother and me. We rented bikes, and because he was five years older, our parents let us go off exploring on our own. We really just rode up and down the Promenade and hung out at the arcades and ate lots of ice cream, but it was fun." She was gazing beyond him now, her face rounder somehow, softer. "It seemed like it rained every night, and every morning when we woke up the ground would still be wet. Outside the guesthouse we stayed in, there was this thicket, I guess, of bushes. We'd head out there while our parents were still asleep, and we'd play a game to see how many snails each of us could spot hidden on the leaves. He always won. And he'd point out these gorgeous spiderwebs, and how sparkly they looked with the leftover rain dripping from them."

Then she paused, jawline tightening, and her smile became fixed. She looked at him suddenly.

"I'm also here because I'm looking for someone." She took a long drag before turning her head away to exhale. "An old friend of mine. His name's Jack. Jackson. I used to call him Jax. Before we lost touch, maybe six or seven months ago, he was living here. I had some downtime, so I figured I'd try to find him." She turned to him again, her chin tilted upward, as if defying him to tell her that she was on a wild goose chase or to say something else, though he didn't know what, that she didn't want to hear.

"The name doesn't ring any bells," he said.

"Yeah, well, with your memory and all." She reached over for the glass ashtray in front of the napkin dispenser and pulled it beside her plate.

"How old is he?"

"Twenty-six." She ran her fingertip along the rim of her dish. "I figured I'd try some of the pubs, see if I spot him, maybe ask around."

"Do you have a picture?"

She shook her head. "Not a good one." She drained her Diet Coke, then squeezed the can with her right hand. "He's blond, thin, not quite as tall as you, kind of pointy features."

Richard tried to summon up some faces. Any faces. Nothing. Forget trying to remember someone fitting that description, he'd have been happy to come up with anyone. Pam. His parents. Nothing. The only image he could see was what was in front of him: this girl Suzanne, her hair still damp near the roots, her sharp chin and her narrow rosebud mouth, her plate empty save for some bread crusts; the ashtray with two cigarette stubs in it; his paper napkin crumpled atop his plate. He could imagine nothing else.

He was breathing faster now, almost panting from the effort of trying to remember. Calm down; he had to calm down, slow his breathing. At least he was in the moment. His name was Richard Sommers. He lived in Billicombe. Today was Saturday—or was it Sunday? Shit. "What's today?"

"Monday. April eighth. Why?" She leaned closer, elbows on the table. "Are you okay?"

He gripped the end of the table and nodded.

"Do you want to lie down?" Her voice was both softer and more gravelly than it had been just seconds earlier. He'd heard that voice before too. Where and when were just out of reach, along with Pam's face, Pam's voice, anything that had been his to remember from before now.

He shook his head. He needed a few minutes, that all. He counted slowly, to steady his breathing. At least no one else was in the snack bar except for the heavy-set, greasy-skinned woman behind the counter at the far end of the room.

Fourteen, fifteen. There it was. Pam's face, with its faint freckles across her nose that she always covered up with powder. The slight gap between her two front teeth. The small dot of a beauty mark on the underside of her chin on the left.

He was breathing easier now. A trickle of oily sweat skidded down the center of his back.

"Sorry about this," he mumbled. His hands felt steadier. He eased them away from the table. His fingers left ghost streaks of heat that quickly faded.

"Why don't you come back to my trailer and rest a bit before heading home?" Suzanne was saying, as if from far away.

He didn't want to. He wanted to return to the cocoon of his flat. But he knew he should go her with.

"I'll be fine in a few minutes," Richard said, but Suzanne ignored him. She made him take off his trainers and stretch out across the bed. She placed a glass of cold water on the tiny tabletop attached to the headboard. She opened the window just an inch or so, enough to let in the grass- and manure-laden breeze and the chanting of the sheep a few fields away, and closed the curtains. She stopped herself from smoothing down his hair. "I'll be right outside," she said.

She sat on the concrete patio in front of the doorway, on one of the two white plastic chairs that came with the trailer. She could hear cows now too, engaging in a call-and-response with the sheep. The sky was a faint gray, streaked with clouds that looked like used, stretched-out cotton balls.

Sitting on guard while pretending not to be, ears straining for the odd gasp or grunt, made her feel less alone, less of a visitor. When Jax had left the last time, to come to England, for nights afterward she'd had the worst time settling down to sleep. She kept getting out of bed to wander from room to room, listening, even though there was nothing to hear but her own breath and soft footsteps against the floor. After years of standing outside Jax's room, checking that he was still breathing, or peeking into the entertainment room, to be sure he hadn't nodded off with a cigarette in hand, she couldn't shake the habit. It was as if, even though she was performing a monologue, she was still waiting for a cue from a phantom actor.

She hadn't planned to lie to Richard about Jax being an old friend rather than her brother. But it just seemed easier, somehow. Easier to go about the town incognito—not that Jax would ever have identified himself as the brother of the girl who'd played Robin on *Lakeview Drive*. Easier to pretend that it was a one-time friend, not her brother, who hadn't made contact for six months.

The first time she'd seen Jax off his head, or at least the first time she was aware of it, she was eleven, which meant he was sixteen. It was just the two of them in the house they were renting up in the hills. She didn't remember where their mum was—probably out hunting for the house they were ultimately to buy. Suzanne had been in her room, supposedly memorizing her scenes for the coming week, but really drawing dresses for her paper doll. She'd made the doll, Emily, herself, out of corrugated board, and she would lay it down on a sheet of paper and sketch an outline around it for each dress. She was filming a movie for a kids' cable channel in which she played the daughter of the woman from whom D'Artagnan, of *The Three Musketeers*, rented a room, and because her character was always following D'Artagnan about she became entangled in one of his adventures. Suzanne's mum said that if the film proved popular, the channel would turn it into a series; she was very excited about that, her mum. Suzanne didn't much care, but she loved designing dresses for Emily in the style of the women's costumes from the film.

She was just cutting out a dress when she heard Jax call. "Zee?" His voice sounded muffled, but there was a thread of electric-blue panic running through it. She clambered to her feet and raced down the hall to his room.

He lay sideways across his bed, his head hanging off the edge. His hair straggled over a puddle of sick on the wood floor. "Zee."

"What happened? Should I call an ambulance?"

"No." He struggled to lift his head onto the bed and to roll onto his side facing her. He curled his knees up to his chest. "I just need you to stay here with me." His eyes closed. "For a bit. If I fall asleep for too long, I need you to wake me up." His words blurred into one another.

She took one of his hands. It was sticky, as if he'd been clutching a half-eaten toffee. She recognized the smell—some sort of alcohol, not beer, something sweeter and thicker. "Are you drunk?"

"Mmm." His lashes flickered as he forced his lids open. His eyes looked runny. "Sort of."

"I won't tell Mum."

He rewarded her with a slow smile as his lids lowered again.

She held his hand and watched him breathe. She counted to fifty, and when he didn't open his eyes during that time, she pulled up one of his eyelids with her forefinger. He muttered something. "You said to make sure you didn't fall asleep," she said.

He squeezed his eyes tight, then opened them. They wandered about before settling on her face. "What were you doing?" His voice was still sludgy.

"When?"

"Before you came in."

"Playing in my room."

She counted to twenty-three before he responded. "How about if we go into your room, and I lay down on the floor while you play? I'll get some kip, and you just make sure I don't get sick in my sleep, yeah?"

She nodded.

Another long pause. "I'm going to need some help getting up, yeah?"

She somehow managed to pull him upright and swing his feet onto the floor. Then she stood up and tugged him toward her. He fell onto her, his neck curving over the top of her head as if it were meant to fit there, but with her help he managed to prop himself upright. He leaned against her, his arm dangling over her shoulders, as she steered him down the hall into her room. He buckled onto her fluffy pink rug like a marionette whose puppeteer had suddenly run off, then curled himself up into a fetal position again. She could see only one of his eyes; the other was smashed against the rug. Self-conscious now that he was watching her, she gathered up Emily and the scissors and the pieces of paper and returned them to the shoebox she kept them in, slid the box under her bed, and retrieved her script from the top of her white-painted desk. Sitting cross-legged on the rug beside Jax, she pretended to run her lines.

"I'm really sorry about this," Jax murmured at one point. She looked over at him. A fat tear was lodged on the side of his nose, too weary to continue rolling downward. With her thumb she flattened it and spread it under his eye. Then she stroked his wispy hair off his damp, pimply forehead.

"I won't do this to you again," Jax said.

But of course he did.

CHAPTER 2

Suzanne was a list maker. Every night before bed she wrote down the tasks she needed to complete the next day, numbering them. Her list for the day before she'd flown out from LAX had included: 1) buy haircolor and dye hair; 2) download and print out maps of Billicombe; 3) find photos of Jax to pack.

Their mum had taken down all her framed photos of Jax some years back, sometime between his first two stints in rehab, when she'd caught him lifting her bank card from her purse and he'd stormed out, returning in a police cruiser with a broken wrist six days later. She'd removed the baby photos from the shelf above the living-room fireplace and the photos of past Christmases from the stairway wall. When Suzanne was preparing to move into her own place she had asked her mother of their whereabouts, as she wanted to bring a few of them with her, but her mother had pressed her lips into a thin horizontal line and shook her head.

Suzanne had a scrapbook, but the most recent photo of Jax was from four years ago, and she was in the picture as well. It was taken on the red carpet of some MTV or VH1 awards show, when *Lakeview Drive* was really catching on, and she was nominated for Best Small-Screen Kiss. The producers of *Lakeview* had wanted her to attend with Davis Jeffrey, who was her co-nominee. By that point she and Davis didn't want to spend any more time together than they had to, so they'd joined forces long enough to put the kibosh on that stunt. And Jax had just returned home a few weeks earlier from his second stint in rehab, and they hadn't been able to spend much time together. She was filming, and he was going to twelve-step meetings in the evenings.

She'd bought him a gray suit with just the slightest silvery sheen, which he wore over a black T-shirt. The jacket was a little large in the shoulders and hung loose, but he looked great, as if he were the one who belonged on the red carpet and she was the guest. Her own dress was nice enough, a black-and-white striped bodice with a black pouf skirt, but her red lipstick overpowered her. The other girls from *Lakeview Drive* had gone all out with bright pinks and neon teals, and Jeannette, who played the resident bitch, wore a dress cut so low in the back you could almost see her butt cleavage. They were all taller than Suzanne, too, and wearing four- and five-inch heels, whereas she'd stuck with lower shoes because she was afraid of tripping, so she looked dumpy and squat in the group photos. But she was so thrilled to have Jax home, and sober, that her concerns about her appearance just buzzed about a bit like a pesky fly that, after realizing there was nothing to feed on, skittered away.

In the red-carpet photo Jax was tanned, and his hair had been trimmed, so that the ends weren't raggedy as they tickled upon his shoulders. And he was smiling, showing his teeth. All of which meant it probably wasn't a good likeness of him anymore, so she hadn't bothered to bring it with her.

Because she'd spent the previous night on what passed for the beach in Billicombe, Suzanne hadn't written a to-do list for today. But she knew what her primary task was: to work her way down the pubs of the High Street, not just observing as she had last evening, but asking around.

Yesterday she'd walked into town—it was only about two miles, all downhill, and after all those years in SoCal, being able to walk from one place to the next was a novelty. But this afternoon when Richard woke from his nap he was bent even farther to the right than he had been in the morning, after they'd finished cleaning, and he was moving stiffly, so she'd announced that she would be taking the bus back into town with him. There was a bus shelter directly across the road from the entrance to the caravan park.

"What else happened to you in that accident?" she asked as he rolled himself a smoke, standing at the far end of the bus shelter from her. "I mean, did you break your leg too, or your spine?"

"Left femur and collarbone, damage to the discs and nerves in the lower back," he muttered. "And you don't have to ride into town with me. I'm perfectly capable of getting home by myself."

Only because she'd thought to write down his address for him to keep in his wallet, but she refrained from reminding him of that fact. "I told you, I'm going to a few pubs anyway. You're welcome to come," she added, knowing he wouldn't.

Although they had to wait nearly a half-hour for the bus, the ride itself took only a few minutes. Richard occupied himself rolling another cigarette. Suzanne stared out the window. Midway down the hill, the road swung sharply to the left, then back toward the right again, at which point you had a perfect view of the steppes of houses leading downward to the Promenade, and the Bristol Channel itself just beyond. As the water came into view, enough sun broke through the clouds to scatter a dusting of glitter onto the lapping waves. The creams and beiges and faded yellows of the stucco homes sparkled white, and the brick terraces winked red and tan. And rising up off the horizon, barely visible between the sea and the sky, was a long thin hump of greenish brown—Wales, on the other side of the channel.

From this narrow, winding road within a faded, near-forgotten town she could see into another country. And that seemed to be some sort of sign that she'd turn up something before the night was over.

She decided to start at the bottom of the High Street and work her way upward. She didn't even bother buying a drink in the first pub, the Prince. Country music was playing, and two older couples were having a meal in a corner.

Beside the Prince was a tea shop, closed now that evening was approaching, followed by another pub, the Dragon. A sign on the front declared it to be the oldest building in Billicombe. The ceilings were so low that most of the half-dozen or so men spread across the front of the bar were hunched over to keep from bumping against the wooden rafters. No one appeared to be under the age of forty. She didn't bother stopping there either.

She climbed uphill—past several surprisingly sophisticated little restaurants that were closed for the day, the season, or in at least one case, forever (a "to let" sign in the window blocked most of the view of a dozen immaculately set tables, stiff triangles of pale turquoise napkins erect in empty wineglasses). The pub she was approaching, Smuggler's Cove, already looked promising. A ruddy bald man stood a few paces from the front door, feet planted nearly a yard apart, listing back and forth. Each time he rocked back his eyes closed, like a baby doll's. He didn't shift to one side or the other as Suzanne drew near but remained soldered in the center of the sidewalk. The alcohol fumes rising from him made her eyes tear.

Inside the pub was choked with smoke. A quick scan showed that she was the only female—and judging by the raised eyebrows of the bulldog-like man behind the bar, the first female to have crossed the threshold in some time. "You sure you're in the right place?" He was missing a front tooth, causing him to lisp.

She peered around again. At least a dozen, maybe almost two dozen, men were scattered throughout the room, but nearly all of them were on their own. Some sat at solitary round tables, a few leaned against the wall beside the cigarette machine, several more stared into a glass while slouched on a stool at the bar. A few were weathered, their tattoos of anchors and arrows faded to weary greens and blues. One or two could have been bikers from central casting: shaved heads, elaborate muttonchops and dense beards, wallets attached to their belts with chains. Most of the others just looked like nondescript losers. Wrinkled, torn, stretched-out T-shirts. Jeans with frayed or mud-stained hems. Greasy scalps. Scabby cheeks. Hands trembling as they grasped their glass. Heads nodding as they sat over a can of Coke.

She dug out her original accent, southeast London. "I'm looking for a mate of mine. Jack. Sound familiar?" She was surprised at the tremor in her voice. She pressed her lips together, because she knew that made her look rougher.

The bartender shook his head, folding his beefy arms over his chest.

She'd made it this far, might as well continue. "Blond, skinny. In his mid-twenties?"

The bartender shook his head again, jowls wobbling. "Look, I don't think this is the type of pub a mate of yours would visit."

She pulled out her cigarettes from her gilet pocket and lit up. "A shot of vodka and a pint of Stella. And yeah, I think it is the type of pub he'd be in."

She tossed down the vodka in one gulp, remembering too late that she hadn't eaten since that toastie at lunchtime. The vodka seared a path through her stomach almost instantly. She took her beer and walked toward the cigarette machine, propping herself against its side. A biker-type stood guard by the machine's other side.

She wasn't sure what to do next. She couldn't very well approach the buzz-cut bloke on the nod at the nearest table and say, "Excuse me. I'm looking for someone who was a junkie too. Do you know where I might find him?" Or the big biker: "Hello, I'm trying to find a scrawny guy you may well have beaten the shit out of at one time or another."

No one approached her as she drank her beer. No one even looked at her.

When she finished she lit another cigarette and headed outside.

By the time she reached the fourth pub—or maybe it was the fifth—Suzanne was finding it simple to breeze in, ask for a shot of vodka and a pint, and start milling about. She knew that this was because she was drunk, and she knew she'd have to stop after this pub, or maybe one more.

For one thing, scanning the faces of the other drinkers was becoming more difficult. She had to blink a lot to clear her mind's eye and keep their features from blurring together. For another, she was beginning to lose control of her accent. For *Lakeview Drive*, she'd had to adopt a full-fledged American accent, the flat Midwestern version, the Yank equivalent of Received Pronunciation. That hadn't been a problem; by the time she was cast, she'd been living and working in America for more than five years, and she'd always been good with accents. But it wasn't until she'd landed at Heathrow last week that she'd realized how much of that American accent had become her own. Now she could feel her vowels slipping and skidding this way and that, being pulled and stretched like a piece of taffy.

She sidled past three women a few years older than her, their earlobes stretched downward from the weight of their heavy gold hoops, toward the snooker table. Settling back against the brick wall, she rested her pint on an empty stool and lit a cigarette. She squinted, trying to imagine Jax bent over the table, eying up a shot like that bloke with a dark ponytail was doing now.

If only she could close her eyes for a moment, enjoy her cigarette in dark solitude, then open them to see Jax coming out of the loo, hiking up the waistband of his jeans, sticking out his lower lip to blow his hair out of his eyes. She wouldn't care if he'd just had a fix, or was so drunk he barely recognized her. So long as she could touch him. She wouldn't ask him why he'd stopped the letters and the calls last autumn. She wouldn't ask him anything, if only she could hear him and wrap her arms around his ribcage and feel his chest rise and fall as he inhaled and exhaled.

"You on your own?"

She opened her eyes. The man next to her was about Jax's age, but already balding, although he shaved his scalp to pretend otherwise. The dark stubble on his chin was heavier than that of his head.

She shifted her London accent into place. "I'm looking for someone, actually. Bloke named Jack. Blond, skinny, about your height."

The man shrugged. "That could describe a lot of blokes. Was he supposed to be meeting you here?"

She shook her head, fighting down a surge of bile as she did so. Please, Lord, don't let her get sick now. "No. I haven't seen him in a while. But I know he was living here at least six months ago or so."

"There was this one geezer, blond, used to come in a lot, but I haven't seen him for a while. From Liverpool, I think. Sounded almost Irish, didn't he?"

Jax couldn't fake accents. He'd never even picked up an American one. "No, that wouldn't be him. But thanks." She shifted away.

"My name's Bart, by the way." He slid in front of her, blocking her view of the snooker table.

She nodded. "I'm Anne." It was the first name she could think of that wasn't her own.

He looked down at her half-empty glass. "What can I get you?"

Bart was standing a little too close; she could see a flake of dead skin on his lower lip and smell the musk mixing with his sweat. She flattened herself further against the wall. "I'm good, ta."

"Come on, let me buy you a half, then." He put his hand up on the wall above her.

She slid out from the arch of his arm. "No, that's all right." She walked the long way around the table and headed toward the door, doubling back when she realized she was still holding her pint glass. She drained her beer, deposited the glass on the bar, and stumbled out onto the High Street. That was enough for tonight.

Heavy drumbeats within her skull, bashing out a song that she neither recalled nor wanted to, woke Suzanne the next morning. A thick film coated her teeth. Maybe it was just as well that she had a hangover, seeing as what her noon task was: a visit to a twelve-step meeting.

"You'd be surprised how many people turn up to meetings loaded," Elisabeth once told her. "Sometimes I'll show up late, and the only seat is next to someone who stinks like he took a bath in cheap wine. Sometimes it makes you sick, but other times it makes you want to run out and get wasted yourself."

Elisabeth played the older sister of Suzanne's character on *Lakeview Drive*. Once when they were going over a scene in Elisabeth's dressing room during the first season, Elisabeth had gotten a call on her cell phone that she said she absolutely had to take, and would Suzanne mind leaving. When they shot the scene late that afternoon, Elisabeth wasn't focused. She muffed her pieces of action—the girls were supposed to be setting the table for dinner, and Elisabeth kept fumbling the plates—and missed a cue. "What's wrong?" Suzanne asked between takes, because Elisabeth rarely fluffed a scene. One of the directors had told them that he liked shooting scenes between the two of them best, because they were the only ones who acted like professionals. Unfortunately he'd said this within earshot of four of the other cast members, who for the rest of the week's filming went out of their way to sabotage any scenes Elisabeth or Suzanne was in. "If I'd wanted to be a high school principal, I would have!" the director shouted at one point. "And I'd have the group of you in detention for a month."

Once they finally nailed the scene, Elisabeth asked Suzanne to come back to her dressing room. "Sorry for all of that," she said as soon as she'd closed the door. "It's just... I'm going to tell you this because I know I can trust you to keep it to yourself. Right?" The call had been from the girl for whom Elisabeth was an AA sponsor. The girl had been sober for more than three months, but that morning she'd snuck a bottle of wine from her parents' cellar and downed most of it. "She was hysterical. Partly because she was shit-faced, but mostly because she just hated herself. She was talking about knives." Elisabeth was wiping her eyelids with a makeup-remover pad, but at this point she turned away from the mirror to face Suzanne. "I've been sober for three years, five months, and twenty-three days, but listening to her just brought it all back, you know?" She still had makeup on her left eye, so that her face looked lopsided, with the right eye insignificant, nearly blind-looking in comparison.

Suzanne had thought then of telling Elisabeth about Jax. For a year or so after his first rehab stay he'd gone straight edge, but then he'd started smoking pot with a few friends. From there he began locking himself in his room in the evenings, refusing to let her in even to say goodnight. Sometimes when she said goodnight through the door he would mutter something that made no sense to her at all; other times he wouldn't say anything.

But something stopped her from confiding in Elisabeth. Her mother had told her repeatedly not to discuss Jackson's problems with anyone at work, but it wasn't that.

"Anyway, I'm going to see her tonight, so I've got to run," Elisabeth was saying. "But I wanted you to know." She smiled, a tight, determined smile.

"Seeing as we're sisters and all."

The meeting was at the Trinity Church, the one on the Promenade. It wasn't strictly an AA meeting, or an NA meeting, but something called an All Addicts Meeting. According to what she'd read online before flying over, they met every Tuesday at noon.

Suzanne arrived twenty minutes early. She stood under the bus shelter across the street from the church, the same shelter where Richard had stood Sunday night. The church was a gray-stone, asymmetrical building, with multiple steeples, each a different height and width from the others, each topped with a cross of a different size and style. She supposed that the circular window below the center peak was made of stained glass, but a sheath of grime encased it, so she couldn't be sure.

She lit a cigarette, cupping the flame against the wind, and waited for people to start walking in. Maybe she could just watch to see if Jax turned up. But she wasn't really expecting him to. More than likely she'd have to strike up a conversation with someone in the meeting to see if he or she knew Jax. Though Suzanne wasn't sure how she was going to do that.

Sometimes when Suzanne was in a situation where she didn't know what to say or do, she tried to imagine how Matthew would write the scene. He was the show runner for *Lakeview Drive*; the program had been his baby. He'd written all the scripts for the first season and most of those for the second. By season three he was writing only the occasional episode, and for season four he simply signed off on the storylines. His scripts had been the ones she'd enjoyed most, because the dialogue was the easiest to say. There were no awkward phrasings, no out-of-character scenes that were almost impossible to carry off.

She had a feeling Matthew would never have written a scene like this. He'd have thought it ridiculous. "Melodramatic," he would have called it. "A writer's version of real life based on other writers' versions of real life."

Maybe her mother was right. Maybe she had no conception of real life anymore.

Fourteen people sat in two rows of semicircles on molded-plastic chairs with metal hooks on the sides so that they could, if necessary, be attached to one another. A radiator hissed, occasionally stopping long enough to cough up a metallic rattle. Suzanne hung her gilet over the back of her chair, then pulled her sweater up over her head, draped it over the gilet, and tucked her long-sleeved silk T-shirt back into her jeans.

A trim, sandy-haired man wearing a Tottenham FC jersey sat facing them from atop a wooden desk. A felt banner tacked up on the wall behind him spelled out, in yellow letters on a red background, "'At the present time your plenty will supply what they need, so in turn their plenty will supply what you need'—2 Corinthians 8:14." She wondered if that banner had been made and hung specifically for these meetings.

Jax was not in the meeting. The windows were wide open, to accommodate the smokers and counteract the overzealous radiator, so the seagulls were as much a presence in the room as anyone.

There were only two other women. One was a grandmotherly type, with metallic eyeglasses that swooped ostentatiously on the sides, crepe-soled shoes, and a soft lap. The other wore her skin next to her bones. Her hair was dyed ink black, and on her right forearm she had a tattoo of a knife plunged into a heart, with blood dripping around it. She swigged from a bottle of Orangina between drags from her cigarette.

The oldest man looked to be in his seventies, close-cropped white grizzle ringing his skull. He had a copy of the *Mirror* folded on his lap. The two youngest guys looked to be just out of high school, one with a precise haircut that left nearly an inch of white skin visible between his ears and his hairline, the other with russet-red curls falling to his collar. Suzanne had to force herself not to gaze at his hair. It was so bright, so rich. When she'd been at the drugstore back home picking out a shade of hair dye, she'd been tempted to go for a similar red. But it would have stood out too much, and the reason she was coloring her hair was to avoid attention.

"Good afternoon." Everyone straightened up and turned toward the man on the desk. "My name is Stu, and I'm an alcoholic and crack addict. Welcome to our regular meeting of All Addicts Anonymous."

Around Suzanne people responded with "Good afternoon." The woman with the dyed black hair spoke loudest.

"Let's begin with a moment of silence to do as you wish, followed by the Serenity Prayer." Stu clasped his hands and bent his head as if to pray. The black-haired woman did the same, as did several of the men. The grandmotherly woman looked out the window, lips moving. The red-haired boy nibbled his thumbnail.

Stu lifted his head. "God grant me the serenity to accept the things I cannot change—" the others had joined in by this point "—courage to change the things I can, and wisdom to know the difference. Amen."

And then it seemed that everyone who wasn't already smoking, except for Stu, lit a cigarette. The sibilance of the lighters and matches was a counterpoint to the shrieking of the gulls.

Someone tapped her shoulder. She turned around. It was the man with the dark ponytail who'd been playing snooker in the final pub she'd visited last night. At least she thought it was him. His hair was slicked back off his face, as had been the man's last night, and fastened with an elastic at the nape, so that it hung between his shoulder blades. The furrows running down his cheeks were deep enough to be scars. "Can I borrow your lighter?"

She handed it to him. He lit his roll-up and handed it back. "Cheers."

Three men in paint-flecked white canvas trousers sat closest to the front. Stu nodded at one of them. "Today Mick will read the Twelve Steps."

Raking his fingers through his shapeless hair, the man on the far left rose and walked to the front, beside Stu. He didn't have a book or a sheet of paper in his hands. Instead, looking straight ahead and above the heads of the others, he recited, "We admitted we were powerless over alcohol and drugs, that our lives had become unmanageable. We came to believe that a Power greater than ourselves could restore us to sanity."

Jax would never tell her what went on in his meetings. "You don't want to know. Trust me. And besides, they're supposed to be anonymous."

"It's only me," she used to say, but still he'd shake his head. Once, though, when she'd said that, when he'd come out back to the pool after a meeting and sat on the lounge chair beside hers as she was studying a script, he'd reached over and rocked her chair, so hard that it jostled the can of soda atop the wicker table beside her, spilling diet cola onto the patio. "Never say that."

"Say what?" She shrank from him.

"'It's only me.' You're not an 'only.' You're more than 'only.'" His blue eyes had been nearly translucent; she'd imagined she could see the nerves behind them.

Mick had finished and was returning to his seat, his face covered with a filmy sheen. "Thank you very much," Stu said. "Now I'll turn the meeting over to you. Does anyone have something they'd like to discuss?"

The russet-haired boy tentatively lifted his hand. Stu nodded.

"I'm Ian, and I'm an alcoholic."

"Hello, Ian," the others responded, as if part of a church service.

"I have a question. How long does it take until you can walk past a pub or the liquor aisle at the supermarket and not think, Blimey, I could murder a pint just now?"

Stu waited for someone else to respond; when no one did, he answered. "I've only been sober for fourteen years, so I don't know." The others laughed, except for Ian, who lit a cigarette. "For some of us, it might never go away. I know for me, it's still something I fight with, if not every day, almost every day. That's why I don't take things just one day at a time, but one moment at a time." Murmurs and nods all around.

She would approach Stu after the meeting. Say that she was looking for a friend, the friend who had suggested awhile back that she attend a meeting. If he couldn't tell her whether Jax had attended meetings, because of the confidentiality aspect, maybe he could at least tell her how to go about finding him.

But after a collection bucket was passed around and the meeting broke up, the grandmotherly woman made a beeline to Stu. Suzanne held back, watching as Mick's two mates slapped him on the back and as Ian followed his friend, nodding slowly at what he was saying as the two of them shrugged into their leather jackets. The black-haired woman touched the old man's shoulder as she passed him on the way out. The ponytailed bloke from the snooker table rolled himself another fag, then asked to borrow her lighter again.

"I can give you my number, if you need to talk." His voice was softer than she'd expected, almost whispery.

She kept her face blank as she shook her head. "That's okay, thanks."

He shrugged. "It's just that, well, I saw you at the pub last night."

"I saw you too."

"But I was only playing snooker."

She looked back at Stu. The woman was making huge sweeping hand motions as she spoke. Suzanne could always come back next week. Now, she just wanted to escape. She grabbed her sweater and her gilet and headed out without saying goodbye to the ponytailed man. He followed her, though, and once outside, placed his palm on her shoulder. She turned to him but said nothing.

"My name's Lee."

She still couldn't tell if the vertical crevices along his cheeks were scars or deep lines. He had a few fine lines radiating from the outer corners of his eyes, but no other hints as to his age. His hands were veiny, with several round, raised scars.

"If you're an alcoholic," she said, "why do you hang out in pubs? Isn't it difficult?" If he wanted to be helpful, he could start by answering this.

His lips curved upward, but the upper portion of his face didn't move. "Alcohol wasn't my drug of choice."

She glanced again at his hands, his arms, which were hidden inside a fleece hoodie. "Smack?" she guessed.

A brief pause. "Yup."

She turned up the side road, Barrow Lane, knowing that he'd tag along. "Maybe you knew a friend of mine. Jack. Blond hair, thin, about your height."

"A junkie?"

She nodded, looking down at the weeds forcing their way through the thin cracks between the bricks of the pavement and the mortar.

"American like you?"

She looked up. Lee's face was blank. "I'm not American," she said. "Though I did live there the past few years."

He nodded, tugging on his left ear. A tiny silver cross dangled from the lobe. "I don't know. I mean, I've come across a lot of people, haven't I, and I have to say that my memory has a lot of holes. Anything really memorable, like a scar or a tattoo?"

She checked her own memory to be sure. "No."

"Well, I guess that's memorable in itself." He smiled. His left eyetooth was shorter than the surrounding teeth, and flat edged, as if it had been filed. "I can't think of anyone like that now. But if you want to give me your mobile number, I could text you if I do remember him, or come across someone who does."

She didn't want to give up her phone number to a stranger. Then again, she was going to have to start doing so if she was to track Jax down. She recited the digits, watching as he entered them into his phone. "Do you have any suggestions as to where I should look?"

Lee flicked his cigarette butt into the grate below the curb. "Riker Road, off the High Street, is where to score. But I wouldn't go there alone." He curved the corners of his lips upward again. "And I can't go there with you, otherwise I'd offer."

She nodded and began heading up the hill. Although the air was crisp, and probably cold, she was slick with perspiration. She wiped her forehead with the back of her hand.

"Wait a second."

She turned.

"You never told me your name."

"Anne."

He strode up beside her. "Wait a second, Anne. Let me give you my number. Just in case." She fished out her cell phone from her bag and entered the digits. "You never know, do you?"

She dug up a smile. "Thanks."

Riker Road was on the other side of the High Street, leading higher into the hills. On one corner stood a letting agent, on the opposite a cash machine. The street was, if anything, even steeper than Barrow Lane—Suzanne had to tilt her head well back to see the top—and like Fortescue Road, it was lined with brick-faced terraces, though these weren't as well kept up. Graffiti scarred some of the facades. The top windows of the house five doors up were covered with planks. Large clumps of dog shit spattered the sidewalks, which unlike the quaint brick pavements of the High Street were made of large slabs of concrete.

She didn't see anyone out and about. Maybe it wasn't till evening that Riker Road came to life. Maybe what she should do was head back to the trailer, take a nap, read a little, then return to town around nine or so this evening. Check out the street, see if it was as bad as that Lee bloke made it out to be, and take it from there.

She set off toward the bus stop at the end of the High Street. A few young mothers, cigarettes dangling from mouths, pushed strollers. Older ladies gripped each other's hands as they bobbled from side to side, stopping to study the windows of one charity shop after another. A bushy-browed, fleshy man with a bloodstained bandage over one ear sat against the front of a now-empty jewelers, nursing a bottle beneath a "to let" sign.

She crossed over to the opposite side of the High Street to avoid the gang of gulls tearing apart what looked to be the remains of a pizza. Fortescue Road was coming up. She wondered how Richard was doing, if his lounge was still tidy, if he would even remember her. She turned down the road.

She pressed the front buzzer to his flat. Nothing. Just as she was turning around to leave he opened the door, his forehead furrowed and brows drawn—whether in wariness or confusion, she couldn't say.

Suddenly, his face relaxed. "Samantha?"

"Suzanne."

He laughed. He had a habit of pulling his lips over his teeth as soon as he laughed, as if ashamed of his smile, though there was nothing wrong with it as far as she could see. "I was rubbish with names even before," he said. "At least, I think I was." He laughed again and waved her in. "What are you up to?"

"I had to come into town anyway, so I figured I'd make sure you were all right." She followed him down the hall.

"As you'll see, the lounge is still clean." He pushed open the door to his flat, which he'd left ajar. "And I scrubbed the bathroom this morning as well."

Aside from a haphazard stack of magazines beside his laptop on the folding table behind the sofa, it did look clean. "Can I get you something to drink?" he asked.

She cocked her head. "Did you clean the kitchen too?"

"No, not yet."

"Then no thanks." She grinned.

He stood in front of her, waiting.

She nodded toward his computer. "You working on something?"

"Not really." He rubbed the back of his head. "I used to be a website designer, so I was just reading some articles, checking out some software updates."

"What kind of sites did you design?"

He sat on the couch, checking by habit to make sure he wouldn't end up squashing a leftover takeaway or crushing a CD. "When I was in London I worked for a midsize agency that did a lot of ecommerce storefronts, a few entertainment sites, things like that."

"Entertainment sites?" She pulled on her bangs, bringing them over her eyes.

"Yeah, for new movies and such like. I can show you a few."

The chances of his having worked on a site related to *Lakeview Drive* or anything else she'd been in were slim. "Sure."

He laughed, a longer, freer laugh than before. "I'm just joking. That would be like a new dad showing off snaps of his baby down the pub, wouldn't it? No one really wants to see them."

She sat down as well, sticking close to the arm of the sofa. "Do you know anyone who lives on Riker Road?"

"Riker Road." He rubbed the top of his head, sending up pieces of his hair in spikes. "That's off the High Street, past the butchers, is it?"

"Between a letting agent and a bank, yeah."

"The junkies' street." He nodded in recognition, then shook his head. "No. Not my type of crowd."

"Oh."

"You think this mate you're looking for got mixed up with that, don't you?"

She clapped her hands. "You remembered!"

He smiled. "Yeah, I remember yesterday pretty clearly, actually. And today so far." Then, as if embarrassed, he shrugged. "So is that where your friend was living last?"

She pulled out her cigarettes, offered him one, which he refused, and lit up. He rose and walked to the folding table to retrieve his tobacco, papers, and filters. His gait was slightly uneven; he held the weight on his right leg a second longer than on his left, but you wouldn't notice unless you were looking for it.

"I don't know." Suzanne was gauging how much information was necessary to dole out. "All I do know is that he moved down here last April, about a month after getting out of rehab in Sussex. He didn't give me his address, just a post office box. And we wrote, and I'd call him on his mobile sometimes. But I haven't heard from him since early November or so. His phone number is out of service, and he hasn't written."

Richard lit his roll-up. "Did you stop by Serenity House? It's the halfway house near the hospital. They also have a drop-in center."

Mentally she scanned the list of hospitals and rehab centers and other facilities that the investigator she'd hired just after the holidays had said he'd contacted. She was almost certain that a Serenity House wasn't on the list. What kind of crap detective was he? How many other places had he missed? "No. I hadn't even heard of it." She twirled her cigarette against the edge of the ashtray atop the round side table between the sofa and the chair.

"They might be able to help."

She lifted the ashtray and placed it on the couch between them. "I went to a twelve-step meeting today. I was hoping to see him there."

"You called around to his friends and family and that?"

The investigator had contacted their few cousins in London and even uncovered some distant relatives on their father's side who lived in Somerset.

She nodded.

Richard raked his hair upward. "I once read about a fire in a circus tent in America. Connecticut, maybe. This was in the 1800s, I think, or maybe the early 1900s. Loads of people were killed. They were able to identify everyone except one person, a little girl about eight or nine years old. They put up posters and bulletins all over, but no one ever stepped forth to say they knew who she was. To this day they don't know."

She stared at him. "I hope this isn't your idea of trying to cheer me up."

"It's just, you wouldn't think it would be that easy to disappear nowadays, would you? I mean, what with Facebook and mobiles and Google and such like."

"I don't know." Suzanne ground out her cigarette. She was thinking how her mother had no idea where she was, nor even Larry, her agent, though she had called him from Heathrow, to let him know that she had decided to go off traveling for a bit, seeing as she had a break in her schedule. He hadn't been pleased; it was still pilot season, he reminded her. But she'd already filmed an episode of a new series a friend of Matthew's was pitching, though Matthew had advised her not to get her hopes up. She'd even committed herself to seven episodes should the pilot get a look-in, which she hoped it wouldn't. Her part, as the college-student girlfriend of the title character, a young man with Asperger's who helped his chief-of-police father solve murders, was so underwritten as to be nearly invisible. Basically she had to feed the main character leading questions, explain his quirks to outsiders, and every so often ask if she could kiss him.

Larry had asked if he could reach her by cell phone, and she'd told him she'd gotten a new number, and that she wasn't going to give it to him. "But I will be back by early May, and I'll be checking in. So hold any decent scripts that aren't pilots for me."

"Should I forward them to your mother?" he asked.

"No. She doesn't know I'm gone."

"What should I tell her when she calls?"

"That I'm off traveling in India."

"Are you?"

"Maybe."

She should call Larry tonight—this morning L.A. time. She felt guilty forcing him to have to deal with her mother, so the least she could do was reassure him that she was okay.

"No one knows where I am," Suzanne told Richard.

"Really?"

She nodded, stupidly proud. "It's kind of, I don't know, liberating."

"Sometimes I wonder, if I dropped dead in my sleep, how long would it take for someone to find me." Richard watched the smoke from his cigarette unspool toward the ceiling.

She shrugged. "It doesn't really matter. Seeing as you'd be dead anyway."

Richard slapped his palms on his thighs. "This is a cheery subject for a nice sunny day."

"It's not all that sunny."

"No?" He peered beyond her toward the kitchen. The room was dim.

"Why don't you come with me to Serenity House?" Suzanne said.

"Why?"

"It would get you out of your apartment. And I don't know, maybe you can help, seeing as you've lived here for—how long now?"

"About a year. I think. But most of that time I was out of commission." Richard did not want to tag around with some kid who was on a wild goose chasing looking for her ex-boyfriend or what have you, like it was some sort of Saturday morning children's program. *The Famous Five Minus Three Go Looking for a Junkie.*

"This'll help you get back into commission." She smiled. She really was pretty when she smiled, pretty in the way of a twelve-year-old girl who was going to grow up to be a stunner but didn't know it.

"How old are you really?" he asked.

"Twenty-one. Really. I can show you my passport if you want."

"And this Jack, is he an old boyfriend?"

"No."

"And you weren't a user yourself?"

"Definitely no." She chuckled without amusement. "I smoked a joint once and hated it. I've drunk more alcohol since I landed here than I have in the rest of my life so far, and even that hasn't been much. My brother used to call me the Vestal Virgin."

He was not going to ask if she was a virgin. He found himself looking at her chest, though. Beneath her pink gilet and the oversize jumper she had on beneath it, she didn't seem to have much in the way of breasts, but that could well be different when she was naked. The first time Pam had stripped off for him he'd been taken aback by how ripe her breasts were. He'd put a hand under each one, delighting in the soft firmness that filled his palms and spilled over his fingers. Her cups had indeed runneth over.

He looked up to see Suzanne watching him check her out. His cheeks burned. "Fine. I'll come with you."

Serenity House looked no different from the B and B's generously interspersed along Caldicott Road, the road leading down from the caravan park to the High Street. Most of these were three- or four-story semidetached homes, pale brick gussied up with wrought-iron balconies and latticework, windowboxes waiting their spring deposits of geraniums, barren birdbaths and brown-rimmed Japanese maples in the front gardens.

The front door was unlocked, but they had to press a buzzer in the vestibule to be let past the second door into the lobby. Near the reception desk stood a wooden pamphlet holder, but instead of glossy color brochures for the local attractions as you'd see in a B and B, these pamphlets were white or marigold copier paper folded into thirds, with titles like "Hepatitis C and You" and "Families in Recovery."

The receptionist had lifeless near-black hair and undereye circles so large and dark they resembled coffee stains. When Suzanne asked, straight off, if she recalled a man named Jack, blond, thin, the woman put up her hand and said she couldn't answer that, but if they sat down she'd have a counselor come out to speak with them.

The chairs had wooden backs with three horizontal rungs. Leaning against the rungs set off rows of short, sharp stabs across his back, so Richard slouched forward. Beside him, Suzanne perched on the edge of her chair, looking around the room. There wasn't much to see. Wallpaper in a small primrose pattern topped with a border of the same pattern enlarged by three. Several more chairs. A floor-standing ashtray from the 1950s, the brass plate flaking in spots.

Another woman emerged from the door behind the reception desk. Her flat blonde hair was cropped just above the shoulders in what Pam would deride as a "no-style style," equally unflattering to all. Being a hairstylist, Pam described people by their hair first and foremost. Before the accident Richard had worn his hair straight just beyond his shoulders. Every month she'd trim the ends and angle the layers around his face.

"My name is Ruth," said the blonde. "Why don't you come with me." She ushered them behind the reception desk and down a short, coral-painted corridor. "First door on the left," she said from behind them.

The office walls were a dark mustard that made the room feel even more cramped than it was. Ruth edged herself in behind a blocky wooden desk, the sort a teacher would have. She nodded at the two folding chairs facing her. Aside from a calendar with a scene of the Billicombe harbor, there were no decorations on the walls. Then again, there wasn't much wall space, what with the rows of putty-colored metal filing cabinets.

"I understand you're looking for someone." Ruth looked from Richard to Suzanne, uncertain of whom to address. Remains of pink lipstick were trapped in the vertical crevices of her lower lip.

"Yes, I am." Suzanne leaned forward. "A friend of mine, named Jack."

"And what makes you think he might have come here?" Ruth sounded neither solicitous nor brusque; she didn't sound anything, other than weary.

Suzanne repeated what she'd told Richard earlier, about Jack moving here after leaving rehab, about the letters that stopped, about the post office box in Billicombe and the disconnected mobile.

"We didn't have anyone named Jack as a resident during the past year. We do run an informal drop-in center, however. People aren't required to give their names, but do you have a photo of him?"

"No, but I can describe him. Blonde, more of a gold than yours, kind of fine and straggly. About average height, maybe a little taller. Thin. Blue eyes that sometimes look bright and sometimes almost gray." She paused. "No tattoos or scars," she added.

Ruth made a steeple with her fingers. "Does he sometimes chew on a piece of hair?"

Suzanne bounced in her seat. "Yes!"

Ruth nodded. "I only remember that because it made me slightly queasy. We had someone of that description who would join us for our midmorning open houses. I thought he called himself Jay, but I could be wrong. For a while we could count on seeing him several times a week, but then he suddenly stopped."

"When?"

Ruth tapped her forefingers against each other. "It was sometime in the autumn, but I can't be certain exactly when. Around the time of the Autumn Carnival, I think, because I remember one of the counselors who used to work here telling me that he was surprised Jay hadn't turned up at the carnival, as he had been looking forward to it. He'd worked throughout the summer on painting the sets for one of the floats, but he'd stopped showing up before finishing. Declan, the counselor, had been worried about him."

"Where is Declan now?"

"Declan works as part of a church-affiliated outreach program in Boutport. I can give you the number." Ruth swiveled her chair toward the outdated computer in the corner of her desk and tapped some keys. The clatter was artificially loud. She waited for Suzanne to take out a pen and paper from her bag before reading out the phone number.

"Do you know if Jack was using?"

Ruth faced Suzanne once again. "I'm afraid I can't disclose that sort of information except to a medical or law-enforcement professional."

"Oh." Suzanne looked down at her lap, her frizzy waves obscuring all of her face except for the tip of her nose and her set jawline.

"But I don't think he was," Ruth added softly.

Suzanne lifted her head slightly. "Can I ask you one last thing?"

Ruth nodded.

"What did the sets that he was painting look like?"

Ruth looked up at the ceiling, as if searching for the answer. "You know, I can't recall."

They sat in the beer garden of the Prince, which was up a flight of stairs outside the back of the pub itself. Through gaps in the shrubbery they could snatch glimpses of blue, though it was difficult to say whether it was the harbor or the sky. Suzanne had insisted on treating him to a meal, but she was only picking at her chips and had had just a few sips of cider. Richard felt guilty chomping away at his burger, but he was famished.

"He must have started using again, and that's why he disappeared." Suzanne lit a cigarette.

"You don't know that. He might have just moved away."

"No." She shook her head, her hair falling further onto her face. "He wouldn't have gone without saying goodbye. He was always very polite like that." She remembered the time she'd had to pick him up at the police station, their mother having washed her hands of him by then. Because he didn't have any drugs on him and hadn't resisted arrest (not that he'd been in any state to), they weren't going to charge him. By the time she arrived he was somewhat alert; tousle-haired, heavy-lidded, but coherent. As they left he turned around to the officers and said, "Thank you." As if they'd returned a lost wallet to him instead of returned him to his sister.

"He didn't say goodbye to you, though, did he?"

She watched Richard chew. His paper napkin, crumpled on the table beside his plate, was streaked with catsup. She felt her nose wrinkle. "Because he'd started using again." She spoke simply, as if Richard himself were simple. "He knew I'd be disappointed."

"But if you were all the way in California and he was here, how would you know?"

"I would have known." She exhaled sharply, coughing a bit.

Richard wondered what he should do now. Before the accident, he probably would have known. Sometimes he felt it wasn't just his memory that had been kicked apart like a jigsaw puzzle and put haphazardly back together, some pieces forced into the wrong positions, a few others missing. Or rather, it wasn't just his memory of even basic facts, but his innate memory of how to act in certain situations. Like this one.

"Are you going to call this Declan bloke?" he finally said.

"No, I'm going to stop by in person tomorrow. It's better if I talk to him face to face." She sprinkled more vinegar on her chips but didn't touch any of them. "Do you know where this Faith Lives organization is exactly?"

"No. But I'm sure you could Google it."

She hadn't brought a computer with her to England. She hadn't wanted to feel obliged to check her email and read the trades online. Jax had never emailed anyway.

"I'll just take the bus to Boutport tomorrow and ask at the bus station. It's not a very big town." She'd come across it in the course of her research on Billicombe, because it was the nearest market town, which as far as she could tell meant it had an M&S, a Boots, and a Primark.

"Do you want me to come with you?"

She looked at him. "Would you?"

"Sure." He was as surprised by his offer as she seemed to be. "Let me know what bus you plan to catch, and I'll meet you on it."

"I know!" Suzanne clapped her hands and bobbed up and down on her bench. "Why don't you stay at my place tonight, and then we can leave together in the morning? It'll be fun, like a sleepover."

"A sleepover?"

She swatted at his hand. "Come on. I won't make you do girly things like manicures or talk about boys." She laughed, showing off square white teeth.

"I don't think there's room enough for me to stay."

"Sure there is. The sofa across from the bed is great for sleeping. I fall asleep on it all the time. You can have the bed, because of your back." She dusted her palms against each other, as she had after cleaning his flat, the matter settled as far as she was concerned.

If he said no, she'd argue her case until he gave in, so he might as well save themselves both the trouble. And let's face it: He didn't have anything better to do anyway. "Fine."

Walking back along the High Street to his flat, she stopped when they reached Riker Road. She looked up the street, craning her neck and even standing on tiptoe. "It doesn't look that bad."

"It's not the Wild West, but it's not Kensington Gardens either." Richard crossed the road.

Suzanne didn't follow. "I'm going to take a little walk. I'll meet you at your flat in a bit."

That suited him. With her constant foot tapping and gesturing, her continual questions—what did that store used to sell before it went out of business? did they have to put a steel rod in your leg? have you ever been to the States?—she was tiring in more than small doses. Spending time with her was like taking care of a friend's preschooler. It was fun for a while, but that was because you knew you could hand the kid back before the end of the day.

Suzanne lit a cigarette before hiking up Riker Road. She had to stop and knead her shin splints before reaching even the first intersection, the inclination was that steep. She passed no one. Most of the windows had the sheers drawn; the ones without curtains looked onto empty rooms, magnolia walls.

When she reached the first crossroad she paused again, rubbing the backs of her calves this time. If this road really was a junkie haven, how the hell did they manage the climb? She crossed the street and continued upward. A dog barked, loud, guttural. She looked around but didn't see it, didn't see anything but more piles of dog shit and crushed cans of Strongbow. Oh, there was a discarded condom; she stepped well around it. She crossed another intersection, passed a building that was completely boarded up. A few doors beyond it another house had "COCKSUCKER" spray-painted in red across the front, the C obscuring part of the ground-floor window and the R covering up the house number. And when she stopped once again to catch her breath, bending down to rub her leg, she saw a bent-handled, blackened spoon lying in the gutter of the road.

CHAPTER 3

Although he'd never tell her as much, Richard felt a little sorry for Suzanne. She must be lonely, out here on her own. In another month, the May bank holidays would kick off the summer season, and there'd be cars parked alongside most of the chalets, and caravans filling the lot beyond. Bicycles would lean precariously against the chalet walls; towels and trousers and maybe even swimsuits, if the weather was warm enough, would flap from the clotheslines that acted as borders between each caravan slot. Kids would be arguing over sweets and racing to capture ladybirds. Older men would sit on the porches, white chest hairs curling over the top of their vests, dropping their cigarette butts into empty beer cans while their wives periodically looked up from their copies of *Let's Chat* to complain about the methane from the nearby cows or insist that their husbands enthuse with them about the red-rimmed sunset.

Now, though, there were just two caravans in the parking lot, and neither showed signs of life: the curtains pulled tight over the small dark windows, the white plastic patio chairs still stacked atop one another beside the electrical connections. The only sounds were the never-ending crying of the gulls and the faint whir of traffic from Caldicott Road. Maybe Suzanne was even a bit frightened at night, encased in the narrow chalet that was nothing more than a caravan anchored to a cement slab, trying to translate the unfamiliar creaks, decode the alien shadows.

She was probably one of those girls used to being part of a crowd, maybe even the leader of her little clique. He imagined her constantly in touch with her friends—traveling with them in packs, forever texting on mobiles, ringing one another to confer on the most minute decisions such as whether to buy the blue blouse or the green.

But so far, at least, spending the evening with her wasn't as tiresome as he'd feared. He hadn't known what to expect, but it certainly wasn't that before catching the bus they'd stop at the Somerfield to buy the last loaf of Italian bread, a few tomatoes, and some mozzarella so that she could grill some bruschetta in her chalet's small oven. She apologized for using margarine instead of olive oil, but he was no gourmet, so it tasted just fine to him. Nor had he expected to see a paperback of *A Clockwork Orange* at the foot of her made-up bed and sections of the *Guardian* in the wire rubbish bin inside the loo. *Heat* or *Cosmo*, maybe.

For the most part she was easy to talk with. Since his accident, he'd sometimes find himself lost in the midst of a conversation, as if watching a film that had skipped ahead by a minute or so, just enough time to be a few sentences behind and uncertain of how to catch up. That hadn't happened with Suzanne. Not yet, anyway.

Maybe it was because for the most part she fired questions at him and waited for his answers. And when he couldn't answer—he couldn't for the life of him remember how fucking old he was, neither what year he was born nor what year it was now—she moved on to another question. After asking his age, for instance, she asked if it bothered him not being able to remember it.

"What do you think?" he snapped back, because the answer seemed pretty obvious. Sitting on her bed, he'd pounded his fist against his thigh and exclaimed, "Shit" when he couldn't summon up his age.

If she was insulted or angry or embarrassed, she didn't show it. "I don't know." She sat cross-legged on the couch opposite him. "Maybe you get used to it. I mean, what if you never get your full memory back?"

"I don't know." He bent over his beer so that she couldn't see his face. He thought about this every night, as he waited for the antidepressants that were supposed to help him sleep kick in. Could he live like this, unmoored, for another forty or sixty years? For even another year? Because it was like standing on a raft that was dipping and rocking, with nothing to hold on to, the bottom continually shifting you off-balance, no matter how much you tried to keep your feet planted in the same spot.

Suzanne had asked Richard to stay mostly because she was afraid he'd forget to meet her otherwise, but also because he seemed so isolated. Not knowing if the person walking by was someone you'd grown up with or a complete stranger. Thinking you weren't worth cleaning your own flat for—what other reason could there be for his living in such a sty?

And maybe she was a little lonely herself. Though she'd grown used to coming home to an empty house. She'd been living on her own since Jax had come to England, and even before then she couldn't count on his being there when she got home, or if he was there, of his being any sort of company. Back then, as soon as she let herself into the house she'd take a deep breath, sniffing for burning fabric. She didn't trust the smoke detectors, not after that time he'd burned a hole in her leather couch with a cigarette while on the nod. And she'd listen for the TV or the stereo. If she heard either, she'd follow the sound, to see if he was in the den, or his bedroom, or even her room. If the TV or stereo was on, it generally meant he was stoned but not in a stupor; she could walk into the room, say hello, make small talk. She'd ask what he was watching. He'd ask how work was. She'd suggest ordering a pizza. He'd say he wasn't hungry, but he'd have a soda or tea while she ate. You might think everything was normal, if you hadn't known how things used to be between them. How Jax used to be.

If the house was quiet, it meant Jax had gone out. Or Jax was out—passed out, nodding in and out. Or if it were one of his periods of sobriety, he was in his room or out by the pool, sketching, reading, doing push-ups, swimming laps, waiting for her to get home and talk to him, asking her question after question about the day's filming, the traffic, what she had for lunch, anything to keep himself from thinking.

He'd attended UCLA for one semester. That had been good. He spent a lot of time studying. He said he had to work harder now to retain information, as he'd killed so many brain cells. He told her about his Newswriting 101 class and the Five W's of reporting: who, what, when, where, and why. They talked about Plato's *Republic* and the Italian Renaissance. He'd usually have dinner waiting for her, something meatless, like spaghetti with garlic and oil, and a salad. His salads were always symmetrical. Atop a bed of red-leaf lettuce and spinach leaves would be a circle of precisely sliced cucumbers, and within that a smaller circle of tomato slices. Above that would be strips of red and yellow peppers, arranged like spokes of a wheel or rays emanating from an invisible sun. His meals reminded her of how, when they were kids in London, he would prepare her breakfast because their mum said they were old enough to get themselves ready for school in the morning. He'd make her toast, because even at seven she was still afraid of the toaster; the ping as the bread popped up startled her every time, no matter how much she braced herself for it. Then he'd pour her milk or, when they were out of it, run the tap till the water was extra cold, the way she liked it.

After his last final of the semester, he'd gone out with some classmates to celebrate. He didn't return home till four days later, minus one of his eyeteeth and stinking of cheap wine and burnt rubber and piss. He cried out when she helped him peel his socks off his feet; he'd developed huge blisters from walking he didn't know how many miles back to the house, and they had opened so that the cotton had melded with the blood and pus and become part of the shredded layers of flesh. He kept calling her Mum, kept pleading, "Please don't tell Zee."

When she thought about Jax, her stomach ached. It didn't matter if she was remembering something good—the afternoon they spent at the Hollywood Bowl flea market, for instance, when he surprised her with a hammered copper choker that he'd bought with money he'd earned walking dogs—or something not so good. She ached with not knowing where he was.

She'd tried to tell him that, one of the last times he'd disappeared before going to the Sussex rehab. He'd called her from Hollywood Boulevard, of all places, on the same block as the Frederick's of Hollywood store, he said. He asked if she'd be able to pay for him to take a cab back to the house. She said she'd come and pick him up, but he said no. "You have work tomorrow, don't you?" She didn't, as it happened, but still he said no. "I better take a cab. Otherwise I might not be here by the time you come."

A few minutes after he hung up, the phone rang again. This time it was a cab driver. He wanted to be sure that she'd pay his fare. When she helped Jax out of the backseat she was surprised he'd managed to call a cab, and that a cab had bothered to stop. A bib of dried vomit topped his T-shirt, a shirt she didn't recognize, and he couldn't stand without clutching on to something— the car door, her.

"I shouldn't have called," he said as she led him into the bathroom.

"What do you mean?" She began running a bath.

"I should have just let you be." There wasn't a scrap of self-pity in his voice. He spoke softly, the matter-of-factness of his tone at odds with his grease-clumped hair, the scabs in the corners of his mouth, the stench of him.

"Don't say that." She hated how shrill her voice was, when his sounded so steady. "I never want you to just let me be, okay? When you disappear like this, I... it's the worst. I'd rather know where you are, I don't care what you're up to. Don't do this again. I don't think I can go through this again." She slumped onto the bathroom floor, spine against the tub, and started crying. The sobs scraped her throat raw.

Jax sat on top of the closed toilet lid. He didn't move toward her. As her crying turned to hiccupping, she heard him sigh, just the slightest escape of breath. She looked up, the tracks of her tears stinging her cheeks. He nodded at the tub, the barest of nods, closing his eyes as if exhausted from the effort. "The water's about to overflow," he whispered.

"You okay?"

Richard looked up, looked around, took a quick mental inventory. His name was Richard Sommers. He lived in Billicombe, Devon. He was twenty-six... no, twenty-seven? Okay, don't get hung up on that one, move along. He was a website designer, currently between jobs. He'd been in a car accident on the twenty-first of October. He was in a chalet with Saman—no, Suzanne. It was Tuesday night. Tomorrow morning he and Suzanne would be taking the bus into Boutport.

All accounted for.

"I'm fine." He polished off his beer.

"So, this accident of yours, how did it happen exactly?" Suzanne stretched out on the couch, propping her head up on her hand, as if waiting for a telly program to start.

"Did anyone ever tell you you're a nosy little so-and-so?"

"Yeah." She waited a few seconds before grinning. Then she waited a few seconds more, still staring expectedly.

Richard sighed. "We were coming home from a party in Boutport—my girlfriend, Pam, and me. It was her turn to drive. We were on the A361, that's the main road between here and Boutport, the road the bus goes on. Everything's fine and dandy, then something comes running out of the shrubs onto the street. Someone. And Pam slams the brakes and, well, there you go." He stood up, shaking the stiffness out of his left leg, and carried his empty can to the scrap of laminate that served as the kitchen counter. He tugged a full can from the plastic rings of the six-pack and returned to the bed.

"And what happened to Pam? She wasn't killed, was she?"

"Christ, no! She was banged up, but otherwise okay." He popped the lid, listened to the clank of the tin, the sizzle of the foam swelling toward the opening.

"So where is she now?"

He took a few long, loud gulps. Suzanne was still watching and waiting.

"She left."

"She left you?"

He nodded, refusing to look up.

"While you were in hospital?"

"No. Soon after."

"Wow. That's cold."

He felt the need to defend Pam. But he wasn't sure how. So he drank more of his beer.

"Did she tell you why?"

"It was because of my scars."

"Your scars?"

He snuck a peek at Suzanne. Her mouth was agape, like a cartoon character's. He almost chuckled, she looked so absurd. "I have scarring on my back, from the surgeries," he said, keeping his tone flat. "Apparently they're pretty bad."

"You haven't seen them?"

"Bits of them, once. I can't see my own back, can I?"

"With two big mirrors you can." She sat up. "Can I see them?"

"No." He sounded like a Victorian spinster responding to a request to reveal her ankles.

"Come on. I bet they're not that bad." She seemed excited. She must like freak shows.

He finished his beer. "No."

"Let me see them, and I'll stop pestering you."

He knew showing her was the only way to shut her up. She really was like a goddam kid. With another sigh, he turned around so that he was facing the window over the bed, its beige curtain pulled tight. He hesitated, then lifted his shirt, wincing a bit.

Suzanne got up, then crouched on the floor behind him. "They're not that bad."

He scoured her comment for some sort of placation, hesitancy, some tell that she was bullshitting him. He couldn't find one, but still he didn't believe her. "Yeah, right."

"No, seriously. You want to know what they look like?" And before he could answer, she was off and running. "There's one large scar that swoops from your right shoulder blade to the center of your spine. Under that you have two short slashes, and then there's like a seam running down along the spine itself. That's the thickest, and it's raised, and a pearly sort of pink. It looks like it would hurt like hell if I touched it." He shrunk away from her involuntarily. "And you can see where they stapled that incision, little dark red horizontal lines. And that's about it." He heard her get to her feet and return to the sofa. He yanked his shirt back down, shuddering as the fabric grazed his back.

"She really said she left you because of your scars?" Suzanne asked as he turned around, shifting his head to avoid her gaze.

He couldn't remember what Pam had said. If she'd said anything. Had she even told him she was leaving, or had she just left? The more he tried to recall, the blanker his memory of the last time he saw her became, as if by trying to get a good look at the image he was actually erasing it. "Not in so many words." But he had the residual memory that this was why, just as no matter what else he forgot, he remembered how to speak English. "But yeah."

"If that's the case, then you're better off without her. I mean, jeez, I've seen a lot worse."

"In all your vast years of medical training?"

Whether she was oblivious to the sarcasm or simply ignoring it, he couldn't tell. She lit a cigarette. "So do you still run into her sometimes?"

He stood up again, again swapping an empty can of beer for a full one. "No. She went to stay with her family down in South Devon."

"Did you try to talk to her after she left?"

"Why do you care?" he growled.

She exhaled, pushing the smoke upward with a thrust of her lower lip. "I don't know," she replied, as if it had been a question that required a response.

"As a matter of fact, I did try to track her down at her parents'. But I can't remember what the hell town they live in. And her surname is Thomas. There are hundreds of Thomases in the phone directory." He slumped onto the bed, defeated by his inability to recall something as basic as the town Pam had fled to and to stop Suzanne's questioning.

She leaned against the back cushions and folded her legs. "What about her friends from around here? Did she used to work here?"

Pam had worked in a hair salon in Boutport. Of course, he added, he couldn't remember the name, only that it had black chairs and sinks and lots of mirrors. Which described half the salons in the town.

He forced himself to finish his beer, drinking so fast it seemed to collect in his chest. "I'm knackered. I'm going to sleep." He made a show of bending over and riffling in his rucksack for his pills, of stretching (even though it hurt to pull his back muscles that way) and yawning, of peeling back the blanket and sliding between the sheets.

Suzanne was still watching him. "You're going to sleep in your clothes?"

He glared at her before turning around, facing the wall like a kid being punished, his back toward her.

He heard her light another cigarette. "Sorry," she said quietly. "I guess I go on a bit when I'm nervous."

He knew that was his cue. He resisted for a few seconds, but then, partly out of pity, partly out of politeness, but mostly from curiosity, he followed up. "What are you nervous about?"

"What this Declan guy is going to say tomorrow. I'm not sure which would be worse: if he says, 'Yeah, I've seen Jax. He's living in some shooting gallery, he's completely fucked up' or 'No idea where he is, he just disappeared off the face of the earth.' Well, the worst would be 'Oh him, he died of an OD months ago.'"

Richard rolled over, then sat up. Suzanne was nibbling on the thumbnail of the hand holding her cigarette, oblivious to the smoke wafting into her eyes.

"If he'd died, you would know by now."

She looked at him. She'd pushed her hair off her face, so he could clearly see her eyes. He didn't know why she hid them; they were her best feature, their roundness softening the harsh angles of her face. Pam would have insisted that she grow out the fringe and brush it off to the side in the meantime.

"I did hire a detective type to call around a few months back," Suzanne admitted. "He said he'd checked with all the hospitals and morgues."

She could afford to hire a detective? He studied her clothes. No designer labels so far as he could tell; even her trainers were nondescript. Aside from a gold ring in the shape of a heart on her right middle finger and a necklace made of irregular chunks of copper or brass, she wore no jewelry. Instead of a fancy leather number with a monogram or lots of metal trim, her handbag was a formless sack made of what he recognized as a Marimekko fabric, bold oversize poppies in shades of blue. If she came from money, she certainly hid it well.

"But what if he didn't have any ID on him?" Suzanne was saying, twisting a sliver of hair around her forefinger. "They wouldn't be able to identify the body." Her eyes widened even more. Their concentric circles of brown, nearly black along the rims, faded by almost imperceptible degrees to amber around the pupils.

"All these social worker types, like that Ruth we met today and this Declan, they always get a call about any unidentified bodies." Richard spoke gently, looking at her straight on, so that she'd know he was speaking the truth. "And if there'd been any unidentified body found, it would have made the local papers. I would have read about it."

She cocked her head and lifted her brows. "Yeah, but would you remember it?"

He laughed in spite of himself. "Okay, you have a point."

Richard did little more than grunt bare-bone replies as they got ready to catch the bus to Boutport in the morning. Suzanne chose to take it as a compliment that he felt comfortable enough with her not to fuss with stiff politenesses, felt no need to be "on." The first few days in rehearsals or on set, you could get swept away by the waves of fake sincerity. *I loved your work in This-and-That. Those earrings are gorgeous. I'm getting a coffee, want one? You can have the seat, I don't mind standing.* Voices filed to a powdery smoothness. Lots of mouth-only smiles displaying freshly whitened teeth. And always one actor who felt it was part of the job description to jolly everyone along: gathering them all round to hear a joke you were compelled to laugh at; bringing in fresh-baked muffins (never mind the continually replenished craft table, and the fact that nearly all the actresses, and most of the actors, forced themselves to avert their eyes from its heaps of M&Ms and mixed nuts and mini bagels for fear of gaining an ounce and facing the scorn of Wardrobe); making a point of asking how So-and-So from your last project was doing, so that you were aware that the two of you knew someone in common, and hey ho, it's a small world, isn't it grand.

Suzanne was usually considered a bit stuck-up at first, she knew, because she wasn't good with the false camaraderie. Turning on the tears when the cameras rolled was easy (at least for the first few takes). Pretending to lust after an actor whose clammy hands and wet lips repelled her was a challenge she prided herself on rising to. Being told to laughingly banter while tilting her head and neck in an ergonomically improbable way to avoid casting unattractive shadows was just another skill set to be perfected. But making small talk with people as they peered past her shoulder in case someone more important strode by, scouring her brain for something about them to praise (I love your hairstyle! Those shoes are so cute!), that was the most difficult part of her job.

Because the questions she really wanted answered were usually those she knew better than to ask, at least at first. Why are you having such a tough time remembering your five lines of dialogue this morning? (Because I did much more than five lines of coke on my way in this morning.) Why do you back away every time the DP approaches? (Because the last time I worked with him, he insisted on feeling my tits to find out for himself if they were real.) Do you really use that skincare regime you rave about in those infomercials? (No, but when my agent received the offer I hadn't worked in six months.)

It was weird, then, how she and Richard had skipped that awkward-niceties phase. Weird, but much appreciated.

He didn't say anything as they waited for the bus, smoking their cigarettes. Once it arrived and they'd settled in to seats near the back, several rows behind an elderly woman with a small hairy dog snoozing on her lap and across the aisle from a splay-legged skinhead busily texting, she asked Richard what he'd be doing today if he hadn't been accompanying her. He shrugged and mumbled something that could have been "Nothing" or "Don't know."

Suzanne sat next to the window. The sun made a few begrudging appearances from behind the clumps of dull clouds, not bothering to bask the rolling fields in brilliance or even to bring out a few contrasting shadows. Cows and sheep chewed in the pastures without looking up.

After a few minutes the bus stopped at a stone shelter on the corner of a lane just wide enough for one small vehicle to get through without having its sides brushed by the outstretched limbs of the overgrown shrubs lining the sides. Several feet up the lane a black-on-white sign emerged from the shrubbery announcing the village of West Downs.

Richard jerked his head toward the even narrower lane—a gravel-and-dirt path, really—on the opposite side of the road. Unpaved, it plunged into an unseen valley, abruptly disappearing just yards away. "See that tree? The big one?" She adjusted her gaze a few degrees to the left, to a trio of huge black-trunked trees. "That's where our accident was. I think."

None of the trees appeared damaged, but they were massive; it would take at least three of her, arms akimbo, to encircle just one of them. She stared at his profile. "Is it strange riding past here?"

The bus groaned into gear and forced itself forward. "Not really," he said. "I don't remember the accident itself. It's more like I remember being told about the accident." As if suddenly aware that she was watching him, he turned to face her. "Just thought I'd point out all the sights." He ended with his barklike laugh.

Faith Lives operated out of an evangelical church that had once been some sort of warehouse or showroom. A low-slung brick building, it was separated by a deep car park from Eastern Avenue, the main thoroughfare from Boutport center to the M5, which continued south past Exeter and east to London. Suzanne had had to ask three bus drivers at the Boutport depot before she found one who had heard of the organization and knew where it was.

It was just a fifteen-minute walk from the station. Richard would have been able to make it in ten before the accident. He was having trouble bending his left knee this morning. Funny how the symptoms of the damage shifted from day to day. Sometimes his knee was fine but then red-streaked pains would set off sparks the length of his thigh when he walked for more than a few minutes. Sometimes he couldn't force his spine to straighten up and he'd spend the better part of a day listing to the right, which in turn made all his other movements off-kilter. The changeability of his physical ailments mirrored that of his memory. All the parts were operable, but not all at the same time. Or, you could argue, all the parts were damaged, in one way or another.

Inside the church, a middle-aged woman sat at a metal desk just beyond the foyer. She was the sort of woman you expected to find handling clerical tasks at a church: shapeless, ageless, her brown hair short and styleless. But she had an impeccable manicure, her long nails polished a deep coral-pink.

No, Declan isn't expecting us, Suzanne told her. Yes, we can wait. Would it be all right if we wait outside so that we can have a cigarette? Thanks so much.

Outside Suzanne paced the length of the church. Lorries rumbled and belched along the avenue. Across the street was a Vauxhall dealership. Tidy huddles of budding plants quivered from the rush of the passing vehicles.

"Hello, I'm Declan. I believe you wanted to see me?" He looked just a few years older than Richard, with a thick head of strawberry-blond curls, and stood only a few inches taller than Suzanne.

Suzanne took a final drag before grinding out her cigarette with the toe of her trainer. Holding out her hand, she said, "Ruth at Serenity House in Billicombe said you might know how I could find my friend Jack. Jay."

Declan nodded. Richard suspected that Ruth had called Declan after they'd left her office. "Come in." He held the door open for them.

His office was at the back of the church, past a small kitchen cluttered with stainless-steel surfaces. Dozens of fliers and memos and lists and schedules were Blu-Tacked to the office walls, which were lumpy with layers of paint. Declan nodded at them to sit on the folding chairs facing his desk, a metal one similar to the one in the entryway, though Declan's had duct tape wrapped around the front left leg.

"Ruth emailed me. I think I know who you're talking about, although I don't know his surname. He told us his name was Jay, and he arrived in Billicombe about a year ago from Sussex. Thin, blonde, very long fingers?"

Suzanne nodded. Her legs were crossed, and her right leg, the one on top, was jiggling furiously, so that the legs of her chair beat a manic tattoo against the lino floor. "Do you know where he is now?"

"What is your relationship to him?" Declan stroked his chin, ignoring Richard, focusing on Suzanne.

"He's an old friend of mine. We grew up together. We'd stayed in touch until last November or so, when his mobile was disconnected and he stopped answering my letters." As Suzanne's voice grew quieter, it also became rougher, raspier.

Declan nodded. "That's around the time we lost touch with him too. I have no idea where he might be. I tried looking for him. In Billicombe, and here, I've always been involved in community outreach. Basically we go out at night and early morning to the areas where the homeless are known to gather. Alcoholics. Drug addicts. We bring them sandwiches and tea, try to get them to come to one of our shelters, get them interested in a recovery program. I thought I'd see Jay during one of those. But I never did." He tugged at the sandy lashes of his right eye, as if something were stuck in them. "I asked. Plenty of people knew who I was talking about, but only one offered a suggestion as to where he might have gone. This person thought he'd maybe gone to Cornwall."

Suzanne leaned forward, her wrists settling on the edge of the desk. "Where in Cornwall?"

Declan shook his head. "He didn't say. He wasn't even sure if that's where Jay had gone."

"Was Jay using?"

Declan wheeled his chair back to the small window behind him. On the ledge a pack of cigarettes sat in a glass ashtray. He retrieved them, slid the ashtray toward the center of his desk, next to a framed picture that Richard could only see the back of. He lit up, then seeing Suzanne pull out her own cigarettes from her bag, passed her the lighter.

"He started drinking again near the end of the summer. Or it could have been earlier, and he'd just hidden it better. The first time I knew he was drunk was during the August bank holiday weekend. He'd come by Serenity House. He was helping us decorate our float for the October carnival. He spilled a can of blue paint over his trainers and couldn't seem to mop it up. He was trying to scoop up the paint with his hands."

Richard glanced at Suzanne. Her face was expressionless as she waited for Declan to continue.

"I tried to persuade him to sign up for the Serenity House residency program. He said no, something about not wanting to take any more money from his sister. I told him that he wouldn't have to worry about the cost, we'd work that out, but he was adamant. He said he'd go back to AA. I even offered to put him up at my flat, but he said no. Thank you, but no."

"Do you always offer to put up drunks and junkies at your flat?" Suzanne asked, not in an accusatory way but with real curiosity, almost as if the drunk in question weren't someone she'd flown halfway across the world to find.

Declan offered a tight smile, his top lip disappearing. "No. But I liked Jay. He'd really seemed to be trying. After a while you can tell the ones who truly want to get clean and stay clean, and the ones who are just going through the motions because it's part of their probation or because that's the only way their family will agree to let them stay or because they think they can game the system. But I didn't think Jay was like that. He talked about how hard it was for him." He shook his head and flicked his cigarette, oblivious to the ash missing the tray and splattering onto his desktop. "I really liked him."

"Do you think he's dead?"

Declan puffed out his cheeks. "If he'd passed away around here, we'd have been notified. Anyone who's found without ID, they call us and the other community groups. Though maybe they'd have contacted this sister of his, but even then I'm sure we would have heard."

Richard thought Suzanne had said Jack had no family. Though that could be his memory toying with him again.

Suzanne turned her head away to avoid exhaling smoke in Declan's or Richard's face. "Do you think I should try Cornwall next?"

Declan raised his hands, palms up toward the ceiling. "It would be like searching for a needle in a haystack, wouldn't it? We do have affiliates in Cornwall, and I haven't heard of anyone coming across him."

Suzanne rattled the cigarette pack in her hand. "So what do you think I should do next?"

Declan ground out his cigarette, staring into the ashtray, saying nothing.

"Who's this person who told you that he'd gone to Cornwall?"

Declan looked up, this time including Richard in his gaze. "I only know him as Valley. I didn't even know he was an associate of Jay's. I think he's still in Billicombe."

"Where would I find him?"

Declan wiped the corners of his mouth with his fingertips. "I think he started showing up at the Serenity House drop-in center shortly before I left in November. And I think you can find him at the Lloyds Pharmacy on the High Street in Billicombe most mornings."

"Lloyds?"

Either Declan hadn't heard her, or he was pretending he hadn't.

"That's where the junkies get their methadone every morning," Richard said.

They just missed the 3 bus back to Billicombe, which meant a twenty-minute wait for the next one. Suzanne didn't suggest getting something to eat, so Richard didn't either, though his stomach was beginning to echo with hunger. They hadn't had breakfast; Suzanne had offered him a diet soda but nothing else.

It wasn't a large bus station, though it was the central point of the bus system for North Devon. Four carrels, each of them sheltered on one side by a long Perspex wall with an intermittent railing about hip height that younger kids jumped up on to use as a bench. Teenagers tended to sit on the ground, while the adults stood with their shoulders against the wall. No one paid attention to the No Smoking signs, including the drivers who wandered about in their fluorescent yellow safety vests between trips.

For a good ten minutes they were the only people at this particular carrel. Suzanne leaned against the shelter, one foot flat against the Perspex, smoking, every so often blowing the hair out of her eyes. Richard hadn't known she could be so still; usually she was shifting her weight from leg to leg or bouncing in her seat or scanning the faces around her. Now she was nearly as motionless as the sky, which was logy and dense with a barely gray, barely moving cloud cover.

A woman holding the hand of a girl who looked about eight, old enough to be in school, joined them. The mother sat her bags from Primark and Iceland onto the pavement but continued to clutch the smaller bag from Boots. The girl scratched her head, her eyes narrowed in concentration. The mother swatted the girl's hand away, but within seconds the girl resumed scratching. She probably had lice, and that was why she was off school. Richard inched away, toward Suzanne.

The girl leaned forward to examine Richard and Suzanne, then tugged her mother's wrist. "Mum, isn't that Robin from *Lakeview Drive*?"

Her mother, reading a sheet of instructions from whatever box was in the Boots bag, didn't look up. "I don't think so."

The girl tugged harder. "Mum, look!"

The woman gave in. "Mmm, it does look a little like her."

At which point Suzanne turned toward them and smiled. "I wish! I get that all the time." She spoke in a full-on London accent, rather than her usual neither-here-nor-there drawl.

"See, I told you," the mother said, returning to the instructions. "Besides, an actress from the telly wouldn't be waiting for a bus here, would she?"

The girl didn't seem convinced. She kept sneaking glances at Suzanne until the bus finally pulled up.

Suzanne headed straight to the back. Richard joined her on the last seat, the one that stretched across the width of the bus. "What's *Lakeview Drive*?"

Suzanne shook her hair onto her face. "It was some telly program apparently, and I guess one of the actresses looks like me." She turned away from Richard to look out the window, even though the bus hadn't started moving yet. "Personally I don't see it. That actress is much prettier, and blond."

She was still speaking in a London accent. "Which is your real accent?" he asked.

"What do you mean?"

"Right now you're speaking like a Londoner, aren't you? But most other times you sound half American."

"Which half?"

He decided to ape her usual approach, and waited.

She turned toward him. "I told you. I'm originally from Deptford, but we moved to America when I was ten. So my accent shifts around a bit."

"Why did you move?"

The bus lurched forward. Waiting until it lumbered out of the station and on to the street, she said, "My older brother was a child actor. He got a part in a U.S. TV show. It only lasted one year, but by then we all liked living there, so we stayed."

He realized he didn't even know her surname. Unless she'd told him and he'd forgot. "What's his name?"

She shook her head. "I'm not going to say."

"Why not?"

She grinned. "Did anyone ever tell you that you're a nosy so-and-so?"

He couldn't help but laugh. "Not really. So, who's your brother?"

She shook her head again, a piece of hair sticking against the corner of her mouth. "I'm not going to say. You can ask me anything else, but this I'm not going to tell you. Because when his show was on, all the kids at school wanted to be friends with me just because of my brother. He was even on the cover of teen magazines for a time. So I just make it a point never to say."

He tugged his fingers through the spiky layers at the top of his head. He knew she was lying. There were no obvious signs—her eyes weren't darting away from his face, nor was she staring too intently at him. She wasn't rubbing the side of her nose or stammering. But he somehow knew.

"Is this Jack you're looking for your brother?"

She shook her head. "No."

"Is he an old boyfriend?"

She laughed. "Christ, no!"

There was something odd about the laughter. "Is he gay? Is that why you're laughing?"

Her smile faded, replaced by absolutely no expression at all. "Depends what you mean by gay."

"Gay. You know, queer."

The bus had sidled to a stop, and several elderly women were heaving themselves on board, leaning heavily on the rail to hoist themselves up toward the driver. Suzanne watched them. "If you mean does he sometimes suck off men for money or a fix, yeah. If you mean does he date men when he's sober, no."

Richard felt his face burn. Looking away from her, he concentrated on rolling himself a cigarette, even though he had another half-hour until his stop.

When he arrived back at his flat Richard headed straight for his laptop. He searched for "Lakeview Drive" on Google, embarrassed by how pleased he was to have remembered the name. The first listing was the program's official website. He clicked through to an overly busy Flash page; upbeat music with an obtrusive drum track startled him. He hated websites that burst into sound without some sort of pop-up or button asking permission for the aural intrusion. A carousel of images of various teenagers, characters in the show he guessed, rotated against the screen. The girl in the fourth image looked like it could be a blond, rounder version of Suzanne.

He clicked on the image. It took him to a page about the character, Robin. "Played by Soozie Northrup."

"Because her older sister, Morgan, has had so many problems with school, drinking, and boys, Robin feels the need to be the 'good girl.' She studies hard, gets good grades, plays violin in the school orchestra, and tries to smooth out any differences between Morgan and their parents. Sometimes, though, she's jealous of the attention that Morgan gets and wishes that she could be a little wild herself. Her first serious boyfriend was Daniel, but she broke up with him when he became too controlling. This year she decided to travel around Europe instead of going to college, but her home will always be on LAKEVIEW DRIVE."

And below that:

"About Soozie Northrup: Soozie was born in London, England, but moved to California when she was 10 and landed a role in 'Ten Acres.' She's acted in more than a dozen films and TV movies, including 'The Youngest Musketeer' and 'Home from Far,' before landing the part of Robin in LAKEVIEW DRIVE. Like Robin, her favorite subject is English, but she doesn't play the violin."

He looked through the photo gallery. The actress who played Robin was much more feminine than Suzanne, her blond hair long and usually held off her face with a barrette. Her face was softer in the photos, the chin not so pointed, the cheekbones not so sharp. But though her lips were heavily glossed, they were the same rosebud shape as Suzanne's. And the eyes, the huge round eyes.

He returned to Google and typed in "Soozie Northrup." An IMDB listing was the first entry. The IMDB page had a gallery of thumbnail images along the top, and below that some brief biographical information. She really had been born in Deptford, and—he called up the calendar function on his computer to check what year it was now—she really was twenty-one. He scrolled down to the "News Desk" section of the page. "Soozie Northrup confirms that this is her final season at Lakeview Drive"; "Soozie Northrup signed to remake of 'Bell, Book, and Candle'"; "Soozie Northrup's brother arrested for disorderly conduct." He clicked that last link. It took him to an article from a wire service:

"The brother of 'Lakeview Drive' star Soozie Northrup was arrested for disorderly conduct on Saturday after he was found unconscious in the parking lot of the Century City Shopping Center. Jackson Northrup, 24, was released on bail."

CHAPTER 4

The misting of rain was cold enough to sting, as if it were pine needles rather than near-invisible droplets being flung into her face. It felt good, though, was keeping her awake.

Maybe setting the alarm for five a.m. and forcing herself to polish off that bottle of cheap wine she'd bought the day before hadn't been such a bright idea. But Suzanne figured that if she was going to be milling about with junkies, she should do her best to fit in. Method acting.

The ground was soggy, and sometimes her foot got lodged in the mud. There were no sidewalks along this part of the road leading down to the High Street, because there were no houses. It was farmland on either side. A few horses in coats the color of shadow chowed down on grass as she passed. The sky was colorless and flat. The sun must have risen, though, otherwise the sky would be black, right?

She stumbled off the grass and onto the street. She'd better pay closer attention. She couldn't watch her feet as she walked, though. It made her dizzy, and queasy.

Some sort of baying in the distance. From the left or the right, she wasn't sure. Or if it was sheep or cows or goats. At least she was growing used to the stench of the farm animals and their shit.

When she got to town she was going to sit out front of the Lloyds and take a nap. She'd fit right in with the junkies, all right.

The rain had dissipated by the time she reached the High Street, but its barbed chill lingered. A group of kids in school uniforms—white polo shirts, navy trousers and skirts, blazers with gold insignia on the chest pocket—their coats tied around their waists or slung over their arms, jostled for cover under the bus shelter in front of the petrol station, sharing bags of sweets and huddling over notebooks. They made a point of looking away as she passed by. Good. That's all she needed, some kid taking a picture of her on his mobile and posting it online. "Soozie from Lakeview Drive wasted @ 8am. LOL!"

A woman in high-heeled pumps clacked past in the opposite direction, staring straight ahead. What did they call those shoes here? She should know this. Court shoes, that's it. An older man, buttoned up in a mac, passed as well, his Jack Russell meandering behind him on a lead.

So this what was it was like to be invisible. No wonder people got high. How invisible could she be? If she walked into this mailbox coming up, would the man across the street sweeping the patch of pavement outside his veg shop look up? Whoa—she almost did walk into that mailbox there. She clamped her lips shut to stop from laughing out loud.

She leaned against the soaped-up window of a closed-down shop to light a smoke. She had to shut one eye to get the flame to connect with the tip of the cigarette.

Right. The Lloyds was across the street. She checked both ways for traffic, checked again before stepping into the road. She concentrated on walking as straight a line as possible, but that only made her stagger. Fuck that, then. Or should it be Sod that. She was going to have to remember to speak in her London accent.

The minimart was open. She hesitated at the doorway. She was thirsty, could do with a Diet Coke. And maybe a sandwich. But that would absorb the alcohol, and she didn't want to sober up just yet. Ever, really. She felt herself smile and moved on.

She passed an alleyway. A man and a woman, both huddled in jackets, were smoking and stomping their feet. Suzanne turned into it. "What time does the Lloyds open?" Her words were taking longer to emerge than she expected. She waited for them to catch up with her.

"Nine o'clock," the bloke said. His hair was grizzled gray around his face, darker along the top.

"Cheers." She rested her head against the brick wall and closed her eyes for a few seconds. The alley smelled of piss. She imagined stink lines, like in a cartoon, surrounding her.

"You have a light?" The grizzled bloke stood so close she felt his words push onto her cheeks.

"Yeah, sure." She fumbled in her back pocket for the lighter, dropped it while fishing it out. He bent down and retrieved it for her, lit his roll-up, and handed it back. Dirt was embedded in his nails and cuticles, and the tips of his thumbs and forefingers were stained nicotine yellow and sludge brown.

"Do you know what time it is?" Suzanne dug her cigarettes out of her pocket as well. Her fingers felt swollen.

The man peered out onto the street. A near-steady stream of people were striding past. "Must be getting on to nine now." He had a Scouse accent. Suzanne wondered what had brought him down here.

"Do you know some bloke named Valley?" she asked.

The man looked back at his companion, who was wiping her nose with her forefinger. "Maybe. I've seen him around."

"Know where I can find him?" The words were slipping out nice and easy now.

"Why do you want to know?" The man took a sharp drag off his fag, exhaled the smoke with an equally sharp burst.

"He's a friend of a friend. My friend told me to look him up."

The bloke nodded but stepped away without saying anything.

Suzanne lowered her lids enough so that she'd appear to be dozing, but from beneath her lashes she watched the pair of them out of the corner of her eye. Once the man finished his smoke they headed toward the High Street. Suzanne counted to twenty, then followed.

A young woman, maybe her own age, was unlocking the doors of the pharmacy from the inside, crouching down to release the bottom lock, then standing on tiptoes to reach the top one. The man and woman from the alley followed her inside. Suzanne leaned against the window, as if waiting for someone. She really had to pee. The pressure on her bladder was sobering her up, not gradually but in chunky increments, like some sort of time-lapse photography. Is that how long a period of drunkenness lasted, just a few hours? She didn't have many memories of her father, but in each of the few that remained, he was in some stage of intoxication. Loosey-goosey, taking long strides, arms swinging with abandon, head thrown back in laughter. Pissed as a fart, short shambling paces, right eye hooded, left eye nearly shut in a squint. Dead drunk, cheek crashed against the kitchen table, white spittle caked in the corners of his mouth. She couldn't recall him without a drink in hand, or to hand, or having fallen out of his hand and puddling on the floor beside him.

Christ, she didn't know how much longer she could wait before her bladder exploded. She'd count to a hundred and watch for anyone else who looked vaguely disreputable to walk by. Then she'd have to find a toilet. The petrol station?

A woman with dyed yellow hair falling out of a messy bun stepped around her. "Excuse me," Suzanne called out, shifting from one foot to the next, "do you know someone named Valley?"

The woman didn't pause as she swung open the door to Lloyds. She jerked her head past Suzanne. "That's him coming up behind you."

Suzanne turned around. Marching toward her, head down, legs far enough apart that a good-size dog could scamper through, was the ponytailed guy from the snooker table and the twelve-step meeting. Lee.

She waited till he was a few paces away. If he recognized her, he didn't show it.

"Hey, Valley!"

He jerked his head up, then reared back, as if surprised to see her. He wore black rectangular sunglasses, even though the sun was making no effort to thrust its way through the dense, soiled clouds. "Anne! I'm glad I found you."

"I found you, you mean." She crossed her legs. Please don't let her piss herself.

He nodded. "I lost your number. But I wanted to ring you."

"And...?"

He nodded at the chemist's door. "I have to go in and pick up a scrip."

"Should I come with you, or should I wait?"

He looked away. "It may take a while."

"How about I meet you somewhere in about twenty minutes?"

He rubbed his nose, then the stubble on his cheeks. The furrows running down them seemed etched in black. "The alley next to the minimart?"

"Fine."

She raced to the petrol station, bought a Diet Coke, an egg-and-bacon sandwich, cigarettes, and a *Guardian*, then after paying asked as casually as she could manage if she could use the loo. The kid behind the counter hesitated, scratching the rash of pimples on his cheek. "Please. I know I'm not looking my best, but it's an emergency. I won't make a mess." Pause. "Come on, I bought the *Guardian*. People who read the *Guardian* don't foul toilets." It worked.

A dull thudding was already making its way to the front of her head. But at least her bladder was empty. She hurried out, unscrewing the soda as she left the petrol station, half running. She crossed the High Street—lots of traffic now, she had to dart in front of a Royal Mail truck on the one side and a camper van on the other. She dashed past the minimart, stopped to look down the alley. Lee wasn't there. She hadn't expected him to be. Hopefully he was still in the chemists so that she could nab him on his way out.

The man and woman she'd stood in the alley with earlier emerged, red faced, as if they'd spent too long in a tanning bed. The man nodded as they passed, the woman's arm around his waist.

Suzanne ripped into half of the sandwich, punctuating each bite with a swig of soda. She felt foggy now, but not intoxicated. All the drawbacks of tying one on without the benefits. She turned to peer into the Lloyds. Even craning her neck she couldn't spot him. Shit. She closed the plastic triangular packaging around the remaining half of a sandwich and went inside. Down the center aisle to the prescription desk in the back. Several elderly people, but not Lee. Up the last aisle, past a woman comparing antacids. Over to the first aisle, with the locked glass cabinets of perfumes. Nothing.

A door in the back, beside the prescription counter, opened. Lee emerged, face flushed and shiny, the skin tight across his features. She met him in the aisle. "Hi." She tilted her head, blinking deliberately a few times, and folded her arms across her chest, letting him know that she knew he'd been hoping to skip out on her.

He pulled his sunglasses down from the top of his head onto his face once more, his shoulders round with resignation.

They walked to the alley. As soon as they got there Lee slid down onto the asphalt and, sitting cross-legged, rolled a cigarette. His hands trembled, but just a little. Several yards away, close to where the alley began its descent toward the Promenade, water coughed out in spurts from a drainpipe. She hadn't noticed before how dank the alley was, pitted with shallow puddles and splattered with viscous globs of white bird shit. She remained standing. "So, what did you want to tell me?"

He patted the ground next to him. "Why don't you sit? I'm getting a cramp in my neck looking up."

"Why don't you stand?"

He barely stifled a sigh. "Because I need to sit for a minute."

She was feeling somewhat shaky herself. Kicking away a cigarette butt, she sat opposite him, hugging her knees. The dampness of the ground seeped through the seat of her jeans.

"I remembered that guy you were looking for. Jack. Only I knew him as Jay." He patted the pockets of his hoodie. "Can I use your lighter? Cheers." After aiming a stream of smoke above her head, he said, "I knew him a bit from when we were both using. But I haven't seen him in months. Since the autumn. When I got clean. I think he said he was heading up to Bristol, he had friends there."

"Bristol? Not Cornwall?"

Another jet propulsion of smoke. "No. I'm pretty sure it was Bristol."

She wished he'd take his sunglasses off. "Did he get clean too?"

Lee wriggled one arm out of his sweatshirt, then the other, finally tugging it over his head, briefly dislodging his shades. He blinked before putting them back on. The collar of his pale gray T-shirt was limp and dark with sweat. "I don't know. I think that's why he was heading to Bristol."

"Do you know who his friends in Bristol were?"

"Nope. I've never been myself."

"When did he start using again?"

"You're not a cop or something, are you?" He clambered to his feet, using the wall as leverage.

Suzanne stood up too, ignoring the way the ground threatened to rise up with her. "I told you. I'm just a friend. I've been worried sick." As if on cue, at the word "sick" she felt the sandwich trying to make its way upward. She swallowed hard.

"I don't know what else to tell you," Lee said.

"When did he start using again?"

He shrugged. "I don't know. I think he was using on and off the entire time he was here."

He had to be lying. Declan said Jax had really been trying to stay straight. And from his letters and the phone calls, she was sure he'd been sober. He'd never fooled her for such a long time before. Though he'd never been away for such a long time.

Lee headed back to the High Street. Suzanne lengthened her stride to keep up with him. "One more thing: Why're you called Valley?"

He stopped short and turned to her. His lips were pursed in surprise, as if that was the last question he'd expected. "Lee Valley—it's a campground not far from here."

"Oh."

He turned right onto the High Street, bolting into the street to skirt past a woman using a Zimmer frame and a bored-looking man pushing a stroller. She headed the opposite way, to the bus stop.

CHAPTER 5

Pam's hand hovered above the scars, but Richard could feel it nonetheless. Feel the air currents from the tremble of her fingers roiling the sliced, diced, tangled, mangled nerve endings beneath his inflamed skin, their coolness at odds with the heat from her hand. And he could feel her staring at the scars.

They sickened Pam. He could tell by the way her hand wavered in horror above them, by the sharpness of her breathing as she stared.

"They'll fade," he said. He was lying stomach down across the bed. His left leg was still in a brace, and he was more concerned about that. The doctors said there was a chance that it would heal up to an inch shorter than his right leg. "And I can keep my shirt on if they bother you." Because he was already thinking about when they'd finally have sex again. She might not want to stroke his back, and to be honest, the nerves that had been severed during the operation were so hypersensitive that he didn't want his back stroked, though he'd been assured that the sensitivity would fade in a matter of months.

Pam didn't reply. She finally put her hand on the bed beside him, but she didn't say anything.

The buzzer rang. "Pam, can you get that?"

Only Pam wasn't there. And he was not stretched out in their bedroom. He stood in front of the kettle, stirring a cup of tea. His vision shattered, as it always did when he was startled out of one time into another, shattered and blurred and then crystallized again.

The buzzer. He squinched his eyes shut. Focus. His name was Richard Sommers. He lived in Billicombe, Devon. He was twenty... fuck, when was he born? Okay, calm down, breathe, skip that one. He was a website designer, currently between jobs.

That goddam buzzer. He stumbled through the lounge, through the vestibule to the front door. The girl at the door, she wasn't Pam. She was shorter. Younger. Wilder, darker hair. He knew her, though. Deep breath, slow down.

Samantha. No, Suzanne. No... He pinched the bridge of his nose and saw her image on his computer screen. "Soozie."

She tilted her head, shaking her hair onto her face. "Suzanne."

"Soozie Northrup," he said, and felt a ping of satisfaction as she bit her lip and turned away.

"Can I use your toilet?" she asked.

He let her in, followed her back to his flat. "Why do you spell it like that, by the way?"

"It was my mother's idea." Her voice was so taut, it seemed to slice her throat. She stalked through the lounge, to the loo.

He was standing next to the blocked-up fireplace, rolling a cigarette atop the mantel when she emerged. Her face was dewy, as if she'd just washed, and she smelled of toothpaste. She stared below his waist. "You might want to put some trousers on."

Shit. He was wearing only his boxers. He checked that his johnson wasn't peering out the flap, then sidled past her to his room, rooting around for a pair of jeans. When he returned she was perched on the sofa, smoking.

"I didn't tell you because the last thing I need is word getting out: 'Soozie Northrup is hunting for her drug-addict friend.'"

"Brother."

She didn't flinch as she flicked her ashes into the teacup he'd been using last night as an ashtray. "Brother," she conceded with a nod. She picked up the cup, her lip curled. "That really is disgusting." She stood and walked over to the folding table behind the sofa, hunting through the piles of bills and papers in search of an ashtray. "Besides, does it matter?"

He scanned the room for his tobacco. There it was, on the mantel. And a half-filled cigarette as well. He licked the papers, fitted on a filter. He could see her point. It wasn't as if they really knew each other anyway. "No, I guess not."

She came back round to the sofa, ashtray in hand. "Good. But you won't go telling anyone, right?"

"I'll probably forget all about it tomorrow." He smiled. She beamed in reply. Odd how elastic her face was. Or how fickle her expressions. Though it was probably all part of being an actress. How could you ever know when to believe an actress?

"Okay. Good. Well, I came here to ask your opinion about something, but—" she waved her hand at the stacks on the table, the cup-as-ashtray, the two empty beer cans on the floor "—you don't seem to be having a good day."

"No, it's fine." Wait, hadn't he been doing something in the kitchen? He had left something there, he knew it. Deep breath. Never mind. If it was important, it would come to him. Stop obsessing. Concentrate on now. He eased himself into the armchair, hands gripping the sides as if they might disappear along with whatever it was he'd been doing or thinking about two minutes earlier.

"Okay. Well, I just met up with that Valley bloke. And he said that Jax had gone off to Bristol, not Cornwall. He also said that Jax had been using off and on for months before he left. But I'm not sure I believe him. I mean, Declan is much more credible, right?"

Valley. Jax. Declan. These were supposed to mean something to him, but he didn't know what. Bristol, Cornwall—those were places, that much he knew. But the rest... Okay, stay calm. Deep breath. And another. Maybe not so deep next time. He was getting dizzy, the here and now receding. This chair—was it his? He didn't remember buying it. Or that sofa. But they were his, weren't they? This was his flat, wasn't it? His name was...

Fuck. It wasn't the room, the place, and the time that were sliding away, escaping his grasp. It was his self. He scrabbled for some simple fact to grab on to, but he couldn't extend far enough into the murk, just as he couldn't seize enough air to fill his lungs, to keep his heart going.

"Richard?" The girl—what the fuck was her name? He'd had it, just seconds ago, he knew he had—she was in his face now, so close he could make out a few tiny freckles below her left eye, could count the individual lashes just above them. She knelt beside him, looking up at him. "Richard, it's Suzanne. We met a few days ago. I came here just now to use your toilet and to talk to you. We're in your flat. It's Thursday, late morning." Her voice was low, calm, rough-soft in the same way as a cat's tongue. Not that he could remember ever being licked by a cat. Did he have a cat?

"I'm going to make you a cup of tea," the girl, Suzanne, said. "Do you like it plain?"

How did he like his tea? "Plain."

"Okay." She curved her palm around his right knee. His good knee. He'd injured his left leg. In the accident. And the accident was why he was having a problem with his memory.

Okay. He was making progress. He was able to scrape together a normal breath this time, enough to inflate his lungs, to keep him going until the next breath. He had a cigarette between his fingers. He brought it to his lips. His hand trembled. Inhale. Exhale.

"I'll be right back." She disappeared behind him. He heard water coming out of a tap. That must be his kitchen. He was in his flat. He lived in Billicombe, Devon. This chair had been Pam's, from her flat, in London, before they'd moved in together. Okay, good. It had been her grandmother's. Pam was always saying she wanted to get it reupholstered because she hated the chintz fabric. But they'd never got around to it. Why hadn't she taken the chair with her when she left him? Because she hated it, probably. She'd been tired of it, so she'd left it. Just as she'd left him.

That he remembered.

Samantha—no, Suzanne, Suzanne returned with a cup of tea on a saucer. He didn't remember having saucers. She placed it on the side table, carefully, then sat on the edge of the sofa, knees primly together.

"I'm sorry about this," he managed to say.

"Don't be. It's okay. Really." She scanned the room. "Do you remember who I am?"

"Suzanne." He looked around for an ashtray. She handed it to him. He saw her image on the computer screen again. "Aka Soozie Northrup. Who spells her name that way because it was her mother's idea." That was better. He was better. Or at least getting better.

She gave half a grin, only the left side of her mouth lifting, then lit another cigarette. "That must be scary, losing yourself like that."

He nodded, sipped some tea. Steady. Inhale. Exhale. Okay. He was in control again.

"It happened to Jax a few times. Different reason, of course." She rubbed her right eye with her index finger.

"You look tired," he said.

"And hung over." She watched the tiny fire eat away at the end of her cigarette. "I don't think you should be here alone right now."

"I'm fine," he said, but she spoke over him: "So how about if I stay with you for a few hours?"

"You don't have to. This happens a lot. I'm fine now." He spoke loudly, to subdue the quaver in his voice.

With her palms she pushed her hair off her face. Her eyes dwarfed the rest of her features. "Okay, then how about letting me crash here for a few hours? I could really use a nap."

She did look shattered. Her face seemed bloodless. "Sure," he said.

She took off her trainers, tucking them under the sofa so that only the toes were visible, and curled up against the armrest like a hedgehog in defense mode, finishing her cigarette. He stood up to pass her the ashtray. She mustered a faint smile.

"Are you okay?" he asked.

"Of course," she said, briskly. "I'm always okay." She stubbed out her fag and leaned forward to put the ashtray on the coffee table.

He remained standing, rubbing the back of his head, trying to remember what he'd planned to do with his day. He spied a magazine, *Web Designer,* on one of the chairs surrounding the folding table. He picked it up and brought it back to the couch. He sat on the opposite end from Suzanne, who was already asleep, her face hidden against her knees.

"Are you sure you're going to be all right here?" Suzanne asked, bending down to tie her trainers.

"Yes, Mum." The exasperation in Richard's voice was only slightly exaggerated.

Suzanne stood up, shaking her hair onto her face. "Where is your family, anyway? I mean, are they okay with you living on your own like this?"

"They live in Cypress." Richard closed the lid of his laptop and stood up as well, rounding his spine forward to loosen his back muscles.

"And they didn't come back when they heard about your accident?"

"I didn't tell them how bad it was." From the moment she'd woken up, it had been like this: fussing, questioning, nagging. "How about your parents?" he countered. "Are they out there looking for your brother too?"

Suzanne grabbed her cigarettes from the coffee table. "I haven't seen my father in eons. And my mum washed her hands of Jax years ago. She doesn't even know he's missing." She stood stock still for a moment, then shook her head again and felt her pockets, making sure she had her keys. She didn't have her bag with her this time.

"You haven't told her?"

She tossed him a grin utterly lacking in mirth. "We don't speak much. It's complicated." Cocking her head, she asked, "Do you talk to your folks much?"

"Oh yeah. They call every other week or so, I think. They're cool."

"You probably didn't tell them about your memory thing because you didn't want to worry them, right?" Suzanne lit a cigarette for the road.

"Yup." He headed to the door, to usher her out.

"That's probably why Jax didn't tell me he was using again," Suzanne said. She looked beyond Richard, beyond the hallway leading to the loo. "But he was wrong. He should have told me."

Walking to the bus stop, Suzanne solidified her plans. Tomorrow morning, before sun-up, she was going to head to Riker Road. She suspected there'd be more junkies out and about at six a.m. than midafternoon. And then she was going to head into Boutport to try to track down Pam for Richard.

First, though, she had to call Larry. It was about 3:30 when she arrived back at the trailer, which meant 7:30 in the morning in L.A. He'd be at his desk by now.

And he was. She and Larry had known each other for years. She'd even spent the occasional weekend at his home, and when she'd sent Jax to rehab that last time, he'd offered to talk with the *Lakeview Drive* producers to get her some time off. "You could take yourself away to a spa for a week. Or the Caribbean. Take some time to regroup." She'd told him thanks but no; if she had too much time on her hands she'd ungroup instead of regroup. So he knew enough not to ask again where she was or what she was doing, for which she was grateful.

Instead he told her about a film the agency was trying to package. They had the script, the director, Davis Jeffrey as one of the leads... "Oh," she said, already disinterested. She opened the minifridge, hoping there was a soda in there that she'd forgotten about.

"You'd be playing brother and sister, not a couple. You'd be slinging insults at him for the most part."

"Oh, that's different!" She giggled as she closed the fridge door. "But wait, you haven't told me what this script is about."

She heard Larry take a deep breath three thousand miles away. "*American Pie* meets Jane Austen."

"You're kidding me, right?"

"I couldn't make up something like that. Actually, it's not bad."

"Larry, if it's *American Pie* meets Jane Austen, it's got to be bad."

"Should I send you the script anyway?"

"Oh, yeah, definitely. This'll be good for a laugh."

"Where should I send it to?"

She paused. "Send it to a friend of mine, Richard Sommers. But address it to Suzanne, care of. Here's the address." She listened to his fingers peck away at his keyboard.

"So you're not in New York, then?"

"No, I told you, I flew into Heathrow, not JFK. Why?"

He chuckled. "According to yesterday's Page 6, you were drunk in a club in the East Village on Tuesday night, dancing on a table and then 'canoodling' with a New York Ranger."

"The Page 6 me is having a much more exciting time than the real me, that's for sure." She giggled again, until she realized... "Shit, did my mum call you yesterday?"

"Yup. So if you could call her sometime today, the entire admin staff would really appreciate it."

She headed to the caravan park's convenience store-cum-reception area, to arm herself with a two-liter bottle of Diet Coke before getting the call to her mother over with. The shelves were nearly as empty as the park itself. Huge gaps between the handful of soda bottles and cereal boxes, the main freezer dark and warm, a lone peach yogurt and two bottles of milk in the fridge.

That was one of the reasons she'd opted to stay here rather than a hotel; she was counting on a near-absence of people. The park had only just opened for the season the week before she'd arrived, to accommodate those hardy souls willing to gamble that the four-day Easter weekend would be gloriously bright and breezy, ideal for hiking in nearby Exmoor and strolling along the Promenade at dusk, rather than sodden and blustery, fit only for shivering in a dank caravan, nose pressed against the windowpane.

The fewer people around, the less likelihood of anyone recognizing her. But that wasn't her primary consideration. The fewer people around, the less likelihood of anyone witnessing her dragging a strung-out, filthy Jax into her accommodations.

During the coach trip from Heathrow to Billicombe—nearly six hours, what with the airport traffic, and the change of buses in Bristol, and the stops in Taunton and a few other towns she couldn't recall—Suzanne had tried to focus on the passing scenery. She'd tried to calculate, when they rode by a petrol station, how much more expensive fuel was here than in California. She'd tried to appreciate the beauty of the green countryside, so garish and profligate compared with the half-dead brush of the hills of Southern California. But her mind's eye insisted on anticipating her eventual meeting with Jax.

None of the scenarios she envisioned were optimistic. She knew she wouldn't come across him as he sauntered down the street dressed in a suit and tie, swinging a briefcase, or clad in a fluorescent yellow vest out with a construction crew. No, she'd find him in a pub, head down on a table in the back, stringy hair splayed across his shoulders, revealing a ring of grime around his nape. Or slumped in an alley, oblivious to the sludge he was seated among, fresh bruises atop older ones. Or crouching amid some shrubs, barefoot as he shot up between his toes, the veins in his arms long since collapsed, thick green pus pulsating from an abscess on the back of his hand.

But at least she'd envisioned finding him. She hadn't allowed herself to imagine that she wouldn't.

Back at the cabin, she lit a cigarette and rang her mother on her mobile (when had she stopped thinking of it as a cell phone?), bracing herself against the front door for support.

"Hi, Mum..."

"So what're you getting up to in New York, then?"

"Hello, Mum. Yes, I'm doing fine, thank you for asking. And you?"

"Larry told me he thought you were in India or someplace godforsaken like that. Where are you?" When her mother strained not to let her anger show, her voice rose a half-octave, and she bit down heavy on her consonants.

"I'm in New York. But not dancing on any tabletops."

"What are you doing out there? And why didn't you tell me you were going? Who's watching your house?"

"It was a spur-of-the-moment kind of thing." She rubbed her eyes, which ached with dryness.

"I tried calling your cell phone and left a couple of messages."

Suzanne said nothing.

"You sure you're okay?" She could picture her mother at her Lucite kitchen table, seated on one of the white-leather and chrome chairs, a kitten-heeled slipper dangling from her toes as she swung her foot back and forth, a cappuccino growing cold in front of her.

"Yes, Mum."

"I read that article and I thought... well, Here we go again."

Again, as in like Jax. And their dad.

"Mum, it's the *New York Post*, Page 6. If Page 6 says it's Thursday, you know it's got to be either Wednesday or Friday."

"You haven't told me what you're doing out there."

She strode over to the ashtray atop the kitchen counter, holding her cigarette upright to avoid jostling the skyscraper of ash onto the floor. "Hanging out. Visiting friends. Taking a break."

"Why did you tell Larry you were in India?"

"Because I don't want anyone trying to track me down."

"Soozie, honey, you can't just skip out of town without staying in touch. What if Martin Scorsese calls wanting you to read for him?"

Jesus. "Martin Scorsese isn't going to call. And if he does, well, he'll have to wait."

"You can't just live in the moment, you know. You've got to be planning a couple of years ahead. How many times have I told you this?" There it was, the whiny siren undertone rising to the surface. "As it is, you're not leveraging yourself. You left *Lakeview Drive*, fine. But what have you done since? A movie that hasn't been released yet. And that play at the La Jolla Playhouse, for Christ's sake. You're not the only blond twenty-one-year-old who used to be on a hit ensemble series. If you don't think long term, there won't be a long term. What the hell is Larry doing for you, anyway?"

Suzanne lit another cigarette from the one she'd smoked down to the filter.

"Soozie, are you there?"

"Mum, when did you stop thinking about Jackson?"

"Why?" Her voice jumped another half-octave, as sharply as a stylus across a scratched record.

"Just curious."

"Is he there in New York? Is that why you're there, bailing him out again?"

Beyond the kitchen in her mother's house, which used to be their house, loomed the huge living room, with the grand piano and the white carpet and the overstuffed furniture with the rococo wood frames. Her mother was probably staring out into it, French-manicured nails tapping against her cup. "No. So far as I know he's still in England. I was just curious is all."

"Maybe you should be a little more curious about what Larry is doing for you and less curious about anything to do with your brother."

"So is the only time you think about him when I mention him?"

"I have better things to do with my time than have this discussion."

Suzanne knew her mother didn't, though. Maybe she had a tennis date to get dressed for, or a hair appointment, or a fundraising meeting for the children's hospital. (To be fair, her mother did help raise a lot of money. Her talents for cajoling and nagging served her well there.) But Suzanne didn't think any of that was more important than telling her daughter whether she still thought about the son she hadn't spoken to in three years and, if she didn't, how she'd managed that feat.

Because Suzanne was afraid that she was running out of roads down which she could chase Jax. That she would never find him. That it wouldn't be a matter of giving up but of facing facts. And she didn't know how she was going to do it. While her mother, who was so eager to give her career advice, was refusing to share with her the information she really needed.

CHAPTER 6

Riker Road off the High Street was just as deserted at 5:30 in the morning as it had been in the afternoon several days ago. The streetlights glowed a pinkish orange on an empty crisps packet scraping along the pavement, on clumps of dog shit, on a fat slug humping a cigarette butt.

Suzanne paused to catch her breath as she reached the first intersection. She'd climb up one more block. If she didn't come across anyone, she'd head back down to the High Street and wait for the first bus to take her back to the trailer. Go back to bed for a few hours, then take another bus out to Boutport and start scouting beauty salons for someone who knew Pam.

She tried to summon up disappointment at not coming across anyone yet. But she had to admit that instead she was relieved. The entire walk down to town from the caravan park, she'd rehearsed how she would approach the first junkie she saw: Excuse me, I'm hoping you can help. Oi, I'm looking for someone. Hey there, do you know a guy named Jay? The rustlings of the tree branches and bushes, the shadows layered upon shadows, the occasional bursts of rain—torrents of bitter pecks, almost like hail, that lasted only a few minutes before stopping as abruptly as they'd started, leaving her hair dripping into her eyes—the unexpected lumps of tree trunks and brambly weeds in her path, the hooting of what she assumed were owls, and of course the shrieks of the seagulls, all had set her on edge. When a van appeared out of the mist, its headlights delineating the rolling clouds of fog, she'd felt an urge to run into its path. Jax had once told her that people who were afraid of heights actually feared that they'd throw themselves off whatever ledge or rooftop they were standing on; she hadn't understood that psychology until now.

Although she was chewing gum, her mouth was still dry. She lit a cigarette. Nothing to see here. One more block, and she was home free.

She crossed the road. And as she stepped up onto the pavement she saw him.

Not Jax. This one was shorter, and even though he was little more than a vague white-gray outline, almost a reverse shadow set apart from the dimness of the fog, she could make out that he was broader across the chest than Jax had ever been. He stood several yards ahead of her, knees bent, swaying in place back and forth. Slowly, in increments, his head and shoulders cantilevered backward and downward, his back arching. Just as he was about to succumb to the laws of gravity and tumble backward onto the pavement, he jerked forward, almost upright, almost still. Then he began wavering again, forward this time.

A junkie on the nod.

When he was living with her and using, Jax would try to fix several hours before she was due home. That way they could almost pretend that he was just sleepy, or maybe hung over, or a little drunk. But there'd been plenty of occasions when he didn't time it right. Once she came home earlier than expected from the day's shoot; a scene they'd planned to film that afternoon had gotten pushed back till the following morning. When she walked into the living room Jax stood several feet in front of the sofa, twisted toward his right, his head at chest level, his hair hanging down to his hips. His lit cigarette had spilled ash onto her polished hardwood floor. When she called his name he managed to lift his eyelids enough that she could make out the lower half of his irises but not his pupils. He started straightening up, took one step forward, then melted downward and rightward again.

"Jax!" She'd shaken his shoulders, his head rattling atop his neck. He was so thin, little more than the balsa wood he used to make planes out of when they still lived in London. She shook him and then pushed him away. He staggered backward but somehow managed to remain on his feet.

Now she stood on the sidewalk, pulling on her cigarette, uncertain what to do next. She decided to cross Riker, continue up on the other side. She'd get nowhere asking this one anything, she knew that much.

She walked around what looked like a puddle of sick in the road. The sidewalk on this side of the road was empty. She took a deep breath and another drag from her cigarette.

The houses were set off from the pavement by knee-high stone walls. A dog growled, low in volume and timbre, but clearly in warning. She looked around, saw nothing, not even a shadow of a dog. Only her own shadow, two of them, one paler and almost purple, both trailing behind her. Should she slow down or pick up the pace?

A fine drizzle enveloped her. She pulled up the hood of her gilet, tugging it far forward so that it wouldn't slip off. She continued walking. The dog growled again, louder, with a serrated edge to its tone.

A shrill whistle. "Barrel, sit." Chuckling. Whispers.

She was in front of the house with the COCKSUCKER graffiti. Except that someone had covered most of the red letters with silvery squiggles, leaving only, out of a misplaced sense of patriotism or as a social indictment, OK UK. On the steps leading to the door she could make out the shapes of five, maybe six men, huddled so close together they formed one amorphous silhouette, like a beachside statue eroded from decades of salty sea air. The man on the lowest step held a pit bull by the collar.

"If you're looking to earn a few quid, you're on the wrong street," said one of men, she couldn't tell which. Another hissed, though whether it was at the speaker or at her, she couldn't tell either.

"You don't have any sandwiches on you, do you?" said yet another man, his *s*'s wet. "You from the outreach?"

She stopped at the walkway leading to the steps. "No."

"You looking to score?"

She took a final drag from her cigarette, cupping her hand around it like a tough guy in a movie would, then flicked it in a high arc into the street. She swallowed, hoping that they didn't hear her shaky gulp. "I'm looking for a friend. Bloke named Jay. Know where I can find him?"

"You blow me, I'll tell you," said a voice thick with phlegm.

"She looks like she's in a hurry." The bloke with the sibilant *s*'s. "She don't have all day to get you hard." Laughter. Then some shuffling, shoving. "Leave off." "Bloody hell, nearly burnt my ear off, didn't he?" "Fuck off." "Oi, pass the fucking bottle, don't fuck the passing bottle."

"So do any of you know Jay?"

"Got any sandwiches?"

"Got a fag?"

"Here, drool over on him."

"I'm gonna fucking cut you, I am. Motherfucker. I'm trying to sleep."

"Where's the motherfucking bottle?"

It was as if she'd unleashed a kennel of minor demons, jeering and cursing. A Greek chorus of derelicts. She took care not to stare directly at them, concentrating her gaze toward her shoes.

More shuffling. "Oi, watch where you're going, mate." "Fucking hell." Heavy footsteps. A storm of stale beer, stale smoke, stale sweat heading toward her.

"What d'you want with Jay?"

She looked up. A scarecrow of a figure, except for a bloated stomach hanging over the top of his jeans, which had slid down to expose his bony hips.

Her mouth was so dry her chewing gum stuck to her palate. She felt like she was about to choke. "He's an old friend of mine, isn't he?" She hit the London accent hard. "We grew up together. I've been looking for him for months now, haven't I?"

"You the old Bill?"

She forced her hands on her hips. "Do I look like a fucking cop?"

He bent forward, whispered in her ear, his breath hot, heavy, thick. "How much money you got on you?"

She fought down the urge to flee. Instead she cased him from crown to feet. Yes, he had a good head, maybe more, on her in height, but a faint rattling wheeze accessorized each breath he drew, and his hands dangled limp from his arms like rusted appendages whose purpose had long been forgotten. She could outrun him if she had to. "Why?"

"You give me a tenner," he whispered, "I'll talk."

She'd suspected she might have to dole out a few quid. She hadn't brought her handbag or wallet, but she did have two fivers in one back pocket, a tenner in another, pound coins and small change in her front pockets, and a twenty tucked into her right sock. "Fine." As she reached for her back pocket, he wrapped his fingers around her wrist. She could feel the jagged edges of his nails against her skin and the quiver beneath his own. "Not here," he breathed into her ear again. "They'll all be wanting some."

He pulled her onto the pavement. His thumb pressed hard against the vein of her wrist but his grip was weak otherwise. He towed her higher up the road, past a half-dozen more houses, before steering her up the walkway to yet another entryway. His palm imprinted a sticky film on the back of her hand. She'd have to pick up some rubbing alcohol before heading back to the trailer so that she could scrub her arm and hand raw.

He sat on the top step. "Got a fag?" She dealt out one for him and one for herself. He wriggled a lighter from his front pocket and, to her surprise, lit hers before lighting his own. The quivering of his hand, now that he wasn't gripping hers, bloomed into a full-fledged tremor. He took a drag, then held out his palm for his cash.

She gave him the tenner, trying hard not to touch him. She couldn't look him in the eyes, focused instead on his mouth. He was missing one of his bottom front teeth. A crooked scar ran from the left corner of his mouth down to the center of his chin, where it faded amid the scuffs of stubble.

"Cheers." He crammed the bill into the same pocket as his lighter. "Right. Jay. Skinny pale bloke, long hair, right?"

The inside of her chest was bruised from the thudding of her heart against it. "Right."

"Okay." He took a deep breath, then paused before exhaling. "Okay, then. My brother, Ian, brought him around. They'd met up drinking somewhere. Not sure where. Our Ian was a drinker, yeah, but not into the H, yeah?" His words thickened. "I'd of killed him if he fucked with that shit." He halted, his head flopping to one side, as if it had grown too heavy for him to prop up. She stole a glance. His eyes were closed.

"When was this?" she asked, so softly she wondered if he heard.

"Last summer sometime." He opened his eyes to a squint.

"So that's it?"

He closed his eyes again, grimacing. "I know our Ian was going drinking with him. Him and some other blokes. But then one night, near the end of the summer, yeah? Or maybe in the autumn? Ian comes round where I'm squatting. It takes me a while to figure out what he's on about, yeah? 'Cause he's so drunk I don't know how he even found his way to me. And 'cause I'm coasting, yeah?" He spoke like someone recounting a dream as it unspooled around him, just as Jax used to when high. "But something happened with him and Jay and this other bloke. They'd been drinking down in one of the valleys off the A361, somewhere between here and Boutport. Something'd happened, and Ian started going off about how he and Jay were gonna get straight, that morning, this was it for them, but could I fix Jay up first?"

"Did you?"

He held his cigarette to his lips without drawing on it. "Fuck no. Didn't have none to spare, did I? So my brother left. But he did get straight. Goes to meetings regular now. Going back to school, isn't he?" He opened his eyes and thrust back his shoulders, took a long last drag and dropped the stub of his cigarette between his feet. Funereal wisps of smoke curled up between his legs.

"What about Jay?" She offered him another cigarette.

"From what Ian told me, he just disappeared that morning. I don't think Ian's seen him again. I know I haven't." He rubbed his eyes with the palms of his hands. "Ian's doing well for himself. He's a good kid, that one." His voice caught on an inaudible snag.

The kid with the thick russet curls at the twelve-step meeting, his name was Ian. It had to be this one's brother. She forced herself to take long, even breaths. She wouldn't allow herself to get excited. Especially as she was going to have wait till the next twelve-step meeting on Tuesday before she'd be able to see Ian and ask him.

But still. It had to be the same Ian.

She looked at Ian's brother. She couldn't make out the color of the scraps of hair clinging to his scalp. They seemed to have a vague curl to them, though. She was about to ask if his brother had red hair, but the man had nodded off, his chin sunk onto his chest. His hand, still managing to hold the cigarette, rested on the step.

She crept away as quietly as she could, on the balls of her feet, down the walkway to the pavement. Then she turned right and continued up the incline of the street, still balancing on the fleshy parts of her soles. Only after she passed a few more houses did she break into a run and somehow race, legs burning, up to the next intersection. Once there she halted, doubled forward, and retched until the muscles of her stomach ached as much as those of her calves.

She headed to the High Street, stumbling a bit because she was suddenly burdened by a lead cloak of exhaustion, but still able to appreciate the irony that, after going to such measures to ferret out a junkie to talk to her, now she was finding them everywhere. As the sky lightened from blue-black to blue-gray, junkies were emerging onto the streets of Billicombe like earthworms to the sidewalks after a heavy rain. She'd passed an old man—or at least he looked old and wizened, forehead furrowed, leaning heavily on an aluminum cane—whose head bobbed as he stood in an alleyway off the road leading back down to the High Street, watching but not seeing. A wraithlike couple propping each other up along the side of the pet-food shop, her head slotting just beneath his chin, his arms around her torso, fingers tucked into her belt buckle. A tousled head just visible beneath a crumple of soiled blankets in the doorway of what had once housed, according to a sign that had been painted over with a thin coat of white emulsion, the Healthy Way natural and organic foods store.

Maybe—she tried not to get too attached to this thought—maybe she was getting closer to Jax after all. She felt lighter, almost giddy, even as her legs grew heavier and more difficult to separate from the ground. Though whether this lightness was optimism, or exhaustion, or simply dizziness from smoking so many cigarettes on an empty stomach, she wasn't sure.

She was so tired that she could fall asleep that very minute, curled up in a doorway herself. But she didn't want to go back to the shoebox of a trailer, where no matter how wide she opened the windows the air remained stagnant and dense. Once she was back there, she knew she'd end up staring at the ceiling, mind racing, unable to close her eyes.

She'd head down to the beach instead. Stretch out on the pebbly sand, let the waves act as a lullaby. People bought sound machines programmed with a recording of waves to help them sleep. She'd be foolish not to take advantage of the real thing while she was here.

Richard did a soft-shoe around some dog shit in the middle of the pavement on the way to the car, putting his hand out to stop himself falling in the process. "Don't forget, you're driving back tonight," he said.

"I know," Pam replied, exasperated. "But you didn't get have to get completely trolleyed, did you?"

"I'm not." Richard walked a few paces beyond their car, then double-tracked back.

They'd gone to a party at the house of one of Pam's workmates in Boutport. Richard didn't know a soul other than Pam, which was probably why he drank more than he'd intended, or even noticed until well into the night. He ended up talking about football to a bloke who was married to another of the hairstylists at Pam's shop. Richard wasn't much of a fan, following it just enough to get by in a pub. When they'd lived in London, West Ham had been his team, but down here Liverpool was favored, for some reason he'd yet to suss out.

In the car now, Pam had both hands on the wheel, gripping so tight that, even in the near blackness, Richard could see her knuckles poking white through her skin. The main road from Boutport to Billicombe, the A361, was narrow, one skinny, snaky lane each way for the most part. When a bus came from the opposite direction you had to skitter off to the side, so that brambles and branches rattled against the roof of the car like sticks being run across a picket fence.

There was virtually no traffic tonight. That didn't necessarily make driving easier. Long stretches of the A361 were bereft of streetlights.

It was silent in the car, but not in Richard's head. He was bobbing up and down to "Ever Fallen in Love" by the Buzzcocks. He hadn't heard the song in years, but it had been playing at the party as they were saying their goodbyes.

The smoldering beams of the car's headlights as they converged at a point on the road in front of them, with the car never catching up to it, were starting to hypnotize him. He shook his head, glanced over at Pam. She was hunched forward slightly, knuckles still white, watching, alert.

A face and body in sharp relief amid the darkness of the road. A face and body, haloed in neon yellow and chalky pink. The zipper of the body's hoodie, the shadows of his pointed beard, the lines etched around his smudged eyes giving him dimension. Mouth open, void black.

Screeching. Thuds. Thump. Thump. "Jesus Christ!" Shatters, high-pitched enough to send an electric current from Richard's ears to his jaw. Then silence, a silence he'd never heard before, a vacuum as he flew...

He wasn't flying. He was sitting. On a hard, damp, sharply aslant rock several meters from the beach. The sea in front of him was gray-green, clashing with the muddled smoke-pale sky. The hues danced before him, zeroing nearer then moving out. He closed his eyes, gripping onto the rock to keep from spilling over. When he opened them again lace-trimmed waves lapped around him, licking the rock a meter or so below his dangling feet.

To his right, just beyond the sea wall was the hill—the mountain, the locals called it—with its zigzag walking path to the Union Jack fluttering at the top. He couldn't see the flag, submerged as it was in fog. But he heard it snapping against the wind. He heard gulls shout as they careened above the larger, farther waves, swooping down low and soaring in huge arcs upward.

Think. Fuck. He must have walked out here during low tide. This must be high tide now, or close to it.

He looked behind him, wincing at the jagged tugging of his shoulder muscles, trying to gauge how steep or shallow the water was, and whether he could walk back to the beach. He couldn't tell whether the water would come up to his ankles, his knees, his hips, or his chest. He didn't know how he'd got here, or why. He didn't know what time it was, or what day it was.

Breathe. Think. His name was Richard Sommers. Good. He lived in Billicombe, Devon. Right. He had been in an accident on the twenty-first of October. And he was seriously sick and fucking tired of his life. If this was his forever, he might as well stay out here on this rock and die of hunger and thirst.

Except that starvation and thirst were painful, drawn-out ways of dying.

He could jump into the water, hope to hit his head on an underground rock and die quickly.

Sod's law, the blow to his head would, like in some crap sitcom, restore his memory—and then he'd die.

But he couldn't keep on like this much longer. Being jostled back and forth in time, leaving behind huge gaps of blankness, not certain where he was or when until he'd already been.

He was sobbing now. Big choking sobs, gusts of anger squeezing out of him, squeezing the breath from him. "I can't take this anymore! I cannot take this anymore!" The words shredded his throat with their ferocity, but they could hardly be heard over the waves and the flapping flag and the gulls.

"Richard! Richard! What the hell?"

He twisted around, a tendon in his back twanging like a broken guitar string. Saman—no, Suzanne, was slipping and skidding along a path of stepping stones toward him. She was just a few arm's lengths away now. "Jesus, what the hell happened to you?" She was biting her lip.

He looked down, making sure he was dressed. He thrust a hand through his hair. Sticky and gritty and thick with saltwater and sand.

She held out her hand, bracing herself with one foot on the rock behind her. "Can you get down?"

He slid down, grabbed her hand, and let her pull him toward her.

"Were you in a fight?" She stood over him in his loo, dabbing at a gash above his right eyebrow with surgical spirit. It stung, and the fumes made his eyes water.

"I doubt it," he said. "If I'd been in a fight, I wouldn't have come out of it this easy."

She chuckled, still dabbing. "So you're a lover, not a fighter, then?"

He closed his eyes. "I don't know what I am."

She tossed the cotton wool into the plastic bin. "I don't think you should be here on your own."

"It's only a cut." He'd checked it out in the mirror before she'd made him sit down on the closed toilet seat and play along with her Florence Nightingale fantasy. It wasn't all that deep, and the blood had already crusted over.

"I don't mean that. I mean the whole wandering off, losing track of yourself thing."

He stood. He didn't like having to look up at her, having her gaze down at him. "I've been living like this for months now."

"And has it always been this bad? There was yesterday, and now this."

He didn't know.

"You have two choices." Suzanne folded her arms across her chest. "I stay here with you for the day, maybe the night. Or you come back to my place."

He couldn't help but grin at the thought of how she'd try to enforce those options. He was no specimen of brute strength, but he'd seen kids on their way to the primary school who were more muscular than she was. "Going to tie me down to a chair, then, is that it?"

She cocked her head and lifted her brows. "Nah. You might enjoy that."

Richard was trying to be tough, but Suzanne knew he was taken aback by this latest memory lapse. His silence on the walk back to his flat, and how he'd let her take the lead, even pausing for a moment at the front door, waiting for her to unlock it, until he realized that he had the keys. How he'd accepted one of her cigarettes rather than rolled his own. The way he'd felt around the cut while staring in the mirror, as if trying to read a message in Braille that would explain how he'd ended up on the beach.

Of course he was going to insist that he was fine, that he didn't need her to stay. So she told him that she was hoping to crash for a few hours on his couch anyway, that she'd been up since stupid o'clock and was exhausted. Let him think she was the one who needed tending. It worked.

She couldn't sleep, though. She curled up on one end of the sofa, forcing her eyes to stay shut, but her mind was mapping out her next steps. Going to Boutport today was out. Tomorrow was Saturday, the busiest day at a salon, and therefore not a good day for trying the patience of overworked stylists. Salons were closed Sunday and Monday, so the earliest she could go was Tuesday.

She really was drained. Even the thought of moving tired her. But she couldn't sleep. She counted backward from one hundred. That had never failed her before.

Apparently there was truth to the saying about there being a first time for everything.

From the table behind the sofa Richard tapped away at his laptop, stopping once or twice to roll and light a cigarette. The snap of his lighter. The occasional gusty exhalation. A few random chuckles at whatever he was reading online. The gulls calling outside.

People who knew Suzanne joked about her ability to fall asleep anywhere, anytime. When she and several of the other girls from *Lakeview Drive* had flown together on a redeye to New York to do some publicity to kick off the third season, she was asleep in her seat before the plane had even taxied off. When she was a kid, she'd spent two weeks filming outside Prague some crappy little movie about a reincarnated spirit. An entire day was spent shooting her death scene; her character was strangled by her uncle, who was possessed by a seventeenth-century mass murderer. It had been intense: running, shouting, pretending to be throttled, falling limp onto the ground. Between takes she'd head to the folding chair with her name written on masking tape on the back, and as the grips and other crew shouted and bustled about, she'd plunge straight into REM. The director loved it: "If only all my talent did that: were up when you needed them, and went to sleep when you didn't."

Jax, though, had suffered from insomnia even as a kid. In most of their flats in London they'd shared a bedroom. Whenever she'd stir in the middle of the night, Jax was awake. Reading with a flashlight under the sheets. Crouched by the doorway, sketching in the narrow light that snuck in beneath the door from the hallway. Once or twice kneeling at the side of the bed, his elbows on the mattress, watching her. "You smile in your sleep," he told her once.

She sat up, uncoiling her limbs. This was ridiculous.

Richard looked up from his computer. "Heading out?" He must have been rubbing the plaster she'd placed over his cut, because one end had come loose and now dangled above his eyebrow. Would he be fine if she left? Just because he'd managed to escape serious harm during however long he'd been on his own so far didn't mean he'd continue to do so. You stop watching a burger on the barbecue for just a few seconds, and that's all it takes for the meat to catch fire. You let go of a kid's hand in a shopping mall just long enough to reach for your wallet in your handbag, and boom, the kid has wandered off. You go a week without talking to your brother, and then you can't track him down.

"I'm making tea," she said. "Want some?"

He didn't even try to hide his annoyance about her continued presence. "Fine."

She filled the kettle and rummaged about his cabinets in hopes of finding an herbal tea. Caffeine was not going to help her doze off. She didn't find any, but she did uncover amid the mismatched dishes another ashtray, a chipped black plastic one; a curled-up two-year-old copy of *PC World*, perhaps used as a spider swatter; a half-filled bag of rock-solid brown sugar; and a dusty bottle of vodka. That at least would help her get to sleep.

"What were you doing down by the beach this morning anyway?" Richard asked. They sat on his couch, each commandeering an end, an ashtray in between, bare feet propped up on the coffee table. When she'd emerged from the kitchen with the vodka, he'd said, "Since you have me under house arrest, I assume you're sharing that with me."

"Of course," she'd said, though she wasn't sure he should be drinking given his memory problems. "It is yours, after all."

Several rounds in, he no longer seemed bothered having her around. His resentment had puddled away. Just as her images of the morning were puddling. The first junkie she'd encountered, tilting backward toward the pavement, seemed almost funny now. The way Ian's brother had lit her cigarette for her, like a suave suitor in a '30s drawing-room film, that was sort of funny too.

"Just taking a walk." Jesus, her vowels were slip-sliding all over the place, from continent to continent. Oh well. She didn't have to keep pretending for Richard anymore. Which was good, because at this point she couldn't remember where she'd left off.

"Just walking? Several miles from the caravan park? Around Billicombe in the early morning?" Some people when they were drunk spoke with extra precision. Richard was one of them.

"Yup. I get up early. Sometimes when I'm filming I have to be at the studio at 6 a.m." She propelled herself forward and poured more vodka into her cup. She knew she had a silly smile plastered across her face for no reason, but she didn't care enough to try to remove it.

"Were you up Riker Road?" He was staring at her. She didn't know why. "Yup. Why?"

Richard bent over the coffee table to roll himself another fag. "I would have gone with you. You shouldn't be going up there on your own, nosing around and such like."

She waved him away, watching her hand trail through the air. "It was fine," she finally said. "I met some bloke whose brother knew Jax."

"And?" He licked the cigarette paper and pinched the ends.

"The kid, the brother, he goes to twelve-step meetings at the church on Tuesdays. So I'm going to talk to him there." Talking tickled her lips. Christ, she was really drunk. The only other time she'd been this shit-faced was that night at Davis's, where she'd gone under the pretense of running lines. That was the night she lost her virginity. Good thing she'd been drunk, or it probably would have hurt like hell. Davis hadn't been particularly tender, or slow. It was whip out the cock, cram it up her cunt, pump for a few minutes, and yank it out.

"And what if he doesn't know anything?"

"But what if he does?"

Richard blew a stream of smoke toward the telly before turning to her. "You may never find him, you know."

She drained her cup, lurched forward to pour some more. "You're a killbuzz. A buzzkill."

"I don't want you to get your hopes up, is all."

"Fuck you very much." She pounded back against the cushions. She felt him watching her but didn't know what to do with that knowledge.

"Why did you move here from London?" she blurted.

He laughed, that brusque bark of his. "Why do you ask?"

"Because I don't know the answer."

He laughed again, a more drawn-out, musical chortle. "You should be a reporter."

"Jax was thinking of becoming one," she almost said, but stopped herself. Why did it always come down to Jax? Today was not going to be about Jax at all. This was going to be about her. Her buzz. "So why did you?" she asked again.

"Well, London's fucking expensive, isn't it? And Pam kind of missed the countryside. And then there was her old boyfriend, which wasn't a main reason. But we were going to move flats anyway, so we figured, Sod it, let's make a big move."

"What's this about her old boyfriend?" Suzanne wiggled her toes.

He shook his head. "He was stalking her, wasn't he? Not really stalking her. But emailing her, then somehow managing to get her new email when she changed it and emailing again. Using different names to try to friend her on Facebook, which is why she's not on there anymore. And then he started sending letters and candy and such like to the flat. So we had to move anyway."

"Elisabeth, she played my sister on *Lakeview*, she had a stalker once. She had to get a restraining order and eventually took him to court. He said that they were really married and that she'd left him but now was sending him messages to come and get her. It was scary. Bodyguards and shit."

"Did anything happen?"

"He's locked up now. Padded cell." She scanned the table for her cigarettes. There they were.

"So how did you get into acting?" Richard asked. He knew it sounded lame, but she was always peppering him with questions, when in actuality she had the better story to tell. And if she was going to insist on playing babysitter, she'd have to entertain her charge.

"My mum. And my brother. He was gorgeous as a kid. Blond hair, big blue eyes, sweet smile. Some agent had noticed him when he was eight or so down at Walthamstow Market, handed my mum a card, started sending him to auditions and casting calls. He did a couple of adverts. But he was too fidgety, at least that's what our mum said, so he didn't get cast much. She used to bring me along, and sometimes when casting for an ad they needed a little girl too. And I wasn't fidgety..."

Richard guffawed.

She drew herself upright and threw him a withering glance. "I can be quite still when I need to."

He threw up his hands in mock defeat. "Fine."

"Anyway, that's it. The rest is Northrup family history."

He recalled their conversation on the bus, about why they'd moved to California. "So it wasn't your brother who got the TV role that brought you to America?"

"No. It was me."

"Do you like it?"

"America?"

"Acting." His roll-up had gone out. He lit the remains.

She wiggled her mouth from side to side as she thought. "Yeah, I do, actually. Plus it's the only thing I'm good at."

"Hell, you're only twenty-one, you don't know what you're good at yet."

"So said the wise old man of... twenty-seven? twenty-six?" Her limbs weren't as loose as they had been. Clearly she needed more vodka. She shifted her cigarette to her left hand so that she could pour some more into her cup with her right.

"Something like that." He wasn't even going to try to figure it out now. He felt good, close to happy, and he didn't want to chase that feeling away. What he needed now was music. The flat was too quiet. "Anything special you want to listen to?"

She shook her head. He got to his feet, weaving just a little, and made it to the stereo. *Laid* by James was already in the CD player. He turned it on. A lone guitar seeped into the background, slowly growing louder.

"Gee, this is cheery," Suzanne said sarcastically. She took another swallow, then wiped her mouth with the back of her hand.

"This album is sort of how I met Pam." He returned to the couch and began rolling another smoke. "I was in a pub with some mates after work, talking about a James concert I'd been to, and she kind of sidled up and asked if they'd performed 'Laid'. I should have known then and there that she wasn't really into James—of course they performed 'Laid,' it's one of their best-known songs, isn't it?"

In fact, as he soon found out, it was pretty much the only James song Pam could name, that and "Sit Down." But by then it didn't matter. This gorgeous girl, with the huge smile and the ass that was an invitation to cup your hands around it, had been impressed enough by him to blag her way into striking up a conversation.

He knew he was nothing special. Oh, he wasn't one of those who ran himself down in hopes of getting others to big him up. He knew he was decent looking, or had been before the accident rearranged his nose and ripped up his back and leg. Even now, with his clothes on, he wasn't a monster, especially with his hair growing back in. He dressed okay. He was told he had a nice speaking voice; one or two old girlfriends had even called it sexy. He wasn't obsessed with any one subject, like *Star Wars* or cricket or global warming; he had a range of conversational topics he could rely on. He'd had a good job, a somewhat hip one if he described it right. He had good hygiene and liked to try different ethnic cuisines and always attempted to make the girl come, if not before him, then after, unless it was an especially exhausting session and he couldn't help but fall asleep. But he wasn't special, the way Pam was. He wasn't someone who drew a room's focus just by entering and smiling.

"If Pam walked into the room right this minute, what would you say?"

"What are you on about?" he asked, partly because he wasn't sure he'd heard her right—her words were slurring together some—but mostly as a stalling tactic.

"Pam. Would you take her back? Kick her out?" In the time it had taken him to put on the album and roll his fag, she'd ramped up from loose to rat-arsed. Right now her hand was wavering about her mouth as she tried to find her lips with her cigarette.

"Why?"

"Curious." She downed the contents of her cup as if it were a single shot, then closed her eyes. He gave her another five minutes, maybe ten, before she passed out. And she was supposed to be taking care of him. He chuckled.

"What's so funny?" She squeezed her eyes tighter before opening them. She reminded him of a little kid who, after uttering a malapropism, grew cross with all the grown-ups laughing at her.

He pointed to the armchair. "I guess I'd ask Pam if she would take that with her."

She shook her head slowly. "No you wouldn't."

"Yeah, I would. Look at it. It's a fucking eyesore, isn't it?"

"I'm serious." And despite her right hand dangling limp from her wrist, and the way she was squinting to keep him in focus, she did look serious.

He started rolling a cigarette, then noticed the one he had just rolled next to his tobacco pouch. "I don't know."

She was watching him, though he wasn't sure what she was seeing. Her eyes were filmy.

"Say something, say something, anything/Your silence is deafening." It spooked him that those exact lyrics were streaming around them right now. They meant something, were some sort of sign, but he wasn't sure of what.

"I still miss her." It hurt to say it, ached in the back of his throat where the words had been stored, dark and flat and overlooked. He continued staring down at the table, because he wasn't sure how he'd react if he looked up to see Suzanne's eyes boring into him, but he knew it wouldn't be good. He'd yell at her to stop pestering her, maybe. Or maybe he'd cry.

Suzanne had known it, of course. She wasn't sure how, but she'd never questioned that he missed Pam, longed for her. Still loved her. After all, that was why she'd decided to try to track Pam down. She tried to enumerate the signs, but almost immediately realized she wouldn't be able to mark them out, not drunk like she was now. Not that it mattered anyway.

What did matter was that she try to make Richard miss Pam less. Because if there were someone or something that could help her miss Jax less, she would be all over it. She even knew, though she certainly couldn't formulate it, that that was what she was going to do now. By focusing on making Richard miss Pam less, she would be focusing a little less on Jax, and missing him less.

She reached toward Richard, put her hand on his thigh. She felt his muscles clench. That was okay. However he reacted was okay, because at least it wouldn't be about Pam. She inched her hand closer to his inseam. As she did so she grew moist herself between her legs. Her labia swelled; she could feel them pink and plump and shiny slick.

He jerked away. Her hand dropped onto the couch.

"What're you doing?" he said, but she knew that's not what he meant. He meant "Why are doing this?"

She placed her palm on his leg again. This time he didn't tense. She slid closer.

A sliver of white showed around his irises on all sides. "Don't. We're drunk..." His voice was husky, musky. He'd forced out those words against his will.

She leaned forward and grazed his cheek with her lips. His stubble sent scores of prickles through her, down the back of her neck and her spine, down to her cunt, which now thumped with a heartbeat of its own. "I'm not that drunk," she said.

He looked at her. She traced the crooked scar on his nose. Its curves made her smile. Then she ran her finger across his lips, wanting him to do the same to her. But not those lips. The lips down below. She wriggled so that the seam of her jeans dug into her crotch. Her panties were already damp.

She tugged his T-shirt out of chinos, gently, making sure the pads of her thumbs grazed his stomach. She slid her hands beneath his shirt, up to his nipples, all the time rotating tightly against the crotch of her jeans. A small, damp groan. She tilted her face upward, knowing that he was bringing his face down.

She slept beside him, only her foot touching him, and that barely, her toes just accidently resting against his calf. The sweat had dried from her back, which faced him; her hair no longer clung to the nape of her neck but floated around it.

He'd never been with someone who rolled over and fell straight to sleep. Wasn't that something women complained about: men closing their eyes and beginning to snore as soon as they'd come?

He thought he'd made her come. She was an actress, so he couldn't be sure, but he didn't think she'd been faking the convulsing of her thigh muscles, the stabbing intakes of breath, the tiny, almost sweet grunts.

She'd been gentle at the right moments, almost ferocious at the right moments. She'd tiptoed her fingers across his back, whispering "Does that hurt?" when she pressed a little harder, when she neared one of the scars. He'd tried to maneuver so that she didn't have to see his back, or his left leg, but she didn't seem to care. As if he wasn't scarred at all. As if he was who he had been.

And by the time he was thrusting inside her, each minute shift and swale of her making his rod stiffer and harder, he felt as he used to feel. He wasn't a stranger to himself. He remembered similar encounters, similar sensations from the past even as he was letting himself be engulfed by the sensations of the present. And afterward, as he fingered her juicy folds and the pillowy gateway to her cunt, he anticipated the future, even though the future was just seconds away, knowing exactly when and where to pinch, exactly how much pressure to exert, so that she arched up off the bed and froze, a sigh caught midway between her throat and the air.

It had been the first time he'd felt someone else's flesh against his since the accident, not counting the clinical pokings of the doctors and nurses. His muscles were drunk with the relief of it. If he got up now, he'd stagger more than he ever had while bladdered.

But—and why was there always a but?—she wasn't Pam. And as exhilarating and exhausting as it had been, and as much as he hoped it would happen again, he still wanted Pam.

CHAPTER 7

Suzanne woke with a start, as if by some inaudible alarm. Richard's back was toward her, and as he slept she again studied his scars. Though the scant light forcing itself through the window was the hue and thickness of oatmeal, she could still make them out, but they weren't stomach-turning or startling. Pam couldn't have left him because of the scars; there had to be something more.

But did she really want to find out? Maybe it was better for Richard to just move on.

Or maybe she was being selfish. Because yesterday with Richard, she'd been... well, she'd had fun. There were whole moments when she hadn't thought about Jax. When she hadn't felt as if a piece of her were missing or she'd left something behind. The only other times she'd felt that way in the past several months had been when she was working. Then it had been because she had so many other things to focus on: hitting her marks, remembering her lines, interpreting what the director wanted and translating it into a performance, observing the other actors and adjusting her reactions accordingly.

But the rest of the time was a wasteland, and she couldn't help but populate it with thoughts of Jax. While driving home from auditions. Cleaning the house. Attending fundraisers. Meeting with Larry. Getting her hair cut. Watching the skaters at Belvedere Park. And of course checking in with the investigators she'd hired—one for England and one back home, just in case Jax had returned to the States. Visiting the missions and the homeless shelters, taking care to hide beneath the rim of one of Jax's baseball caps. Trolling through Facebook and MySpace and Bebo. Scouring Google and Yahoo! and Dogpile.

Yesterday, though, had been filled to capacity, and not with Jax.

She eased out of bed, slipped into her clothes, tiptoed to the toilet, breathing shallowly so as not to wake Richard. But wake he did. As she glided past the bedroom toward the front door, he called out, "Where are you going?", his voice thin, as if part of it were still submerged in sleep. She froze.

The bedsprings creaked and the sheets rustled. "You're coming back, aren't you?" His tone wasn't plaintive so much as resigned, as if he expected her to leave and not return.

"Of course I am. I'm just going back to the trailer to fetch my toothbrush and some clothes." Which wasn't what she'd intended to say, but when she said them the words felt right.

Things she hadn't realized she missed until spending a few days at Richard's: Cooking a meal for someone else. Eating with someone else, even when sitting in front of the telly watching *Top Gear* while doing so. Someone asking her opinion about a news story or where the ashtray was. Having to close the bathroom door. Hearing some else's footprints, someone else's fingers pecking on a keyboard, someone else singing along to a CD, someone else breathing.

If she stayed many nights longer, she could just get used to it. As could he.

He was good in bed, so far as she could tell. He was only the fourth guy she'd slept with, and he was the first one who made her come even when she hadn't had a few drinks. And he was sweet afterward, lighting a cigarette for the two of them to share. He was funny as well, in a quiet, dry way. She couldn't call to mind anything particularly humorous that he'd said, but she remembered laughing with him.

Except for the actual moments of orgasm, though, she remained fully aware of what she was doing. Take last night. She'd been reading the script that Larry had express-mailed over, and Richard had been fiddling with the computer, putting together some sort of animation, and she had thought, We should have sex again. Just like that, a complete sentence, the same way she might say to herself, I really should defrost the fridge, or I must run through those lines once more. It wasn't as if she didn't want to have sex with him—she'd grown warm between her legs as soon as she had that thought—but even so, there was almost a sense of obligation. Time to administer his medicine. Time for another bicycle lesson. Maybe he'd soon be ready to lose the training wheels.

And that image turned into a lump in her throat, because it was Jax who had taught her how to ride a bike. That week they'd spent down here in Billicombe on holiday.

Richard, Suzanne knew, still wanted Pam. She knew by the way he'd completely stopped talking about her. While rifling through the drawers of his wardrobe for a T-shirt this morning—she'd asked first—she came across a pink camisole with lace straps. She'd brought it out to the lounge where he sat flipping channels on the remote. "Cross-dressing, are we?" she asked. He shot out his arm to grab it, then dropped his arm just as quickly, pretending that he didn't really care. "Whose is this, then?" He shrugged, but refused to say Pam's name. Because it clearly still pained him to do so, but now he didn't want her to know.

So she was going to track down Pam. Instead of traipsing about Boutport, though, she was going to call around first before going to the twelve-step meeting at noon. When Richard got up from the couch to take a shower, she asked if she could borrow his computer to check her email. He said yes, of course. As soon as she heard him close the bathroom door she searched for hair salons in Boutport, jotting down the names and phone numbers on the inside cover of the copy of *A Clockwork Orange* she'd brought from the trailer. When he emerged, a towel wrapped around his torso, raking his hair upward with his fingers, she told him she was going to do a spot of research at the library on Georgian manners and mores, following up on the script she was reading.

It was a relief to get out of Richard's flat, although the wind was so raw she curled her hands into fists, crossed her arms tightly across her chest, and wished she had a jacket with sleeves or at least a thick scarf to wind several times around her neck. Even so, shivering against the gray gusts as she walked down to the Promenade was preferable to staying in the room with Richard, knowing that, though he wouldn't admit it, to her or to himself, he was comparing her with Pam. It was like flubbing an audition but being forced to sit and watch everyone else read the same scene, and read it better.

When she was little, still a toddler really, she had to accompany her mum to Jax's auditions, as there was no one to leave her with, and they couldn't afford a sitter. They'd be seated with a dozen other towheaded boys Jax's age and their mums and the occasional tagalong sibling in a waiting room. Some of the boys would occupy themselves reading or doing schoolwork; one or two would be kneeling on the floor, playing with toy soldiers or trucks, their mothers hushing them sharply when they raised their voices above a whisper.

Jax would slouch in his seat, legs swinging; then, when their mum nudged him to sit up straight, he'd hop to his feet and wander about, studying the promo posters of TV programs and films on the walls, standing over the boys playing on the floor, hopping on one foot to the inevitable water cooler in the corner, then switching to the other foot before hopping back. A few times, she remembered, he brought a notepad and colored pencils, but their mum put a stop to that after the time he'd been called in for his turn to audition and he'd said to the woman in the pale pink twin set who stood at the open door, hand on the jamb, "In a minute, I have to finish this drawing first."

He landed only three jobs from all those early auditions and go-sees: modeling pajamas for one catalog and summer clothing for another, and a commercial in which he had to say, "Mmm, good soup." But at one of his auditions—another commercial, this one for a stain remover—the casting agent, after escorting him out of the private room where he'd read for the director, spotted Suzanne sitting beside their mum. Suzanne still recalled how mind-numbingly bored she'd been. Only a few other children were in the anteroom: a boy who moved his lips as he read *The Beano*; a girl who squirmed as her mother brushed her hair, clucking her tongue and squealing each time the mum tugged especially hard. So Suzanne had busied herself playing museum: She pretended she was a statue and couldn't move. The casting agent spotted her and asked their mum if she would be interested in trying out. She couldn't read yet, so the director fed her the lines and had her repeat them. Apparently she repeated them well enough; the commercial was her first job.

For a while after that, both she and Jax went on auditions. Some for him; some for her; a few, particularly the modeling jobs, for the pair of them. But as she landed several more jobs—an advert for hot cocoa, five lines in a *London's Burning*, a featured part in an episode of *Children's Ward*—fewer of the auditions were for Jax. Then none of them were, and it was his turn to tag along. Sometimes he brought a notepad and pencils, but other times he forgot, or their mum took them out of school early and they didn't have time to stop home for them. Then he'd slouch in a chair, his feet dangling, their mother no longer bothering to nudge him to sit up straight. He was redundant, as she'd been in Richard's flat that morning.

She'd just passed the Bastille when the rain began streaking down in sheets. She pulled up the hood of her gilet and ran to the bus shelter opposite the church. She checked the clock on her mobile. Not even ten-thirty yet. Rain pelleted the shelter's Plexiglas roof. The few cars that passed made subdued squelching sounds. Even the gulls were dispirited, gloating less frequently and less loudly than usual.

She mentally rehearsed once again how she was going to approach Ian after the meeting. She'd use her London accent and her softest tone of voice. And then she forced herself to stop, because in addition to practicing what she was going to say, she couldn't help but anticipate his reaction. "Jay? Yeah, I just heard from his last week. He was in an outpatient program in Bristol, and now he's got a job down there." No, it wouldn't go like that.

"Jay? Yeah, the poor bastard's locked up down Exeter way. Got caught with several balloons of junk."

No.

"Jay? Never heard of him. And I don't even have a brother."

Ten-thirty-seven. She could stop in at one of the cafes on the High Street, nurse a soda and some eggs for a while. But the thought of eating made her stomach churn, and the thought of sitting down made her muscles tense.

She pulled *A Clockwork Orange* out of her bag and looked over the list of Boutport hair salons. Most of them had ridiculous puns for names: Cool for Cuts, Hair Force, Mane Attraction, Curl Crazy. She hoped Pam worked at one of the more somberly named ones, like Serenity Beauty or Options.

She'd start ringing the salons now. Maybe she'd luck out, find Pam straight away, and be able to book an appointment for tomorrow or Thursday.

She'd alphabetized the list. She was a stickler for alphabetizing: books, CDs, DVDs. She'd picked up the habit from Jax. When she'd moved into her own house they'd spent one day putting away her music and books in alphabetical order by artist and writer. They still hadn't finished by dinnertime, because they kept stopping to leaf through a particular book or check out the track listings of a particular CD. Calling out to each other, "I forgot I had this!" and "So that's where my copy of *Fateless* went—you nicked it." Over pizza, they'd laughed about what wonks they were, to enjoy sorting and filing so much.

Cool for Cuts was first on the list. She entered the digits on her mobile and, in her best Received Pronunciation, asked for an appointment with Pam. Oops, no one named Pam worked there? So sorry.

She had no joy till she rang Elite Salon. Yes, she could have an appointment with Pam. Oh, Pam Thomas? No, it was Pam Tolliver. But there was a Pam Thomas at Options. No worries, people confused the two of them all the time.

Suzanne lit a cigarette and called. Yes, Pam Thomas worked there. She had several openings tomorrow, at 10:30, 3:30, and 4. Of course, half-ten would be fine.

Yes. This was going to be her lucky day. She knew it.

The same cast filled the same room of the church, in the same seats. Many of them seemed to be wearing the same clothes. Mick and one of his friends, for instance, again wore paint-splattered white trousers. Stu wore his Tottenham jersey. And just like last time, Lee didn't slide in until Stu was calling the meeting to order. When he spotted her, though, he walked around to the other side of the room and sat behind the older man with the *Mirror* on his lap.

This time the woman with the dyed black hair, Tiffany, read the Twelve Steps. She kept tossing her head back, like a bridled horse. When she came to step eight, "Made a list of all we had harmed, and became willing to make amends to them all," her voice shook. She had to pause midway through step nine. "Made direct amends to such people wherever possible—" she swallowed hard, veins pressing against her throat "—except when to do so would injure them and others."

When Jax had been in the program while living with her and enrolled at UCLA, he'd joined her in the den one night directly after a meeting. He wore the blazer he'd picked up at a Salvation Army shop and a dark gray V-neck jumper, although the evening was a warm one, even by SoCal standards.

"Are you doing anything Saturday?" He spoke down to the floor, rather than facing her as she sat the couch, watching some nature show and pretending that the plain yogurt she was eating was French vanilla ice cream.

"Not yet." It was only Wednesday. "Why?"

"Will you come on a picnic with me?" He wouldn't tell her why, just that he'd arrange for the food.

On Saturday he had a cooler packed before she had even showered. "Where exactly are we going?" She'd have to drive, as his license had been suspended.

"Not far."

It was, in fact, the basement of the house. The previous owner had stuccoed it and added some English cottage-style beams, but Suzanne didn't use it. She hadn't even finished furnishing the living and dining rooms yet.

Jax had laid down a blanket on the parquet floors and hung from the rafters a dozen or so clouds cut from cardboard and covered with cotton balls, the sort of clouds a grade-school class would make for their end-of-year play.

"I wasn't sure if they were corny or kitsch," Jax said, blushing.

"They're perfect." She meant it.

They sat on the blanket, and Jax unloaded the cooler he'd lugged down the flight of stairs. Gherkins, not the fat American-style pickles, and slaw and a hero sandwich brimming with salami and pastrami and corned beef, her favorites. A salad for him. Brie and crackers. Diet Coke and apple juice. She clapped her hands like a little girl.

He lit a cigarette and took several drags before he spoke. "I'm working on step nine in my program." A few beads of sweat emerged on his forehead, a strand of hair sticking to one of them. She sat on her hands to keep from wiping it free. "That's where we ask forgiveness of all the people we hurt. And since I hurt you the most, I'm starting with you."

He'd probably hurt their mother more. He'd thrown her against the wall once, when she'd confronted him about some money he'd stolen. Suzanne didn't think a brother could hurt a sister as much as a son could wound a mother. But she didn't say anything.

He was facing her but couldn't raise his eyes to meet hers. "I'm sorry for stealing money from you, and that gold necklace they gave you after filming *Tim and Me and the Terrible Three*." He spoke in a rush, as if afraid of being interrupted before he could finish. "I'm sorry for taking your car without permission and banging it up. I'm sorry for burning a hole in your new Marimekko duvet and for getting blood on your pink rug. I'm sorry for making you have to clean up my sick and get me out of my trousers when I pissed myself and was too wasted to notice. I'm sorry for all the times I lied to you. I'm sorry for all the times you needed me to listen to you and help you and I couldn't because I was too fucked up. I'm sorry for not being a decent brother, let alone the brother you deserve."

Only then did he lift his eyes, and as he did they overflowed. He clambered to his feet and stumbled to the far corner, where he stood facing the wall, his shoulders heaving.

She sat on the corner of the blanket and cried, as quietly as Jax. At one point she bit the fleshy part of her palm, just below the thumb, to keep from making a sound.

Then she felt his arms around her shoulders, just as so many times she had wrapped hers around him. "I don't know how to make it up to you. I can't, not really. But..."

"You can, by..." She wiped her cheeks with her fists.

"By staying straight. I know," he whispered into her hair. And he had stayed straight. For another six weeks.

Six goddam weeks. That's all he could make amends for. Fury swept through her now, a white swash of it. Her fists clenched, and she trembled with the effort of staying seated, staying silent. She pressed her lips shut and closed her eyes. Counted by threes, just as she did before auditions to calm herself down.

It wasn't until she reached sixty-three that the anger had flowed from her—or, more likely, had been reabsorbed, waiting to resurface. She opened her eyes. Tiffany was now seated and swigging her Orangina, and several of the men were discussing something to do with pubs. She had missed a good chunk of the meeting. Christ, she was getting to be like Richard.

She lit a cigarette. She was smoking way too much. Thinking way too much. She needed to get back to L.A. and work.

She needed to find Jax and get back to L.A. and work.

The meeting was breaking up. Lee was first out the door. Suzanne hurried out as well, so that she'd be waiting outside when Ian and his friend emerged.

The rain had stopped, and the wind had died down. The sky was the same wan shade as pussy-willow buds, and water burbled in the gutters. As soon as Ian and his friend made it to the damp-darkened sidewalk, she stepped in front of them. "Ian, hello." She spoke quickly. "I was talking to your brother the other day, and I think you can help me with something. Do you have a few minutes?"

Ian looked at his friend, who shrugged. He turned to her. He had a prominent lower lip, and right now it was wobbling just slightly. "I guess so. But I'm not in with my brother's crew."

"I know." She made her voice as gentle as possible. "I'm trying to find a friend of mine." His eyes widened.

"Why don't we go across the street and sit down?" she said.

Ian looked at his friend again. "You can come too," Suzanne said. "It's no big secret. No big deal." She trotted out her red-carpet smile, top teeth visible, cheeks pushing upward to create crinkles around the eyes.

Several alcoves had been carved into the side of the waterfront hill across the Promenade, to shelter benches from the elements. They picked their way carefully, as the pavement was slick from the rain and moss, to the alcove on the same level as the Pavilion so that they didn't have to climb one of the paths.

She offered her hand as they sat down, Ian in the middle. "I'm Anne, by the way." They shook hands and mumbled their names. Ian's friend was Adam.

"I'm looking for Jay. Your brother said you used to go drinking with him last summer."

"You spoke to my brother?" Ian folded his arms in front of his chest and tilted his head to one side, challenging her. "What's he look like, then?"

She'd spent so much time avoiding looking at him that she wasn't quite sure. "He's missing a bottom tooth near the front. He was on Riker Road Saturday morning, sitting with four or five other blokes in front of the house that used to have COCKSUCKER written on it."

Ian gave a small concessionary nod. "And what did he say?"

"That for a while last summer, before you got sober, you went drinking with Jay. Jay's an old friend of mine, and I came to town to track him down because I've been worried about him. I haven't heard from him since last autumn."

Ian nibbled his thumbnail. Adam, sitting on the other side of him, rolled a fag.

"I only hung out with Jay a few times, really. Don't ask me how I got to know him because fuck me if I can remember, yeah?" Ian waited for her to nod before he continued. "I ain't seen him since that last time in October, down the valley, with the accident. I got myself into a program the next day. I thought he was going to come with me, but he didn't show, yeah? And I never saw him since."

"What accident?" She took note of how steady her voice was, how chalky dry.

Adam handed Ian a fag and proceeded to roll another. Suzanne lit Ian's cigarette and one for herself.

Ian stared out at the Promenade. She followed his gaze. Two women her age were pushing strollers and passing a roll-up, or maybe it was a spliff, back and forth. Their babies were hidden beneath plastic rain coverings and wads of blankets. "We'd gone down to one of the farms off the A361, me, Jay, and another bloke. We were already rat-arsed when we got on the bus, yeah? I even slid out of my seat onto the floor when the bus made a turn." His lashes cast purple shadows beneath his eyes. "We each had a bottle with us. We somehow made it down the dirt road, yeah?, to this little cabin. Not even a cabin. It only had three walls left and part of a roof. I guess it used to be a shelter for the shepherds or something."

He stopped. Suzanne made an encouraging noise.

"So we're drinking, and I don't know, Jay and the other bloke start arguing or something. And then the bloke starts chasing Jay, out the shelter and up the road. I follow. It seems like we're tearing ass, but of course we aren't, we can barely walk, can we? I'm blind drunk, I can't see where I'm going, I can't see them, I'm just following their voices." Ian continued staring straight ahead. "The path's curving upwards. Then the other bloke stops dead. But Jay, he keeps running, yeah? He's running into the road. And then there's a huge screech, skidding tires, glass crashing. A car must have swerved to avoid hitting Jay, and it ends up smashing into a tree. I'm just standing there off the road, Jay's just standing there in the middle of the road. We don't know what to do. Jay starts patting himself down, looking for his mobile. He can't find it. He asks if I have one. I do, yeah, but I can't make out the numbers, so I walk out into the road to give it to him. I don't know how long all this takes. The car's completely still. No noises. I don't think to go over and look inside, though. I don't know why." He stuck out his tongue to remove a flake of tobacco. "Yeah, I do know why. Because I'm too fucking bladdered to think." His voice was rising in anger. His eyes narrowed.

"So Jay rings 999. It seems like it takes him awhile to get across that there's been a car accident, because he's so rat-arsed too. But he manages, yeah, even manages to tell them it's across from the bus shelter outside the sign for West Downs. All this time he's in the middle of the road, and not a single car's come by. He hangs up, hands me the phone. Then without us saying another word we both run. And next thing I know I'm at my brother's squat." Ian dropped the remains of his cigarette and with the toe of his right boot ground it into the cement, kept grinding long after it had been scraped into shards.

Suzanne grabbed his hands. She wasn't normally touchy-feely. She hated when cast and crew members hugged her at the end of a shoot, even those she liked and considered friends. She loathed the cheek-kissing that went on at parties and other events. She'd never held hands with any of her boyfriends as they walked and talked. But Ian needed her to grab his trembling hands and hold them steady. He needed to be reminded of where he was now, and that now was okay.

Ian started at her touch, his face breaking out in red blotches. He stared down at her hands clasped over his fingers, then glanced up at her face briefly, turning away before she could decipher his expression.

"It's all right," Suzanne said. "It made you get clean, so maybe all this happened for a reason." She'd never believed that sort of rationalization herself, but she sensed that Ian did. She waited till she could no longer feel his veins throbbing beneath her palms before she lifted her hands.

"Shit, there's one more thing." Ian gulped some air. "I told you I never saw Jay again, yeah? But I did go looking for him, because I'd read about the accident in the *Gazette*, and it ends up one of the passengers had to go to hospital, but no one died. I figured he'd want to know, in case he hadn't read it himself. Anyway, I couldn't find him. But I heard he was looking to score some H, him and the other guy we'd been drinking with. But then that was it. I never heard nothing else."

Somehow Suzanne was certain of the answer, as if this moment were a scene from a film that she'd shot months ago but was now viewing for the first time. She asked the question anyway. "Who was this other guy?"

Ian looked over at Adam. Adam nodded. Ian lowered his voice to just above a whisper. "You know the dark bloke at the meeting, the one with his hair pulled back? His name's Valley. It was him."

They sat in silence for a few minutes. The blotches faded from Ian's face, leaving it so pale that every freckle across his cheeks leaped out in contrast. His eyes were half-closed, and his mouth was slack with exhaustion. A drizzle had started up, fine sparkles animating the otherwise still, empty Promenade.

Adam nudged Ian, muttered something. They stood up. "We've got to go," Ian said, wiping his palms against his thighs. "Good luck finding Jay, yeah?"

She dredged up a smile. "Cheers."

The boys headed toward the Pavilion, but after a half-dozen steps Ian turned around and walked back. "About my brother, yeah?"

She nodded.

"How is he?" He winced as he said it, bracing himself for the answer.

She forced her mouth to curve upward. "He's really proud of you," she said.

She didn't return to Richard's flat but instead took the bus back to Caldicott Cross. She couldn't face him just now. He'd want to know how it had gone, and she didn't want to have to summarize the conversation. She didn't want to think about it at all. Whenever she began rerunning Ian's words in her mind, she yanked away from it, drove herself to think about what she would make for dinner that night, or establish her schedule for tomorrow. Ian's account was like a hangnail, though: You tried not to pick at it, you folded your hands or sat on them to keep from doing so, but as soon as you relaxed your vigilance there you were picking at it again.

It wasn't till she was back in the trailer, showering, letting the shampoo trail down her back, that what she'd been trying to avoid smacked her—almost literally, sending her swaying against the tiled wall. The accident on the A361 just outside Billicombe. October. Just the one car. No fatalities.

Jax had caused Richard and Pam's accident.

Richard had fallen asleep while reading an article about overwriting URL codes with SEO-friendly alternatives and didn't wake until midafternoon, so it took him awhile to realize that Suzanne hadn't returned from the twelve-step meeting. He checked his mobile, but she hadn't phoned or texted either. He couldn't remember her mobile number, of course, but after a few minutes he did recall that she'd written it on a scrap of paper that he'd tucked into his wallet. He rang her, only to get voice mail. "It's Richard. Just checking to make sure you're all right." Within minutes she texted him back: "Sorry. Tired. Came straight 2 trailer & bed. Will ring 2morrow."

That had been this afternoon. Now it was evening. His bed seemed to have expanded now that he was alone in it once again. The crowing of the gulls sounded louder and shriller without Suzanne's soft breaths to muffle them. Maybe he should get a dog. A dog to nestle beside him and snuffle as he slept. A dog wouldn't leave him. And he wouldn't be beholden to a dog, other than to feed it and walk it. He wouldn't have to worry about what a dog was thinking and plotting, what a dog really wanted from him, and whether he could give it to him.

He stretched out on his stomach, his right cheek against the pillow, waiting for sleep. Suzanne's text had been so terse, and "terse" was one word that he'd never have used to describe her. She must be angry at him, or disappointed by him somehow. What was it she wanted from him? Surely it wasn't for him to say the "l" word? To talk about their feelings, their future?

She was young. For all that she was independent, supporting herself—hell, she was a bloody TV star—he didn't think she'd had a lot of boyfriends. She didn't talk about her exes, or even joke about the uselessness of men the way that women who'd had a few bad experiences did.

But she hadn't said the "l" word—shit, was he such a pussy he couldn't even say the word in his mind?—either. And they'd only been sleeping together a few days. He was being ridiculous. Just as he'd forgotten what year he was born, he'd forgotten how to act and react when you started sleeping with someone.

He'd first told Pam he loved her during an especially intense orgasm. He was thrusting on top of her; she was licking the few hairs that ran down the center of his chest, tugging them just enough with her teeth, and "I love you" escaped his mouth just as his dick expanded within her and his cum exploded against her walls. But he didn't regret it. He repeated it afterward, as she nestled against his arm, the two of them watching the lazy tendrils of smoke from their shared cigarette drift upward. He repeated it, and because it felt so good to say it, he repeated it once more besides.

He couldn't imagine saying it to Suzanne. The thing was, he did feel something for her. Thinking of her now, wondering what was up with her, he felt a certain warmth inside, like when you drink hot chocolate on an especially cold day. He liked having her around. The way she cleaned the flat, so methodically, one area at a time, sorting things into piles, making sure the front of the lounge was shipshape before moving on to the back. How she cooked, like the tuna pasta bake she'd made last night: checking that all the ingredients were to hand, lining them up on the counter. He liked how he took care of her, he had to admit.

He'd even grown to like her continual questions, because sometimes they were so unexpected, you had to stop and try to puzzle out her thought processes. Take last night, when they were stretched out on the couch, his feet dangling over the edge, hers resting on his chest; *EastEnders* or *Coronation Street*, he wasn't sure which, was on the telly; she was leafing through one of his old computer magazines while he was reading a new one. And just like that she asked, "You know how some people have different-scented cleaning products in their house? Like lemon-scented dish soap and rose-gardenia air freshener and coconut hand soap? Why don't they think all those scents clash? If they were different colors or patterns, they'd clash horribly. So why don't people mind about scents clashing?" He'd laughed, and when she'd pouted, her lips puffing out slightly, he'd laughed harder.

Or early this morning, while he was still half-asleep: "Why did you decide to become a website designer? If the web hadn't been invented yet, what would you have done?"

He wasn't sure if he'd even answered her; he might have just gone back to sleep.

He liked her. He even liked living with her. But he didn't love her. He couldn't imagine saying the "l" word to her.

Maybe she knew it. Maybe that's why she'd left in such a hurry this morning. She hadn't even mentioned when she might be coming back. She'd arrived out of the blue, and now she'd left the same way.

She couldn't stay in the trailer. It was closing in around her. She grabbed her cigarettes, a soda from the fridge, and the script. She'd sit outside and finish reading it. Larry had been right: It wasn't awful. Her character, Cathy, got off some good lines at the expense of Davis's character. It would be fun. She needed fun. She'd finish reading it, ring Larry, and book her flight home.

Because if she'd thought she was climbing up her own arse before, what the hell did she call her situation now?

Shit stirring, that's all it was. She wasn't going to find Jax. He didn't want to be found.

She lit a cigarette, staring up. The clouds were so thick they formed one unending, impenetrable mass. If you were an alien landing on earth right now, you'd assume that the sky wasn't blue but the color of grubby hot-sheet hotel bedding, that there was no sun, that there was nothing up there but a soiled, solid scrim.

Beyond her stood several more rows of trailers, unoccupied so far as she could tell. The curtains drawn in all the windows. No cars parked next to them, no laundry hanging from the clotheslines, no bicycles leaning against them, no dirty wellies lined up outside the doors.

From the outside all the trailers looked like hers.

Faraway bleats punctuated the gossip of the unseen gulls.

She wasn't going to tell Richard what she knew about Jax and the accident. That would simply be more shit stirring.

But she would keep her appointment with Pam tomorrow. Tell her how Richard was doing. Tell her Richard still missed her.

And then she would book her flight and get the hell out of here.

CHAPTER 8

To kill time before she had to catch the bus to Boutport, Suzanne walked down to the High Street. Only a few clouds floated above, and they were the plump, billowy sort you saw on postcards, providing a picturesque contrast to the full-on brilliance of the sun. This was one of the few purely bright days since she'd arrived in Billicombe. The air was still cool, the breeze still strong enough to send the grasses rustling and her hair skittering about her face, but it didn't matter. The cows and sheep were more verbal than usual, their calls piling one atop the other, while the hoots of the wood pigeons overwhelmed the moaning of the gulls.

Once in town, she was reminded of another sketch of the High Street that Jax had included in a letter, of the upper portions of the buildings. The drawing had stretched across the entire width of the paper, one narrow structure against another, with no two the same. Each building was a different height, with different sizes and configurations of windows, some with balconies and windowboxes, some with flat roofs, others sloped. Dormers, gables, pediments, eaves, finials, brackets, all sorts of other architectural details she didn't know the names of—each building had a wealth of them, in different styles and numbers and sizes from every other building. Below this drawing, Jax had copied the Oscar Wilde quote "We are all in the gutter, but some of us are looking at the stars." His script was small and tight; in primary school he'd been scolded for writing too small and ignoring the lines on the pages.

She wondered whether, if she had the drawing with her, she'd be able to pick out the exact buildings Jax had depicted, or if he'd combined details to make up his own, heightened depiction. She lit a cigarette and pressed herself against the former health-food store with the "To Let" sign in the window so that the dog-walking pensioners and pony-tailed mothers with their strollers could pass as she stared up, studying the buildings opposite. "You know those pictures we used to like when we were kids, Spot the Difference?" he'd written. "In Billicombe you could do Spot the Similarities. Except there are none. You could make a picture book of it and drive a generation of kids mental."

She had to look away, back down to street level, before she'd even finished her cigarette. It was partly because the sun was so bright, even semiobscured as it was by the buildings. But it was also partly because Jax was right; staring too long to find two windows or two gingerbread balconies that were identical would drive you mad.

Options salon was tucked in one of the lanes off Boutport's High Street, between a SpecSavers and a fair-trade clothing and jewelry shop. With its black sinks and counters, mirrors framed in brushed silver, knockoff Eames chairs in the waiting area, copies of British and American and Italian *Vogue* fanned out on the low-slung glass table that the chairs surrounded, Options apparently catered to an aspirational clientele. Suzanne was glad. She'd have hated for Richard's girlfriend to be someone who spent all day painting thick yellow highlights on brown-haired women or administering poodle perms.

Only two other customers were in the shop. Both looked to be in their thirties, maybe early forties. One had dozens of silver squares folded about her head that stuck out like miniature solar panels. She was reading a hardcover book. The other gestured around her wet hair, no doubt telling the stylist, a swarthy man whose gray tank top clung to his six-pack, exactly how she wanted her cut to look.

Barely two minutes after Suzanne had identified herself to the receptionist and sat down, a tall woman with an asymmetrical short bob dyed the palest shade of blonde walked over. "Are you Anne? I'm Pam."

Suzanne stood up. Pam was nearly as tall as Richard. She wasn't beautiful—her nose was too broad, her eyes too small for that—but she nonetheless managed to be gorgeous. Her white jeans hugged what Davis would have described as an ass you could bounce a dime off of. The V of her black T-shirt revealed a tease of cleavage. Suzanne felt boyish in comparison.

Pam guided her to a chair opposite the woman in foils. "So, what can we do for you today?" She ran her hands through Suzanne's uncombed waves. "Your hair is colored, isn't it? Did you do it yourself?" She tucked the side sections behind Suzanne's ears and raked the fringe off her forehead. Looking in the mirror, Pam stopped. "You know, you look a lot like that girl from the American TV show—what is it?—*Lakeview Drive*, I think. Though she's blond."

Suzanne looked down at her lap. "Yeah, I get that a lot." She spoke in her London accent.

Pam removed her hand, letting Suzanne's hair fall back onto her face. "She's not all that pretty. We can make you look better." Suzanne had to fight to keep from smirking.

Pam continued staring into the mirror at her. "So, what were you thinking?" she said to Suzanne's reflection. "A big change, go really short?"

This was it. Deep breath. "Actually, I wanted to talk about Richard."

Beneath her carefully applied foundation Pam turned pale. She almost seemed to shrink away from the makeup, so that a fine buffer of nothing sat between the powder and blusher and mascara and Pam herself. "My Richard?" Pam said. And with that, Suzanne knew that Pam still loved him.

"Yes. I'm a friend of his. Is there somewhere we can..."

"Is he all right?" Pam rested an arm on the countertop beneath the mirror to steady herself.

"He's fine. He doesn't know I'm here, by the way."

Pam glanced around. She walked over to the receptionist, who was now sweeping the floor, and spoke too quietly for Suzanne to hear. Then she came back, took Suzanne's hand, and walked with her to the door. "We can get a coffee around the corner."

"What did you tell the receptionist?" Suzanne asked as they walked past the SpecSavers and turned right onto an even tinier, cobble-stoned alley. As if to confirm that the enveloping coffee aroma wasn't an olfactory mirage, a metal stand outside the alley's lone door advertised cappuccino and espresso. Pam directed her in, nodded at the middle-aged woman behind the counter, and sat down at a small square table in the back.

"I told her you'd come in to get a haircut because you'd broken up with your boyfriend, but that you'd started getting really upset and said you couldn't go through with it and just needed someone to talk to." Pam pulled out a pack of cigarettes from the fashionably oversize black-leather bag she'd grabbed on her way out of the salon. "Do you mind if I smoke?"

Jesus, did everyone in Devon smoke? "Not at all," Suzanne said, rummaging around her own canvas bag for her cigarettes.

"So how is Richard? And why are you here?" Pam drew the flimsy tin ashtray from the end of the table to the center. Her hand holding the cigarette was clenched.

"I'm visiting Billicombe, met Richard, and we struck up a friendship. Like I said, he doesn't know I'm here."

"But he's okay? His leg is healing?"

"He's fine, out and about."

"What about his memory?"

The middle-aged woman, her hair tucked into a white cap, came by the table. "The usual?" she asked Pam, who nodded. Turning to Suzanne, "And you?"

"A Diet Coke, please."

The woman left, her white nursing shoes leaving a trail of soft squeaks.

"I don't know what his memory was like before." Suzanne rolled the tip of her cigarette against the edge of the ashtray. "I've only known him for a couple of weeks. It's still spotty, I guess." She waited, watching Pam through her lashes.

Pam waited too. After another silent drag of her cigarette, she said, "So why are you here, then?"

Suzanne knew she should have spent the bus ride rehearsing what she was going to say, rather than admiring the scenery. "He thinks you left him because of the scars on his back. I've seen the scars; they aren't that bad. I don't think you're that shallow a person. Something seems off."

The woman returned with their drinks. They thanked her; once again she squeaked away.

"Has he told you what happened, the accident and that?" Pam was looking not at Suzanne but at an invisible companion beside Suzanne.

Suzanne nodded.

"Who exactly are you?"

"I told you; I'm a friend. I'm only in Billicombe for a few more weeks, but I just felt that I couldn't leave without getting to the bottom of this." Christ, she sounded like she was in a straight-to-DVD flick. "Richard seems like a good guy. Though he thinks I'm a little nosy." She smiled, the same close-lipped one she used in *Lakeview Drive* when Robin was trying to worm out of a minor scrape.

"How did you see his back scars?"

"We were talking, he mentioned them, I asked him to lift up his shirt." Now Suzanne got it. "We're not dating, if that's what you mean. He's still in love with you, to be honest. Which is why I'm here."

Pam's face crumpled. Suzanne yanked a wad of napkins from the metal dispenser and passed them to her. Pam dabbed at her face, shading it from Suzanne with her hand.

"When he finally came out of hospital, Richard was a mess." Pam blew her nose quietly. "I'm surprised they even let him out. He'd be fine for a couple hours, listening to music, chatting like normal. But then he'd just stop and stare. And you'd say something to him, like, 'Are you okay?' and he'd look at you like he had no idea who you were or even who he was. 'Whose house is this?' 'Do I know you?'" She stubbed out her cigarette.

"They had nurses come by every day so I could go back to work. Usually he was asleep when I came home. When he woke up sometimes he was fine, almost back to normal. But other times it was, 'What's my name again? Shit, I can't remember my name,' all panicky. The doctors had said his memory would heal over time, but I wasn't seeing it."

"It's gotten much better since then."

"He told you about the accident, did he?" Pam straightened up and stared at her full on, almost defiant. "He told you I was driving?"

Suzanne nodded.

"So basically all this was my fault, wasn't it?"

Before Suzanne had time to respond, Pam rushed on. "I'm not sure he'd thought about it that way yet. But he's a smart guy, Richard. Maybe he was already thinking it and just didn't want me to know." Pam wiped under her eyes with her forefingers. They came away smudged with mascara. "But it was only a matter of time before he started resenting me, wasn't it? And me being around reminding him of what had happened, and how he was all effed up but I'd walked away pretty much scot-free, hadn't I? Almost like... like a taunt, I guess. 'Ha ha, I'm fine, and you're effed.' So I figured, the best thing I could do for him was let him heal and start fresh. You know?" Again Pam looked directly at her. Mascara was clumped in the inner corners of her eyes and streaked beneath them. Her nose was red and shiny. Her hair remained perfect, however, which only made the rest of her look more bedraggled.

Suzanne didn't know what to say. She knew what she was thinking, but she wasn't sure saying it was the best tack to take.

Screw it. She might as well. "That has to be one of the stupidest things I've ever heard."

Pam's brows rose, disappearing beneath her bangs. "What?" Her voice was equal parts hurt and outrage.

"Did you ask him if he resented you? Blamed you? Did you tell him you felt guilty?" Suzanne lit a fresh cigarette from the stub she was about to grind out. "I didn't think so. So you left Richard because of what you thought he was thinking."

"Because I thought it was best for him," Pam hissed. "And really, if he was missing me so goddam much, he could have rung me."

"For one thing, he couldn't remember the town you'd gone to. Did you even go back to your folks?"

Pam glared at her, but finally answered. "Yes, I took a month's leave. I went to stay with my parents in Torbay."

Suzanne refused to look away. "Also, I think because of that stalker ex-boyfriend of yours..."

"He told you about that?" Pam said in wonderment.

"... he was afraid of tracking you down. Hunting you down. He didn't want to spook you. And he figured if you wanted to come back you would have called."

Pam scooped her hair off her forehead with both hands. Her fringe had been hiding a cluster of tiny white blemishes. "Bloody hell," she muttered.

Suzanne smoked in silence. Pam's cappuccino grew cold. Pam stared into it but showed no inclination to drink it.

"Would you be willing to have lunch with him?" Suzanne asked.

Pam lifted her eyes but not her head. "Would he be willing to have lunch with me?"

Suzanne shrugged. "I don't know. But I can ask."

Pam nodded. Suzanne rummaged through her bag, pulled out a creased matchbook with just one match left. She wrote down her mobile number and slid it across the table to Pam. "You ring to tell me when is a good time, and I'll take it from there." She wondered why she didn't feel sympathy or empathy for Pam as she had yesterday for Ian. "I have to go. Are you going to be okay?"

Pam nodded, snuffling. She brought her handbag up onto the table and retrieved a compact. Seeing her reflection, she groaned. "Jesus, I'm a bloody wreck." From her bag she pulled out a smaller, purple zippered bag and began plucking out mascara, an eyelash curler, cotton swabs. Suzanne scraped back her chair and stood. Pam looked up. "Sorry for being such a mess."

Suzanne smiled politely. "No worries." Then she remembered what she'd wanted to say earlier, but hadn't had the chance to amid Pam's flow of words. "It wasn't your fault, you know. It was just an accident."

Pam sighed. "I don't know. Maybe if I'd been driving slower..."

"The guy ran right out in front of you on a dark deserted road." She was surprised by the intensity of her tone. "There was nothing you could do."

Pam sighed again, a shakier sigh. Her shoulders were slumped, her head wilting on her neck. She was never going to believe that, not completely.

For the first time, Suzanne hated Jax.

No matter how many cigarettes she smoked while waiting for the bus, no matter how much soda she guzzled while riding back to Billicombe, Suzanne couldn't get the bilelike taste of her hatred out of her mouth. She knew her face was contorted in a sneer, but she couldn't unfreeze the muscles. She couldn't unclench her fists or her toes. When she tracked Jax down—and she would, never mind what she'd thought yesterday, she was closing in on him, all she had to do was talk to Valley one more time—when she tracked him down she wasn't going to be all soft and understanding and allow him to cry and promise to do better.

She didn't think she'd been an enabler—how she hated all that recovery jargon. This last rehab stint, for instance, that had been an ultimatum. When the police had called that last time, she hadn't rushed to bail him out; she'd made him stay overnight in jail and most of the next day. She'd refused to pay for a lawyer, made him rely on a public defender. And when the charges (disorderly conduct, destruction of property) were dropped, she'd sat him down at the dining room table and told him he could either go to rehab in England or move out. She hadn't sat next to him, but at the head of the table, with him at the foot. She'd chosen the center in Sussex, Jaywalker Manor, because she felt he needed to get away from his environment—not just his user buddies and his coterie of dealers, but also from her.

He listened, chewing on several strands of hair, slouched over a mug of orange juice that she knew he'd poured some vodka into. Which was just as well. She wasn't equipped to deal with a full-blown detox.

He listened, and when she was finished he nodded.

"So what's it going to be?" She didn't dare light a cigarette. She didn't want him to see how unsteady her hands were.

"Rehab. When can I go?"

They had four days together before he left. They avoided each other. He drank in his room, maybe cooked up a few bags for all she knew. She went out and about: costume fittings for a film that later fell through, dinner with Elisabeth, a meeting with Larry. Hours spent at the Barnes & Noble in The Grove.

She booked a cab to take him to LAX. The flight was scheduled for 5:35 in the evening. She had the cab come at one. Even if traffic was especially snarled, he'd have a few hours to check in, find a bar, have a few drinks. He'd probably stash a bottle in one of his bags and be half-loaded by the time he arrived at the airport, not enough to stagger about or slur, but enough that it would take him longer to get his bearings, find the right gate. She hoped he didn't drink so much at the airport itself that they wouldn't let him on the plane, but if he did, and he called, she had steeled herself to say no, he couldn't come back here.

She sat on the couch, waiting for the cab, rubbing at the spot where he'd burned a hole. It had been repaired, no one would guess it had been damaged, but she knew. She didn't even pretend to read. She sat, cross-legged, and smoked.

Jax dragged his duffel bag into the living room at a quarter to one. His hair was wet. He smelled of sandalwood and cigarettes; a half-smoked one hung from his chafed lips. His eyes were red-rimmed. He'd had gorgeous eyes once, huge, round, the blue of the Pacific on an especially vivid day. Now they were puffy and faded, the whites resembling cream gone bad and crisscrossed with broken capillaries.

He stood before her, examining the scuffed-beige toes of his brown boots. "I'm not going to say sorry, because you've heard it so many times before. It probably doesn't mean anything anymore, does it?"

She stared into the ashtray on the table in front of her. "No."

He let go of the bag. It made a soft thump as its full weight fell to the floor. He walked over to the table, stiff-legged, and flicked his ashes. "Thanks for this." He trembled, all over. He must not have had anything to drink since yesterday.

She remained seated. He remained standing.

The cab came several minutes early. Even though she'd been expecting the doorbell for hours, she jumped when it chimed.

Jax carefully stubbed out against his fingertip the cigarette he'd just lit, then tucked it behind his ear. "Thanks," he said again, picking up the handle on one end of his bag. "I love you," he said without looking at her.

She ran to him, wrapped herself around him, tried to hold him tight enough to stop his shaking but failed. "I'm going to miss you." She managed to keep her voice steady. "I love you too."

Jax let her hold him for a moment, then eased himself away. "I know. But maybe you should learn not to." He opened the door, nodded to the driver, and left without looking back.

That had been nineteen months ago. September fifteenth. A week shy of three months later she flew out to visit him. She'd paid for him to stay in rehab for three months. He, and his care team, had suggested he stay another three.

She hired a car at Heathrow, even though she'd never driven in England and was nervous about being on the opposite side of the road and negotiating the roundabouts, and headed straight to Jaywalker. The facility had once been the seat of a now-dead line of nobility. From the B road up to the circular drive in front of the building was nearly three miles of crunchy gravel.

Jax had put on a few pounds, which suited him. His skin didn't look to be hanging off his bones anymore. The ends of his hair were neatly trimmed. His eyes were clear. Not as bright as when they were kids, but focused. His nails were short and clean.

He still smelled of sandalwood and cigarettes.

They walked the grounds. The frost-hardened grass snapped beneath their feet. White puffs of breath punctuated their speech.

They made small talk at first. You look good. What are you working on? How's the food?

"I don't know if I can ever pay you back. The dosh for this place, I mean."

"I don't want you to." She'd banked a nice bonus for agreeing to a fourth season of *Lakeview Drive* the previous year, which was covering his stay and would help him out once he left. That's why she'd signed on again for that last year; she'd suspected even then that he'd need another stint at rehab sooner or later. He hadn't settled in to his sobriety. He'd kept himself busy—working in a call center, then in an art-supply store; studying tae kwan do; picking up another book the moment he closed the one he'd just finished reading—but it only served to distract himself from using when he should have been concentrating on staying sober.

"I want to pay you back, though. I just don't know how or when."

"Okay." She stared at his profile. Golden stubble glistened on his cheeks. "We'll work something out."

They passed an older, well-fed man walking with a careworn woman. Jax and the man nodded to each other.

"I know I'm not ready to leave just yet." Jax removed the half-smoked roll-up tucked behind his ear and stopped to light it. "And I'm scared shitless."

He'd never told her he was scared. She'd known it, but he'd never said it.

"I know this is it for me." Crisp clouds hung on his words. "I fuck this up, and I'm done."

The air was astringent. Her skin and scalp tingled.

"I don't think you know how much I appreciate everything."

"Of course I do..."

"No. You can't." The fresh pink of his cheeks deepened to a rough red. "However much you think it is, it's more."

She took her cigarettes out of her back pocket and lit one.

"The thing is..." He paused to lick his lips. He opened and closed his mouth several times before continuing. "The thing is, I love you, I love seeing you, I'm so glad you came."

He paused. She braced herself.

"But being with you makes me feel like shit. Because I've been a shit to you. And because compared with you, I am a shit."

"Stop it," she snapped.

He halted, so she did as well. All around them lay nothing but white-rimmed grass, except for the pebbled walkway parallel to them a few yards away. Far off the silhouettes of bare-branched trees stood flat against the faded blue sky and a few anemic clouds.

"Hear me out, okay? I'm not saying this to get a rise from you, I'm not saying this because I'm feeling sorry for myself. I'm saying it because it's true, for me." He turned toward her. His face was all sharp, piercing angles, and his skin sheer enough to be bruised by a gust of wind. "I don't want you feeling, I don't know, guilty. Or angry. But the thing is, I could get out of here tomorrow, stay sober the rest of my life, and I could never catch up with you. Or undo the shit I've done."

"It's not a competition."

He took a last drag, then pinched the lit end of the cigarette between his fingers before putting the stub in his front jeans pocket. "I know that, here." He rapped the side of his head with his fist. "But not in here." Now he thumped his chest.

"Jax, if you stayed sober, that would be better than anything I could do."

He lifted one corner of his mouth. "For me, yeah. But let's face it, most of the world manages not to become junkies or drunks, and they don't walk around expecting praise for it." He mustered a grin. "Obviously this is something I still need to work on."

She gave a half-grin in response almost without realizing it. Finishing her cigarette she dropped it to the ground and stamped it out. Jax bent down to retrieve it and slipped it in his pocket.

He took her hands. His felt wonderfully dry. "I must have done something amazing in a previous life to get you as my sister." He coughed up a chuckle. "And you must have been a real arsehole to get me as a brother."

Suzanne missed her stop. She got off at the next one, about a mile downhill, and trudged back to the caravan park. It had started to rain sometime during the bus ride, a steady but unexceptional downpour. She didn't bother putting up the hood of her gilet; she'd just end up soaked anyway.

As she walked, she mapped out her next moves. Tonight she'd head back to the pub where she'd first seen Lee. If he wasn't there, she'd wait for him at Lloyds Pharmacy tomorrow morning.

And once she found Jax, she wouldn't confront him about the accident. That's not what all this effort and time was about. It wasn't even about Jax, not really. It was about her. Because she missed him.

Suzanne fell asleep on the sofa within minutes of peeling off her drenched jeans and socks and boots. She didn't wake until nearly half-ten that night. The rain rattled against the sides and roof of the cabin and the wind throttled the windows, demanding to be let in. She'd skip the pub but definitely head down to Lloyds in the morning.

While she was asleep Pam had texted her. Friday noon was best for her, but if need be, she could work out something for later in the day.

Richard had texted as well. "Everything okay?"

She set the alarm on her mobile for 7 a.m. and went back to sleep.

CHAPTER 9

Suzanne waited outside the Lloyds for over an hour. The couple who'd been in the alley with her the last time shuffled to the door a few minutes before it opened. They didn't acknowledge her. The woman with the badly dyed bun came shortly after as well. Each left about twenty minutes after entering, faces flushed and damp.

A woman with severe scoliosis, her neck and shoulders nearly parallel to the ground, struggled with the door. Suzanne opened it for her. She also opened the door for several young women with strollers. When they emerged their faces were the same pale color as when they'd entered, a bloodless hue that reminded her of raw chicken and that had seemed so foreign when she'd first arrived back in England, such a contrast to the perma-tans of L.A.

She continued to look up and down the street, across the street. Maybe Lee had seen her waiting for him. But she was certain she'd have spotted him turning away, slipping down a side road or an alley.

Maybe he'd worked his way up to being allowed to get a week's worth of methadone at a time to take home, rather than having to come down to the pharmacy every day but Sunday.

Or maybe he was using again.

She checked the time on her mobile periodically. A few minutes past ten she called it quits. She was tired of avoiding the stares of everyone who walked by. And she needed to talk to Richard.

When faced with what she felt was an unactable scene, Suzanne would prepare by making up an imaginary scene that led up to it. She'd had to do this a lot that last season of *Lakeview Drive*. Like when Robin had to tell Eric, her boyfriend, that she wasn't going to go to college in Boston after all; she was going to take a year off and travel through Europe instead. The entire previous season had been setting things up so that Robin would get into

Harvard and be just across town from Eric, who had already enrolled at Tufts. But when Suzanne refused to renew for a fifth season, except for a few guest appearances, the producers had decided they needed to bring Eric back to Lakeview from Boston as a regular character, and the way to do this was to have his heart broken by Robin so that he would drop out of college and return home to pull himself together. It had been nothing short of ridiculous: Robin was the last character on earth who would give up a partial scholarship to Harvard, and arrogant Eric was the last character on earth who would fall to pieces after being dumped.

So to make sense of it, Suzanne had made up a scene in which Eric began laying out their entire future, and when Robin balked, he all but dared her to come up with some sort of alternative. "What're you going to do—go hitchhiking across Europe for a year? That's not you, and you know it!"

"Maybe. You don't know..."

"Oh, come off it, Robs. You don't even like coming to Boston by yourself."

"Oh, I do." Making up these lines in her bathroom, facing the mirror as she ran a cold shower to drown out her words in case Jax could hear her talking to herself, she'd shoved her shoulders back and lengthened her spine. "What I'm beginning to realize is that I like coming to Boston, but not seeing you. Traveling by myself, riding the T from the airport out here by myself because you're too selfish to meet me, that's the best part of the trip."

As a scriptwriter she was a pretty good actress. All the same, creating that bit of backstory and acting it out, even though she was alone and in her bathroom, gave her enough of a reason to be able to say with some sort of conviction the lines that had been written.

So she'd done something similar this morning on her way to the High Street. She'd crafted a scene that would lead to Richard agreeing to accompany her to Boutport for lunch tomorrow. Hopefully Richard would stick close to the lines she had written for him, although he didn't even know a script existed.

She stopped by the convenience store to buy two bottles of Diet Coke for herself, then at the bakery to pick up two frosted buns, one for each of them. She let herself into his flat with the spare set of keys that they'd found over the weekend while cleaning out his bedroom—Pam's old keys, no doubt.

Richard was making a cup of tea. She stood in the doorway to the kitchen. "Sorry for not returning your text. I was exhausted. I slept straight through the night and only saw it this morning."

"No worries." Richard avoided looking at her. Could Pam have contacted him? No, she'd know straightaway. "Want a cuppa?" He seemed to be working to keep his voice level.

"No thanks." She set her bags down on the folding table on her way to the loo. When she returned Richard was seated at the head of the table drinking his tea in front of his laptop. She went into the kitchen, found two plates, washed them (they looked greasy), and brought them out. She perched on a chair along the side of the table, placing the buns on the dishes and sliding one over to him.

"Cheers." His smile erased the furrow between his brows. He hadn't combed his hair yet, so it stuck up in patches like a lawn overdue for mowing. "You didn't have to do that."

"I know. I'm a nice person." She grinned. "What did you do last night?"

"I was trying out a new code for an animation. But it wasn't compatible with..." He broke off. "I won't bore you with it. But I'm thinking of maybe putting an ad in the local paper, seeing if any of the small businesses around here need a website built. I won't charge much, in case..." He shrugged.

"In case you take a job and then forget about the deadline?"

He lowered his head. "Something like that."

She bit into her bun. "So you haven't forgotten anything you knew about web design from before the accident?"

"No." The surprise was evident in his voice. "In fact, I apparently picked up information that I don't remember learning. Like there's an add-on that was introduced around Christmastime. I saw an article about it last night and I started reading it, and I knew everything that was in it. It should have been new to me, but it wasn't. I must have read about it sometime in the past few months but not remembered reading it. But I still remembered the information in it." He shook his head. "Weird, isn't it? Though apparently there's a name for this sort of amnesia. I checked it out on Wikipedia this morning." He paused for effect. "Of course, now I can't remember what it's called." He laughed.

Suzanne rubbed her teeth with her forefinger. The bun was so sweet, her teeth were sticky with sugar. "Can I be your first client?"

"You?"

"Yeah. Larry thinks I should have an official website. I think it's a load of crap, but it might be a way for you to ease back into it."

"Yeah?"

She liked how he lifted his eyebrows when especially pleased. She couldn't help but smile in response. "Yeah. Nothing too fancy. I'm not going to be blogging to my three fans or anything. Just a few pix, a bio, a news section. I guess that's it."

"You sure?" He sounded disappointed.

She pushed the rest of her bun away and pulled out her cigarettes. "Well, unless you have any ideas. You're the expert."

"I'll have a think." He closed the lid of his laptop and moved it off to the side, then pulled his bun in front of him.

"So," Suzanne stroked the side of her soda bottle, "are you doing anything tomorrow for lunch?"

He waited till he finished chewing to reply. "I don't know. I'll have to check my busy social calendar."

"I'll take that as a no. Which is good because I'm meeting someone for lunch in Boutport at noon and I want you to come."

"Something to do with your brother?"

She'd hoped he would assume as much. "Yup." If he pressed for details, she had at the ready a story about how this person she was meeting sounded a bit intimidating on the phone, so she'd feel much more comfortable having a guy come with her. But he didn't press. "So you'll come?"

He snorted. "You're actually asking? Usually you just tell me."

"I haven't known you long enough for anything to be 'usually.'"

"Maybe it's only been a week or two, but that's definitely been long enough for me to say that you 'usually' tell me to do something instead of ask me."

She laughed. "If I didn't know better, I'd think you were suggesting that I'm bossy."

"Oh, I'm not suggesting."

Suddenly she wished they could continue this give-and-take in bed. They were good together. They always had fun. And he knew exactly which spots to tease and which to caress at exactly which times.

But they couldn't, not when she was getting him ready to reunite with Pam. She finished her cigarette and stood up.

"Well, I have to go."

"You do?" He reached out for her hands and gently tugged her toward him.

She'd planned for this as well, but now she didn't want to follow through with the scene she'd plotted out. All the same she broke away. "I promised Larry I'd finish reading the script today and get back to him about whether I want to go for it."

"Why don't you come back here tonight, then?"

She'd intended to return tonight to the pub where she'd first seen Lee. But maybe it would be less awkward, less obvious, if she had Richard with her. And then she could stay at Richard's flat and they'd catch the bus to Boutport together in the morning. He'd probably want to have sex, but she could easily come up with an excuse. Cramps or something.

"Okay. How about I come by around seven?"

They went to Emperor's Court, the Chinese restaurant just a few doors down from the pub, for dinner. Suzanne couldn't eat more than a few bites. Which was not good, as it meant that by the time she finished her second cider at the pub, she was already developing a buzz.

"So did you like the script?"

She could barely hear him. Their booth was beside the snooker table, and the clacking of the balls and the whoops of the players and the thumping of the speakers hanging above the booth behind them overwhelmed his words.

"The script that you were reading—any good?"

Oh. She nodded. "Yeah, it is kind of cute. So I told him to pursue it. Which means I'll probably have to fly back in a week or so." All of which was a lie. Except for the script being okay.

"Who are you looking for?"

"No one. Why?"

"Because you keep craning your neck and looking around. Are you supposed to be meeting someone?"

"No." She looked down into her empty pint glass. "Though I'm hoping someone might show up."

The set of her jaw warned Richard not to ask anything else. He drained his pint, took her glass as well, and headed to the bar. Something was up with her. She was more fidgety than usual. Shifting in her seat, drumming her fingertips against the table, saying she wanted to cut down her smoking one minute and lighting another cigarette the next. It would be presumptuous to think it had anything to do with him. It must be something about her brother.

He'd seen one picture of him online, with her at some awards show. If Richard had spotted him around Billicombe, he'd have assumed Jax was a surfer from nearby Croyde or Saunton. He saw the family resemblance straight away, especially because Suzanne had also been blond in the photo, though a darker shade than her brother. They had the same thin face and pointy chin, the same large eyes, though while hers were a chocolaty brown, like a Labrador's, his seemed to be a run-of-the-mill blue. But even in that one photo, you could see that she had the charisma for both of them. You didn't even notice him at first. It was as if they weren't together, that he was just some random bloke who'd stepped into the frame. Suzanne, though, she glowed. Like Pam did when she entered a room.

He carried their pints back to the table, raising his arms over the heads of a sudden throng crushing toward the bar. He and Suzanne would finish their drinks and he'd try to persuade her to head home. Head to bed. He felt a twinge of guilt for using sex with her to forget about Pam, but it wasn't as if she didn't enjoy it. He'd grown certain that she did. Some things you couldn't fake, could you? He didn't mean the actual orgasms, a girl didn't need to be a professional actress to fake those. But the rest: her sliding her calves against his afterward, the slow smile that overtook her face as he stroked the hair out of her eyes. He'd take her to bed, really focus on relaxing her. She was probably nervous about this lunch tomorrow, is all.

While Richard was at the bar Suzanne slid out of the booth and walked over to one of the snooker players waiting his turn. "Excuse me. Are you expecting a bloke named Valley to be coming by?"

The snooker player, a weedy guy with rounded shoulders whose hair looked to be plastered to his crown with either sweat or too much gel, shifted his cue from one hand to the next. "I'm not in with Valley."

"But he comes here a lot, doesn't he?"

The guy, who looked to be about her age, stepped back. "I don't know. I'm not into that shit."

She spied Richard returning with their pints. "Cheers, then."

"If you tell me what this person you're hoping to see looks like," Richard said after a few moments, "I can keep an eye out as well."

She nibbled on her lower lip. "He's dark. Dark hair pulled back in a ponytail. Big creases down his cheeks. Taller than me, not as tall as you."

"That part doesn't narrow it down very much," he said. She didn't laugh.

Watching her so keyed up was making him edgy. He dug out his wallet. He had just enough for one more round, and that was only because she'd insisted on paying for dinner. He didn't even know if he had enough coins on the kitchen counter for tomorrow's bus fare.

As soon as she finished her pint he went back to the bar and returned with two sambucas. He slammed his down in one go and nodded at her to do the same. She sniffed the contents of the glass, shrugged, and drank up, spluttering afterward.

"What the hell was that?"

"Sambuca. You didn't like it, did you?"

She grinned for the first time that evening. "I loved it, actually." She paused as if to catch her breath, then stood up and went to the bar for two more.

He draped his arm around her shoulder as they walked down Fortescue to his flat. She was leaning against him, but holding herself rigid. Still, at least she was talking, and laughing.

He kept his arm around her even as he unlocked the front door and then the door to his flat. Steered her to the bed and gently pressed her shoulders to sit her down. Without taking off his jacket he knelt in front of her, ignoring the pangs in his left knee, and kissed her, separating her lips with his tongue. She reared back. "Not tonight."

"Yes tonight." He smoothed her hair off her face. "I know you're nervous about tomorrow. I'll help you relax." He sat beside her and leaned over to nuzzle the nape of her neck. She tasted of anise from the sambuca and salt.

She pushed herself up, and several lengths away, toward the foot of the bed. He leaned toward her. "What's wrong?"

She shook her head, her neck hunched into her shoulders. Her legs dangled over the side, several centimeters off the ground.

He wrapped his arm around her again, gently, as if afraid of squeezing too tight and shattering her. "It's all right," he murmured. "Just tell me what's wrong, so I can help." He meant it. He didn't care if they had sex. Well, of course he cared, of course he still wanted her, his dick was chafing against the confines of his trousers and boxers. But more than that, he wanted her to smile.

Her back remained stiff and her body still except for her legs, which swung back and forth. After a moment, though, she placed one of her hands on top of his, stroking the raised veins. He lifted her hand and pressed it against his lips. She inched toward him and allowed herself to melt beneath him, then allowed him to melt around her and, finally, within her.

Afterward, when she curled over and pretended to be asleep, she was able to rationalize it. She didn't want him feeling insecure about his sexual prowess before meeting with Pam. She wanted him to feel confident. If she'd refused, he'd have insisted on knowing why, and she would have had to tell him the truth about tomorrow's lunch, and then he'd have stayed up worrying the whole night.

But having lived with an addict for so many years, she knew bullshit when she heard it, even when she was the one dishing it out. She'd made love with him because she'd wanted to, one last time.

She was already growing accustomed to his body—the areas of his back to avoid, the small slightly raised mole on his left shoulder. She'd learned that he liked her to nibble on his earlobe but not run her tongue around it. Knowing that this was the last time, she found herself elaborating her caresses, trying to brush against every part of him.

She hoped he'd remember tonight for years to come, and that when he did he'd smile, and feel a comforting, reassuring warmth. Because she knew she would.

CHAPTER 10

"Why aren't you dressed? We have to catch the bus in twenty minutes."

Richard looked up from his computer, pausing the video he was watching. Suzanne had just come in the front door, but he didn't remember her leaving. Or getting dressed, for that matter. Or why they had to catch a bus in twenty minutes or where they were going.

Fuck, not again. He turned away so she wouldn't see the panic on his face. Faded yellowish light was pushing through from the kitchen, so it was daytime. He was in his flat. He remembered being in bed with Suzanne, watching her ribcage rise and fall as she slept. He remembered tangled sweaty limbs slipping and gliding against each other...

Right. He was accompanying her to lunch in Boutport. They were going to meet someone who had some sort of connection with her brother. He sighed in relief, then leapt to his feet as he realized, Shit, he'd better hurry.

They had to run for the bus, Richard's run more of a lopsided hop favoring his left leg, but they made it. They sat in the last row. Suzanne jiggled her foot. "Nervous?" he asked. He put his arm around her shoulder, but she leaned forward so that it dropped off, as a silk shawl might. "Just rehearsing what I'm going to say." She flashed a smile before turning to stare out the window.

As they neared the curve in the road leading up to the spot of the accident, Suzanne asked suddenly, "Why don't you ever see any baby seagulls?"

"Eh?"

She leaned her back against the window. "In the city you never see baby pigeons, and by the seaside you never see baby seagulls. It's like they're born full grown, like that Botticelli painting of Venus rising from the clam."

Why was she talking about baby birds all of a sudden? As they rolled past the West Downs sign, it came to him that she was going out of her way to distract him from the scene of the accident. Which was sweet. She really was a sweet kid.

Not that he'd thought of her as a kid last night. Though now, revisiting certain moments—or rather, as certain moments flashed through his mind—there'd been a credulity, or maybe incredulity, to her. One moment in particular: She'd been above him, supporting her weight on her arms, and she'd looked into his face as if trying to memorize it, because she couldn't quite believe the moment was happening.

Or maybe he was projecting. Because really, here he was, scarred, leg still gimpy, Swiss cheese for a memory, jobless, banging a TV star. Okay, a TV star he'd never heard of until a few days ago. But still. If it had been a year ago, if he were still in London, still working at the agency, still going out to crowded pubs with his mates, even then it would have been pretty damn unbelievable. But here and now...

He had to force himself to think of her as a Hollywood actress, though. To think of her as Soozie Northrup. Aside from the occasional moment like now, or last night as he was entering her, she was just little, skinny Suzanne. Like the sister of a friend of a friend, or something like that. Odd, wasn't it?

They got off the bus at the penultimate stop, down the street from the Pannier Market and across from Wood's, a cafe-slash-coffeehouse with none of the charm that either noun implied. Wood's had a plastic-looking facade painted in an unappetizing cross between yellow and coral. It looked all the more uninspiring for being sandwiched between The Three Pigeons, whose hand-lettered wooden sign swaying above its heavy oaken door would not have been out of place when the pub was founded four hundred years ago, and Turpin's Meats, in whose front window a butcher in the traditional red-and-white striped apron, bow tie, and straw boater was adjusting the display of chops and steaks.

Suzanne leaned against the brick wall beside an estate agent's window and lit a cigarette. "About who we're meeting." She paused to turn her head and exhale away from the elderly woman chugging past in an electric scooter. "It's Pam."

"Pam?" The only Pam he knew was... "My Pam? What does she have to do with your brother?"

Suzanne continued to look away. The breeze blew her hair across her face, but she didn't tuck it behind her ears. "Nothing. I kind of lied about that part."

He joined her against the wall, supporting himself with one arm so that he could face her, watch her, though her wind-strewn hair screened her off. "You and I are here in Boutport to meet with Pam? Pam who moved out this past autumn?"

"Yup."

"How...?" He was missing something, not just a gap of hours or days, something bigger.

"I tracked her down. I knew she couldn't have left you because of those dinky little scars, there had to be something else. So I called around a few salons here, found her, met with her on Wednesday, and, well, here we are." Finally she pushed her hair out of her eyes and mouth, but her face still wasn't giving anything away.

He pulled his tobacco out from his back pocket, dropped it on the pavement. As he rose from retrieving it, Suzanne handed him her pack of Marlboro Lights and lighter. He took one and lit up. He could barely feel it in his hand; he was numb.

"And whose idea was this lunch, then?"

"Hers." She seemed to be trying to hide how proud of herself she was; she wore a crooked little smile and her cheeks were carnation pink. "Look, she was really worried about you, wanted to be sure you were okay, was really happy when I told her you were."

"And did she wonder who the hell you were?" A woman bent from the weight of several canvas shopping bags glared at him as she passed. He must have been shouting, or near to it.

"I told her I was a friend. That's all." She waited till a woman pushing a double-stroller had passed before tossing her cigarette butt toward the curb.

"You didn't think to tell me what you were planning? To, I don't know, give me a choice as to whether I wanted to see her? Or at least prepare myself?" He yanked his gaze from her and stared down the street, watching the shoppers stroll into and out of the Pannier, biting into fruit, gesturing while talking into their mobiles, examining the contents of their bags and their wallets.

"Look, in America they're big on 'closure.'" She made quote marks with her fingers. "I thought you two definitely needed some closure. And I didn't want you worrying yourself sick ahead of time." He tried to interrupt, but she spoke over him. "So just have lunch, and if you still hate me afterward, you can tell me."

He turned back toward her and tried to anticipate the tenure of the meeting from her face, but it was blank. Damn, she'd be a good poker player. "Am I going to hate you afterward?"

"I don't know." She shrugged. "Hell, I thought this was a good idea, so apparently I don't know much." She dug out her mobile from her bag. "It's two minutes to noon."

"What's Pam going to say?"

She smiled, a close-lipped, sweet smile that rounded all the angles of her face. "I don't know. Why don't we go in and see?"

He saw Pam through the window as they crossed the street to the restaurant. Her hair was shorter than it had been when she'd left, so her bare nape was visible as she sat, back to the outside, curved ever so slightly forward. It was lighter too, a shocking near-white, but still he knew it was her. Even if he'd forgotten her name and everything they'd shared during those nearly three years together, his body would have remembered her, and his chest would have still seized up in recognition and longing.

Pam looked up as the door swung open, then stood as she saw them. She smiled—that huge smile that almost seemed to break her face in half—and edged out from behind the table. But as he came almost within touching distance, she stiffened, and the smile faded. He wiped at his nose. Maybe it was runny, and that's why she'd gone cold.

He nodded. "Hey."

She was examining him. He had to look away.

"You look good," she said, so softly he almost missed it.

He looked at her again. She was smiling again. "So do you."

From behind him Suzanne said, "You know what? I've got a few errands to run. How about I come back in forty-five minutes or so." She was opening the door by the time he turned around.

They sat opposite each other. Pam eked out an awkward laugh. "Hungry?"

He wasn't, but he wasn't going to let her know that his stomach had pulled so tight upon itself that the sharpest sewing needle wouldn't be able to pierce it. "I can eat. You?"

She shook her head. "I'll just have a coffee." She craned her neck to attract a waitress. He made a show of studying the laminated menu.

"You've been okay?" Pam pulled a cigarette from the pack on the table. Two stubs, trimmed with her deep red lipstick, lay in the ashtray.

"Yeah, good. Started getting back to work and such like." He couldn't look at her.

A waitress came, her overbite almost distracting from her severely overplucked brows. Pam ordered a coffee, and Richard a fried egg on toast. Pam took a huge breath. "I've been so worried about you..."

"So that's why you left, is it?" He'd been hoping for a wry delivery, like Pierce Brosnan's James Bond. Instead he sounded more like Sean Connery's, harsh and angry instead of charming.

Pam finally lit that cigarette she'd been toying with. "I left because I didn't want you to hate me."

He gritted his teeth to keep from shouting. "Ah, that explains everything."

Pam rubbed her palm against the tabletop, leaving streaks of sweat. "I couldn't handle you blaming me for the accident, for getting you in the state you were in."

He gaped at her, knew he was doing so, but it took him a few seconds before he could do anything else, and then it was to blurt, "I didn't blame you for the bloody accident!"

He hadn't. Had he? Had he said anything to her, any little digs, any muttered asides? He didn't remember doing so—but of course that meant nothing. "I didn't blame you," he repeated, softer, less certain. "The only person at fault was the fucking knob who ran in front of us."

She nodded her head toward one side, as if that were a point of discussion for later. "Well, I thought you did. And, well, I did. And so, I thought you'd be better off without me around as a constant reminder."

He continued to stare. "That's got to be the dumbest thing you've ever said."

Pam rubbed under her right eye with her forefinger. "That's pretty much what your friend Anne said too."

"Anne?"

"Your friend. The one who brought you here." Pam nodded toward the door, as if she were still there. Her eyes widened, in slight alarm, an expression that seemed vaguely familiar to him.

"Her name's Suzanne."

Pam frowned, tilting her head skeptically. "I could have sworn she said her name was Anne."

"Well, you're wrong. And you were wrong about the other thing too." He reached over and helped himself to one of her cigarettes and her lighter. "I... I needed you."

There, he'd said it. He had let her know just how weak he was. Well, surely it hadn't been a secret. Christ, he'd barely been able to wipe his own arse, literally—the pulling of the muscles along his spine when he reached his arm round his back used to make him light-headed. He'd had to be reminded to shave, to wash his hair, to eat. He would sleep in odd stretches—four hours here, twenty minutes there, then out for twelve hours at a stretch—and each time he woke he was convinced it was the morning of a dateless day.

"And you just skipped out on me, didn't you?" He had never allowed himself to even imagine saying this to her. Now that he had, he felt neither unburdened nor satisfied. If anything, he felt shittier for having to actually say it, for having to admit out loud that it was fact.

Pam nodded. "I know." She spoke to the table. "I know that now. I guess I knew it even then. I mean, after I left, I used to call the flat almost every night, just to hear you pick up so that I knew you were all right."

His breath caught in his throat. "You did?"

"Yeah." She leaned forward and looked up, her eyes searching his face. "You don't remember?"

"No." He stared down at her hands. On the back of her left one, just below the knuckle of her forefinger, she had a lone freckle. He'd always loved that freckle. At night, when there was just enough moonlight sneaking in between the gap in the curtains, he used to seek that hand out and bring it close to his face so that he could see the freckle.

What a goddam sap. "You could have said something when I picked up the phone. You could have said, 'Hello, it's me, how are you doing?' You could have said, 'The real reason I left is because I couldn't stand what a pathetic mess you'd become.'"

She slapped her palms on the table and half-rose from her seat. "That wasn't why I left." Aware of the other customers staring, of the waitress hesitating to come forward with her coffee, Pam sat back on the edge of her chair and ground her cigarette into the ashtray. After the waitress slid her cup in front of her, coffee slopping onto the saucer, she continued, in measured tones. "I explained to your case worker Aggie that I thought I was holding you back. She said..."

"My case worker is Gillian." Christ, this whole escapade obviously meant so fucking little to her she couldn't even get the name of his case worker correct.

Pam shook her head. "No, Aggie. Frizzy light-brown hair, Scottish."

Frizzy light-brown hair... Fuck. He remembered now. His case worker before Gillian. She had completely escaped his memory. But now, now he couldn't avoid seeing her: Pam used to say that she'd love to get her hands on the woman's mop, slather it with a hot-oil treatment, and let it soak for a full day. She'd had an octagonal age spot on her cheek. "Gillian replaced her."

She studied his face. "And you misplaced the piece of paper I left with your medicines that had my parents' address and phone number on it, didn't you?"

He didn't recall any such paper.

"And you had my mobile number in your phone. You could have called me, couldn't you?"

Something was shifting. Now he was in the wrong, somehow. "If you'd left me because I was such a burden, why the hell would I ring you?"

"That's not why..."

They stared at each other. It didn't matter what he remembered or didn't remember; everything was askew, as if he'd trained his binoculars to zoom in on the branches of a far-away tree when what he was seeking was hiding in the bushes in front of him.

The waitress slid his order in front of him with the same lack of care she'd taken with Pam's coffee. One of the triangles of toast dangled off the edge of the plate.

"Fuck," he said.

"Fuck-a-doodle-doo," Pam agreed.

He pushed his toast back onto the plate.

"So," Pam addressed her coffee cup, "what do you want to do now?"

"Eat my eggs," he said, because he hoped it would make her laugh. It did.

"Are you... seeing Anne? Suzanne?" Pam asked.

He willed himself to forget last night. Lord knows he was able to forget so many other, important things. "No, of course not. Why? Are you seeing someone?"

"Jesus, no."

He reached across the table and with his thumb stroked the freckle on her hand. Though Pam continued to stare down, he thought he detected the corners of her mouth curving upward. "So, what now?" she asked again.

For whatever reasons, she'd walked out on him. Surely he shouldn't simply open his arms to her and let her glide back into him.

But he wanted her in his arms. For months he had been attacked every day by uncertainty of the most basic elements of being: What was his address? Was this the present, or was he stuck in a memory again? What had he been doing just five minutes ago? For the past five hours? Even now, he still didn't know what year it was.

What he did know was that he wanted her. He knew it with a sureness that felt strange, but that he was certain he'd once taken for granted concerning so many matters, large and small: his birthdate, the website he was working on, that Pam would be lying beside him in bed at night. Somehow, even now, in this restaurant, surrounded by the smell of coffee and fried breakfasts, bland instrumental renditions of pop hits wafting above them, the blur of shoppers and strollers on the other side of the window serving to put Pam in sharp, close relief, that sureness and Pam were linked. He wanted her to come back to him and stay with him and not leave him again.

"Monday night, then?" Suzanne said. "That's good—-it gives you enough time to spruce up your flat..."

"What's wrong with my flat?"

"... and cook her something impressive, something she'll be surprised you know how to make. Unless there's a favorite meal of hers you want to cook instead."

Pam was coming into Billicombe on Monday evening. She was doing the hair and makeup for a friend's wedding in Bude tomorrow night, traveling down with another friend early tomorrow morning and then making a weekend of it. "But I'll see if we can leave a little earlier than planned on Monday," she'd said to Richard after he'd hesitantly, gulpingly, heart-hammering-in-spite-of-himself-ly asked if she wanted to do something with him over the weekend. "Even if we can't leave early, you'll definitely see me Monday night." Then, outside her salon, after he had walked her back to work, she'd whispered into his ear, "Looking forward to Monday night" just before kissing him on the cheek and then letting her lips skate against his.

Suzanne had kept a respectful distance behind them, leaning against a streetlight on the High Street and leafing through the *Mirror* as he and Pam turned down the alley leading to the salon. As Richard strode back toward her, he thought Suzanne looked like a bad detective in an even worse police program. "I hope you're never cast as a spy," he'd said as she lowered the paper upon hearing him approach.

"Why not?" She pretended to sound aggrieved, but her grin made it impossible for her to pull it off.

She'd continued grinning—or was it smirking?—as they waited at the bus stand and now that they were on the bus.

"One question," he said to her, as the bus rumbled at having to slow to a crawl behind a smoke-belching tractor. "If you knew Pam and I would, as you put it..."

"Enter into a rapprochement."

"Fine. Then what was last night about?"

Her grin faded, and she pressed her lips together, cheeks darkening from pink to dull red. She forced a chuckle. "Yeah, well... if you'll recall, I was resistant."

"Come on, I hardly forced you against your will."

"No, you didn't." She looked beyond him out the window on the opposite side of the bus, taking a keen interest in the smattering of lambs that had joined the sheep in the fields unrolling as they passed. Some of the lambs suckled their mothers; others stood within the ewes' shadows, looking up frequently from the grass they were nibbling to make sure they hadn't been abandoned.

"Let's think of it as a pep-rally fuck," Suzanne said.

"What?"

"No, let's make it a friendly fuck. Or a goodbye fuck."

He wanted to grab her shoulders and force her to look up at him.

She sighed. "Oh hell, I did it because I knew it would be my last chance, and I wanted to." She shook her hair onto her face.

They sat in silence. The tractor turned left at the next lane, freeing the bus to pick up speed.

"Well, this is awkward," she finally said.

He murmured in agreement. He was flattered, of course. Nonetheless a scrim of guilt began to fall over him.

"We don't need to tell Pam," he said.

"Oh, Christ, no. Definitely not."

The bus was heaving up the hill toward the roundabout that preceded the caravan park. Suzanne slung the strap of her bag over her shoulder. "I need you to let me out."

"So, this is it, then?" She was just going to disappear like some fairy godmother who, having rescued her charge from danger, flitted away to the next mortal in distress. "Are you leaving?"

"Billicombe? No. I still have a few things to do." She rose, forcing him to slide his legs over to the side of the bench so that she could sidle out into the aisle. "And I've got to hear how things go Monday night, of course." She grinned again.

"Right." He was too off-balance to smile back. He was going to miss having her around, he realized with a stab. He considered asking if she wanted to come by his flat tomorrow afternoon, but something about the way she was standing, one arm folded across her chest as the other held on to the back of the seat in front of him, persuaded him not to. "Well, if you need help with, you know, your brother and such like this weekend..."

"Thanks." She pressed the button to signal that she needed the next stop. "And I'll ring you Tuesday morning." She turned and skidded down the aisle toward the front, not bothering to wait for the bus to grind to a halt or even to slow down.

CHAPTER 11

Before heading to Boutport with Richard on Friday morning, Suzanne had slipped out just before nine to wait again outside the Lloyds. Again Lee didn't show up.

He was probably using again. Jax too, that's why Ian hadn't seen him for so long. If Lee was using again, he'd know where Jax was. Lee wasn't part of the same crew as Ian's brother, so Jax hadn't been either. Which was why Ian's brother hadn't known Jax.

But Billicombe wasn't that big a town. Someone on Riker Road would have to know, if not Jax, Lee. In fact, plenty of people did seem to know Lee, even if they didn't know Jax. But Lee knew Jax. So all she had to do was find Lee, and force Jax's whereabouts out of him.

It sounded simple when she put it like that.

Had it been just this morning that she'd escorted Richard to his meeting with Pam? Technically it had been yesterday morning, as it was now just after two a.m. on Saturday. She'd been awake for nearly an hour now. Something must have disturbed her—a strong gust of wind rattling the windows, backfire from a lorry—because she'd jolted upright, pulse pounding against her temples, a rivulet of sweat coursing from her nape along her spine.

She'd forced herself to lie down again, on her back, one forearm over her eyes to ensure that they stayed shut. But she couldn't shut down her mind.

Richard had asked if she was leaving Billicombe. And really, the time had come. Forget what she'd thought earlier. It was childish to imagine that hunting down Lee once again meant she'd find Jax. Just as it had been childish to come traipsing all the way over here expecting to find him at all. Life wasn't a movie, with all the loose ends sewn up somewhere around the two-hour mark. Never mind happy endings or unhappy endings; sometimes there were no endings at all, and you just had to plod through a mire of uncertainty until it became a landscape as familiar as any other, with landmarks of some sort revealing themselves to keep you from treading in the same circles. Jax had once told her that if you were abandoned in an unfamiliar forest with no marked trails or signposts, you'd inevitably find yourself walking in a circle. You might think you were walking in a straight line, from point A to point B, but it would be an illusion, and you'd just end up right back where you'd begun.

That's what she was doing in Billicombe. It was time to go home. Monday she'd ask Richard if she could use his computer to book a flight back to the States.

She sat up and swung her legs over the edge of the bed. First, though, she'd get dressed, call a taxi, and head to Riker Road one last time.

She had the taxi drop her off at the beginning of the High Street. Groups of three and five were still swaggering down the pavement, shouting, yelping, occasionally helping each other up.

She turned off the High Street and walked down one of the back lanes toward Riker. She had the hood of her gilet pulled up and her hands slung in its front pockets. The dampness of the night burrowed into her muscles like a full-body tick and refused to relinquish its grip.

The cackles and whooping from the High Street were muted by distance but still audible, even above the warnings of the gulls. The shattering of glass, followed by a raucous cheer. On this street, though, not a single light shone from behind the sheers that were closed against every window.

The road veered toward the right, and uphill, before dissolving into another street and heading back downward. The slabs of pavement were uneven, some of them rising as much as an inch above their neighbor. Suzanne coughed, a soggy smoker's hack, and it reverberated against the sidewalk and the brick terraces.

About a block from Riker she spied a man pissing against a car. She slowed her pace. He finished and zipped up, stumbling back a few steps before lurching across the street.

A dog howled. Another dog responded with several sharp, shrill yaps.

Her heart was pounding so fast and with such ferocity, a cudgel against her eardrums, that she wondered, for a few seconds, if she were having a coronary.

When she reached the corner of Riker, where she'd had the dry heaves a few mornings ago, she stopped to light a cigarette and look around.

Straight ahead, across the road, someone was on his knees on the sidewalk, heading nodding just inches from the pavement. To her right, uphill, a cat scurried out from under a car onto the sidewalk and skittered away. To the left, downhill, she heard words she couldn't make out.

She walked toward them. They grew louder before becoming distinguishable. "Fuck, man, get off me!" "Where'd he get that shit?" "Gimme the fucking bottle, you fuck." "I ain't seen your sister." "He don't even have a sister."

She came to the former COCKSUCKER house, which was still the OK UK house. Again five or six men clustered against each other on the steps. She recognized the dog, who uncurled himself from the ground and sat on his haunches as she approached. Walking up the pathway toward them, she said, "I'm looking for Valley."

A wad of spit flew toward her. She jumped to the side to avoid it.

"That fuck owes me a tenner."

She didn't look up to see who was speaking. She avoided looking at the men, at the dog, at the yellow-green globule of spit beside her. She stared at the toes of her boots. "Do you know where I can find him?"

"I want my lady, man."

"Hey, it's the blow-job ho. Gimme a blow job and I'll find him for you."

"You're not my lady."

She lifted her head. Other than the eyes of the dog, glinting flat, she couldn't make out any of their features. Most of them had hoods pulled over their heads. One seemed to be nodding on the shoulder of the man next to him. Another was necking a bottle.

"Look, I just need to find Valley." The exasperation in her voice startled her. "If you don't know where he is, just say so."

"You talked to Ian, yeah?" Ian's brother lifted his head from the other man's shoulder. His words, like his movements, were thick and halting.

"Yeah, I did."

He placed his hands on the shoulders of the bloke in front of him to push himself upright. Wavering, he shook his head, then tried to step over the men sitting on the stair. They parted for him, grumbling, except for the one on the end, who mewled, "That's not my lady."

He tumbled toward her. She put out her hands to break his fall, but he caught himself first. "Come on." He lurched from side to side as much as forward. At the pavement he stopped, drifting into a nod. She lit another cigarette from the one in her hand. His lids fluttered open, but all she could make out were the whites of his eyes. "Got an extra?"

She handed him one. He nodded off, but only for a few seconds, then examined the cigarette in his hand. She lit it for him.

He exhaled in stuttering coughs. "See that car up there?" He pointed with his head.

She squinted. "Which one?"

"Gray."

With the clouds obscuring the remains of the moon, all the cars looked gray. "Okay."

"He's in there."

She'd just have to peer into each car until she saw him. "Cheers." She started off.

"Wait."

She pulled out a tenner from her back pocket. But his hand wasn't out. "I'll come with you." He shuffled beside her. "He's a right bastard."

He stopped just short of the third car and again pointed with his head. She squinted through the front window. Someone was in the driver's seat, slumped forward.

She pressed the money into Ian's brother's hand. She couldn't avoid touching him this time. His palm was sticky.

He folded his fingers around the bill. "Is Ian all right?"

Her eyes ached suddenly. "He's good. Sober." She waited, then started walking.

"Ta," he said without moving.

The body in the car didn't move at all as she approached, not even a bobbing of the head. He'd better not be dead. She tried the passenger-side door; it opened.

Inside smelled like the water-dowsed remnants of a fire, acrid and dank. She examined the passenger seat for sharps before getting in. Lee slumped toward his right, away from the gear shift. A bent, blackened spoon was on the seat beside him. He muttered. She could hear the clacking of his tongue against his dry palate.

She chucked her cigarette butt into the street and sucked in a lungful of cool, salt-cleansed air before slamming the door shut. On the pavement Ian's brother nodded forward.

She smoked another cigarette. The fresh smoke wrapped around the stale, murky fetor of the car, dressing it up but also pulling it closer around her, pulling her closer to Lee. She looked over at him. He wobbled forward, banging his head against the dashboard. It then listed toward his right shoulder.

When she finished the cigarette she opened the door, dropped the butt into the gutter, siphoned up another dose of fresh air, and slammed the door again. On the sidewalk Ian's brother was making his way back to the others, zigzagging from one side of the pavement to the next. Lee shifted upright.

She didn't know how much longer she could stay in here. She could almost see the smog inside the car thickening and darkening, could feel its dampness clamping onto her hands, slithering up the sleeves of her jumper to paw her arms. "Where's Jay?" Her voice loud but thin. "Where's Jay?" Deeper this time.

Lee nodded forward, lids fluttering. He turned to her, eyes slitted. "Who the fuck are you?"

"Where's Jay?"

"Fuck." He closed his eyes, swallowing hard, his Adam's apple all but slicing his throat.

"Where's Jay?" she shouted, slashing through the fog.

No reaction. She shoved his shoulder, hard enough to send him thudding against the driver's-side door. "Where the fuck is Jay?"

"What the FUCK are you playing at?" His eyelids were wide open now, so wide she could almost see their undersides.

"Where is Jay? I know you've been with him."

He stared as if translating her words to a language he understood. "I ain't seen Jay in months."

"I know you're lying." To keep the shrillness from her voice, she had to lower the volume. She spoke in a soft growl. "You're using, I know he's using. Where is he?"

"He ain't using." Lee bent forward and felt around his feet.

"So where is he, then?"

Lee resurfaced with a bent cigarette in hand. Now he was feeling around his jacket pockets for a lighter. She passed him hers, keeping her hand out for him to return it.

Smoke trickled out from his mouth, as if he were too exhausted to exhale properly. "Last time I saw him was down in the valley by West Down." He barely bothered to move his lips. "Across the bus shelter, there's a road." He tilted his head back, eyes closing. "There's a little stone... structure... building... something there. That was the last time I saw him. We went there to get high." He nodded off, ash dropping on his thigh.

"When was this?" When he didn't reply, she jabbed his arm with her elbow. "When was this?"

"What?" He took a breath to gather his thoughts. Then, bending forward, he coughed up some phlegm, spat it onto the floor. "Shit. This was in autumn sometime. I ain't seen him since."

She was sick to death of going round in circles. "I know you have."

"I haven't." His shout set the car rocking, or maybe that was just her shaking. "I haven't, because he fucking died out there. He fucking OD'ed, man."

She listened to the echo of his words before they were swallowed up by the smog, replaced by the sound of her breathing. In and out, like normal. No heavier, no shakier, no quicker or slower.

"Now get the fuck out of the car."

She didn't have to believe him. He could just be saying this to get rid of her.

But she knew it was true.

When Jax had disappeared in the past, every phone call brought a shiver of fear. In those seconds between the first ring and when she managed to pick up the phone and say hello, her mind told her, Jax is dead. Yet she never truly believed it. Although her mouth dried up, saliva replaced with a thick sourness; her heart raced; her hand trembled; her voice quavered; she knew—not just hoped, but knew—that the call was Larry, or her mum, or the police telling her Jax was at the station, or Jax himself. And she was always right.

And now she knew that Lee wasn't lying. He wasn't in a state to, for one thing. And it all made sense. More sense than any other possibility.

Drunks and junkies, Jax once told her, adhere to Occam's Razor: The simplest answer is usually the correct one. When you're dope sick, he said, the simplest answer is to get more dope. When you're hung over, the simplest way to rectify the situation is to have another drink.

He'd been high, of course, when they'd had this conversation. She didn't know on what. His consonants elided into each other, and he'd had to prop his head up with his hand, his arm resting on the dining room table, to keep it upright, but with his other hand he'd waved his cigarette with dramatic flourishes as he spoke.

That he was dead, had been since October, was the simplest, most logical explanation. That she now remembered this long-ago conversation was Jax's way of letting her know the search was over.

Funny how aware she was, of every detail, of exactly what she was doing. Taking herself out of the car: She didn't scramble or scurry; she kept her back ramrod-straight. Opened the door as if she had all the proverbial time in the world (which she did now, of course), then deliberately kept the door open as she walked up Riker Road, back still straight, still in no hurry.

She elected to walk up, and away from the High Street, because she did not want to pass Ian's brother and his mates again. Once she reached the next intersection, she turned right and continued on till she reached a road perpendicular to the High Street—Fairbrass, according to the metal sign screwed into the brick facade below the first-floor window of the corner house—and walked down.

A mist had developed in the time she'd been in the car. It wasn't the dense fog that she'd just left, but more like a filter over a camera lens, creating a watery halo around the pinky glow of the street lamps, around the misshapen moon, even around each individual star.

Nothing hazy about the rest of the night, though. Look how well delineated every crack in the pavement was. That one reminded her of the California coastline; when she was in junior high she'd had a homework assignment that entailed drawing a map of California and including all the major cities. And that wad of gum, a fluorescent green. It really stood out among the beige and faintly pink wads also stuck to the pavement.

The High Street was barren now, except for several lager cans rattling against the curb and the seagulls pecking about for scraps. One gull stood on top of a rubbish bin, craning forward so that its beak, yellow with a small spot of red on the bottom, could root around inside. Another whooshed overhead, dropping a thick white projectile that landed with a pulpy splat inches from her right shoe. Two more gulls engaged in a tug-of-war over a pebbled scrap of kebab. Oh, there was someone, leaning against the metal window guard of the video store, a black-haired woman with a good inch of gray regrowth running down the center of her scalp so that her head resembled a skunk. A peasant skirt hung loosely around her legs as she bent forward to suction her lips around the neck of a nearly empty bottle of wine.

Three storefronts down, Suzanne knew, was a variety store. She recalled that in one of its windows, taped from the inside, was a flyer urging passersby to Rat on a Rat. Call the number on the bottom of the page to report any drug dealers; you wouldn't be asked for your name, and there might even be a reward. How would they get the reward to you if you didn't leave a name? Not that she cared about a reward. She headed to the storefront, stopped long enough to read the phone number, then repeated the number to herself as she walked on, back still straight, still in no hurry. She crossed the High Street and proceeded to Barrow Lane, turning left onto it and walking a few feet until the Bristol Channel was in sight. She retrieved her mobile from the inside pocket of her gilet, called the number, and told the deep-voiced woman on the other end that she had reason to believe the body of a junkie had been abandoned several months back in a shelter on a field in the valley opposite the West Down bus shelter, down the winding dirt-and-stone lane.

The sea was almost indistinguishable from the sky. She could make out the slightest difference in tone between the two, the sea just that much blacker. And in lieu of fuzzy-rimmed stars, the sea had frilly horizontal jags of white interrupting its surface, resembling the artfully torn and fringy edges of expensive invitations to weddings and bar mitzvahs. She walked down Barrow Lane toward the Promenade, not allowing the steepness of the hill to speed her pace, refusing to bend forward.

She crossed the Promenade and pulled herself onto the waist-high iron rail that separated the paved edge of the Pavilion from the beach below. Her hands curved around it; the metal was smooth and cool. She slotted the soles of her boots onto the parallel rail below, so that its curves fitted in to each arch. The top rail dug into her arse, where the fleshy part gave way to the tops of the legs, but she didn't mind. The roar of the waves throwing themselves onto the rocks failed to drown out the drone of the gulls or the half-hearted flapping of the British flag hoisted on the top of the so-called mountain.

Her eyes were gritty with want of sleep, but she wondered if she'd ever sleep again. Oh, of course she would, but the details of when and where were too much to imagine.

Each wave brought in another rush of salt spray and the stench of decaying sea life, briny and musky and mildewed. She lit a cigarette. She expected her hand to tremble, to have to flick the lighter several times before it caught, but neither was the case. She smoked and stared ahead.

Jax had tried to take up yoga. His problem, he'd told her, was that when they were meant to empty their minds of conscious thought, he couldn't. "It's like trying to sweep out the garage when it's windy. You keep shoving out the dirt with your broom, but the wind keeps blowing more dirt back in."

Right now her mind was as empty as it had ever been. There was nothing soothing about the blankness, though. It was terrifying, having this emptiness with nothing to fill it.

She felt him first. Felt his breath stirring up the small hairs of her neck, even though he was much too far away to actually be doing so. Then she smelled him: days-old sweat beneath stale smoke beneath a burning cigarette, a shadow of piss, a whiff of shit. Next she heard his footsteps, more of a shuffling really, the actual tread so faint as to be weightless.

"Oi, Anne!"

Maybe he had come after her to tell her that it wasn't true. That he'd made it up because he was angry at having his high disturbed.

She didn't believe that, of course. But maybe...

She refused to turn around. She kept her back straight.

"Sorry." His voice was devoid of apology, of regret, of any emotion, any shading.

"What the fuck do you want?" She sounded like she was the one on H: every word an effort.

"You call the cops, did you?"

The stink of him was making her gag. She lit a cigarette to block it out. "Yeah. But I didn't mention you."

"Cheers."

His tone was still flat. She wondered what sort of expression, if any, he wore, but she'd be damned if she gave him the satisfaction of turning around to look.

"You didn't have a baby off Jay, did you?"

She shook her head.

"The thing is, yeah, he knew exactly what he was doing." She could hear Lee lick his lips. "He meant to kill himself, didn't he?"

Sudden fury swelled within her, fury at the English with their way of ending simple declarative sentences with a question. He was telling her what he thought, so why pretend he was doing her the courtesy of asking? Fuck him. Fuck this town, this country. She was never coming back to this motherfucking island again. "I don't know, did he?"

Lee clicked his tongue against his teeth. "Yeah. He'd only started using maybe a couple of days before then. He'd been drinking, but no H. And he hadn't been shooting. We'd been chasing the dragon, and he got off on a much smaller amount than he ended up cooking that last night. When we were in the hut, I was watching him cook up, and I even said something like, Hey, that's for the both of us, right? He didn't say anything. He jacked the whole fucking lot. He did it on purpose."

The demarcation between sea and sky grew more apparent as a faint, formless, colorless light sidled between them. "Why are you telling me this?"

She heard a scratchy shift of fabric against fabric. "I don't know."

The light on the horizon solidified into an elongated yellow-tinged oval, then divided into two, the slightly larger, brighter one against the sky, its echo below it merging onto the sea.

"Do you know someone named Dee?" he asked.

She searched her memory to be sure. "No. Why?"

"Just that, as he was strapping up, I think he said something like, Don't tell Dee. Maybe not. He had his works between his teeth then. And I'd just been smoking myself. But yeah, that's what it sounded like."

She threw her cigarette stub toward the sea. It fell somewhere onto the rocks. She couldn't see where. "Zee? Did he say, Don't tell Zee?"

More scratchy muffles. "Could have done."

So it really was true then. Lee couldn't have made up that part.

The only thing she felt now was the fullness of her bladder. She hoped she could make it to the petrol station in time. But she wasn't going to leave before Lee did. "What will it take for you to piss off?" She crossed her legs.

"Got a fag?"

She pulled out her cigarettes, plucked one from the box, and held it over her shoulder. His fingertips touched hers as he took it. She wiped her fingers against the thigh of her jeans, up and down, harder and harder, even after she felt and heard him shuffle off.

CHAPTER 12

The buzzer rang three times before Richard concluded that he was neither dreaming nor lost in some past time but that, yes, someone was trying to come in at—what time did it say on his clock?—6:04 in the morning. On a Sunday—no, Saturday, Saturday morning. Probably one of the upstairs neighbors who'd lost his key.

Or Pam? Maybe Pam stopping by before heading down to Bude. No, that was ridiculous. He stumbled, eyes still crusty with sleep, out to the front door.

Suzanne. "What are you doing here?"

"I need your toilet. It's an emergency." She dashed past him, into his flat and to the loo.

He hoped she didn't want to chat. He wanted to head straight back to bed. As he heard the toilet flush he remembered to look down and make sure everything was tucked into his boxers.

She reemerged. "Thanks." Suzanne didn't look like herself. More like a wax figure—a good likeness, but not lifelike.

"What's wrong?" he asked, though even before she answered, he knew.

She was so... businesslike. As if she had a checklist of chores she had to complete before she could allow herself the luxury of crying. She asked if she could make a few phone calls from here; of course, he said, hovering about her while trying not to appear to be doing so. Could he get her anything? Tea? A beer? No, she was fine, thanks. Would she like to go into his bedroom for some privacy? No, this was fine. Would she like him to leave? No, not unless he wanted to; she wasn't about to kick him out of his own lounge.

As she tapped the buttons of her mobile he slipped into the loo, thinking he had a box of tissues there. He didn't. He probably hadn't had tissues in there for months, since whenever he'd run out of the last box Pam had bought. He took the loo roll off its hook and brought it into the lounge, placing it onto the couch beside her. She looked at it, then at him, mobile to her ear, uncomprehendingly.

The first call was to her solicitor apparently. "Lawyer" was the term. She left a brief message, and a few minutes later he rang back. From what Richard could make out from Suzanne's side of the conversation, he was going to get in touch with another lawyer, one whose specialty was more in line with what she needed, and he'd ring her, get the details, sort things out. The same lawyer who had represented her brother in court a few times, from what Richard gathered.

He stood by the dining table, waiting. When she hung up he asked, "Everything okay?", then winced as soon as the words hit the air. She didn't answer, just lit a cigarette. He brought over the ashtray, relieved to be able to do at least that much for her.

She checked the clock on her phone once more, subtracted eight hours once more. It was just after eleven p.m. in L.A. Surely if Aarons her entertainment lawyer had been willing to ring her back at eleven on a Friday night, her mother wouldn't mind her calling now.

"Hello, Mum?" Her voice wavered.

"Soozie, what's wrong? Where are you? Are you all right?"

She must have sounded even worse than she thought. She cleared her throat. "I'm fine. I just rang to tell you that—" a deep breath; you can do it "—that Jax is dead."

Silence. She strained to pick up the slightest sound: a sniffle, an intake of breath. Finally, "As far as I'm concerned he's been dead."

"No, Mum, really, he's dead. He died six, no, eight months ago. I just found out." Now her voice was under control. Strange that she was able to enunciate these words so precisely when she'd had such trouble summoning up "Hello, Mum."

"In New York?" Surely the frostiness of her mother's voice was just masking something else.

"No, I'm in England. Devon. Billicombe. Remember we came here once on holiday when we were little? Jax had been living here." A minute pyramid of ash fell onto her right thigh. She tried picking it up with her thumb and forefinger, but all that did was disperse the particles into a pallid stain.

"What on earth are you doing in Devon?"

Suzanne stared at her ash-smudged fingertip. "I came looking for Jax."

"I could have told you that would be a wasted trip."

"It wasn't wasted. At least I found out..."

"You found out that he was dead. Just like I'd told you he was for years. All that money and time you wasted—I told you it wouldn't matter in the end, didn't I?" Her mother's voice was heating up now. It had bypassed warm and stalked straight from frigid to inflamed. Suzanne could see the jagged blue vein of her mother's right temple distending toward the surface; could see the thin strands of saliva bridging her top and bottom teeth as she spoke. "Whether he was cold in the ground or the walking dead, it was all the same." As the temperature of her voice rose, so did the volume. "And why the hell did you call me about this at midnight on a Friday night?"

"It's not midnight yet."

"It's like ringing me to say, Water's still wet..."

"I'm sorry." Suzanne sliced through her mother's rage, speaking with precision. "I thought you might care. I won't make that mistake again." She cut off the call. Staring down she saw that she'd managed to drop even more ash onto her lap. The cigarette in her hand was now nothing but a burnt scrap of paper wrapped around tar-stained fiber.

Richard hadn't meant to listen. He'd hid in the kitchen, busied himself with the kettle. He couldn't help but overhear, though. Not that he understood the conversation, not really. But he did understand that Suzanne hadn't called her mother to tell her the news; from the querying, tentative way she'd said hello, it was apparent that Suzanne had called in search of comfort from her mother. And her mother hadn't been able to provide any, or willing to, or didn't know that she was meant to.

And he knew, somehow, without being aware of it, that Jax had been the person Suzanne had gone to for comfort in the past. When she broke up with a boyfriend, or flubbed an audition, or had a bad day on the set, or before all that, when their father had left, it had been Jax she'd talked with, nestled against, cried to.

He made two cups of tea and carried them out to the lounge. As he handed one to Suzanne she said, "Gee, that went well" with a grim gaiety. She picked a magazine up off the floor and placed it on the table, then put her cup on top of it. "I guess I should have waited till morning. Their morning." She lit another cigarette. It took a few tries before she'd sucked hard enough on it for the flame to catch.

Richard sat in the armchair, hands wrapped around his cup.

"I shouldn't have expected anything different from her, really. I mean, she is what she is."

"She sounds like a right bitch." He inhaled sharply. "Sorry. That was out of line."

Suzanne threw him a small smile. With that smile she aged decades; Richard knew exactly how she'd look thirty, forty years from now, Dorian Gray in reverse.

"That's just how she is," Suzanne said. "We just accepted it, Jax and me." She looked down into the ashtray. "That's why it was always just Jax and me." She pulled long and hard on her cigarette, then released the smoke with a gust. "And now it's just me." She bit on her lower lip.

"No, it's not," Richard said, so softly he wasn't certain he'd uttered the words rather than thought them. "No, it's not," he said, louder, though this time they sounded stilted to his ears.

She turned to him, willing the corner of her mouth to turn upward into a lopsided grin.

He put down his cup, stood up, and sat beside her. Wrapping his arms around her, he brought her head onto his chest. She shivered against him but didn't break down into sobs.

She let Richard think that he was comforting her. It was the least she could do after barging into his flat at daybreak on a Saturday. Oh, and there's the matter of it being her brother who caused the accident that landed him in hospital, left him with half a memory, and almost cost him the love of his life. Let's not forget that.

But the thing was, nothing could comfort her. And in a way, she didn't need any comforting. Because she didn't feel like weeping or wailing. She didn't feel much of anything. It was as if with Jax gone, her ability to feel was gone too. As if he'd taken it with him, some sort of superpower that he'd absconded with.

She wondered if she'd ever get that power back, if the ability to feel again would regenerate. It hadn't for their mother, that was apparent.

She should have prepared herself better for this possibility—or eventuality, as her mum would have said. All these months, by and large, she had blithely assumed that Jax was still alive. What a fool. If she'd assumed the worst six months ago, when her concern about Jax's lack of contact had expanded into worry, then she'd now be wherever she was going to be six months from now in terms of-—what? Acceptance? Resignation? Healing? Feeling?

She was exhausted. That's why she wasn't making any sense. That's why she was numb. She didn't even have the strength to shift herself away from Richard and curl up on the end of the couch. Thoughts spun in her head so quickly, like a foil pinwheel in the winds before a summer storm, that she couldn't follow them without getting sick.

She'd close her eyes for just a few minutes, enough to recharge. Then when she reopened them she'd have herself a good, cathartic cry and get on with things.

CHAPTER 13

Back when Jax was just smoking weed, when he was fourteen or fifteen, Suzanne would know he was high when he played the same song on a CD over and over. One day it would be "Before They Make Me Run" by the Stones; three days later "Isn't It Time" by the Babys; a week might go by, and then it would be Squeeze's "In Quintessence" on an endless loop. She once asked him why. "Because each time I hear something different in it. It never sounds the same way twice," he said, looking up at her from his bed through his long pale lashes as if she'd asked what one plus one equaled.

Throughout the weekend she replayed her last conversation with Jax over and over. While ironing Richard's bed sheets ("Who the hell irons sheets?" he'd said in something close to horror as he watched); between phone calls from her lawyer, who was dealing with the police on her behalf; while shampooing the carpets in Richard's flat ("Told you they were filthy. What do you mean, you don't see much of a difference?"); while researching airfares online (she couldn't book a flight home yet, the police still wanted her nearby, but this way she would be ready). That last conversation was a song stuck in her head, gouging a deeper and deeper rut into her mind, until it lodged itself in there so firmly she'd never be able to extricate it.

And each time she listened to the conversation in her mind, she discovered possible hints and clues that she'd overlooked.

"Jax! Hey, it's me." She'd been on the highway, traffic at a standstill and nearly bumper to bumper. Agents and managers hoping to squeeze in a bit of time in the gym or at their desks before their breakfast meetings; grips and other techs working early shoots; shift workers going home or going in. The sun not yet up, but the sky no longer inky with night; smoky clouds mingling with fog; rows of winking headlights in the rear-view mirror; rows of glaring red taillights straight ahead.

"Hey, Zee. What's up?" Jax sounded as if caught off-guard. Or maybe furtive. Or was that guilt icing his words?

"Nothing much. I'm stuck in traffic, and since I haven't heard from you in a while, I figured I'd call."

"It must be, what, five in the morning there?"

"Six. All this time, and you still can't get the time zone thing right." He knew the time difference. He'd been stalling. Maybe she'd caught him as he was swigging from a bottle.

"You know maths wasn't my strong suit." Was he slurring slightly? Were his *s*'s more sibilant than when he was sober?

"True." She laughed. He didn't.

"So where're you going at six in the morning, then?" The way he'd jumped in with a question, as if to deflect attention from himself. Like after his first stint in rehab, when she'd catch a whiff of alcohol from his breath, his skin; "Were you drink—" and before she could finish, he'd leap in with "So, how was work?" or "Have you seen my blue notebook?"

"Early call. We're shooting on the beach this morning, and the permit's only good till eleven or something."

"They making you wear a bikini?"

"Yeah. I've been living on apples and celery for a week. I'm telling you, once this scene is wrapped I'm heading to the craft table and gorging myself on M&Ms. But what have you been up to?"

"Oh…" A long pause, as if grappling for an excuse, a lie. Or had the pause been Jax struggling, but failing, to work up the nerve to admit that he'd started using again? "Nothing much. Was doing a bit of painting and that, but that's dried up, so I'm looking for work."

"Any luck?"

Defensively, "If there was, I wouldn't still be looking, would I?"

Even then she'd been hurt by the sharpness of his voice, but she hadn't let on. "True. Sorry. That was stupid."

"No. I'm sorry I snapped."

"So, I was thinking: How about if I come to visit?"

Another pause. "Visit here?" So clear from his tone that he wanted her to do no such thing. And was that an undercurrent of panic, fear that he'd be caught out?

"I could come down to Billicombe, or you could meet me in London, or we could go someplace different altogether. Want to go to Paris?"

"Paris?"

"Just a suggestion. I don't care where, really. It's just I haven't seen you in almost a year and I really miss you."

"I miss you too." An obligatory response.

"You could at least try to sound like you mean it." She should have probed his hesitancy, not just made a joke of it.

"I do." He did sound as if he meant it that time, with a dash of contrition as well.

"I know. So what do you say?"

A sharp intake of breath. Was he having a drag off a cigarette, or about to confess something, or just embarrassed? "Well, I can't really afford to go anywhere right now..."

"My treat."

"Don't you think I've taken enough dosh from you?" Yes, embarrassed at being indebted to his little sister, who'd paid for his rehab, and his phone cards so that he could ring her sometimes instead of her always having to phone him, and who before that had let him stay rent free at her fancy SoCal house.

And she'd disregarded his embarrassment, placating him instead. "This would be a gift. And it's as much a gift for me as for you. I really want to see you. And I could use a vacation." Trying so hard to persuade him that he was doing her the favor. He never could see that it was at least partially true. And she had refused to see how small it made him feel.

"Listen to Miss America. 'Vacation.'"

"Okay, I could use a holiday as well."

"Everything okay?"

"Oh yeah. It's just that I haven't been anywhere non-work-related since I came over to see you last December."

"Yeah." A forced chuckle as he remembered how she'd had to sign for him at the front desk before he was allowed off the grounds. "And that was a right little holiday, wasn't it?"

"It was for me. Jax, I miss you. I miss hanging out with you. I miss all the stupid shit we do together. I even miss your stupid dog imitations."

"Hey, they're not stupid." Even now, despite everything, she smiled each time she heard the mock affront in his voice. "It took years of practice to master that portrayal of Lassie."

"So I can come? Don't make me beg like a pesky little sister: 'Mum, Jax won't play with me.'"

He sighed. Capitulation. "Okay."

"Really?"

"You tell me when and where, and I'll be there." Sometimes when she replayed the conversation the resignation was more marked than other times, but it was always evident. Christ, why hadn't she noticed?

"I'm thinking the week of Thanksgiving. We have a break from filming then."

"Let me know the date and what airport to meet you, and we'll do it."

"Really? Oh my God, I'm so excited. I cannot wait to see you! If we meet in London we can go to the Tower. Remember when we went when we were little, and you told me that sometimes visitors were followed out of there by the headless ghost of Anne Boleyn, and I kept looking over my shoulder the rest of the day, and Mum thought I had some sort of twitch in my neck?"

"Yeah." He was humoring her now. Or maybe his lack of enthusiasm was because he couldn't even recall that visit.

"I can't wait!" A horn honked from behind. She'd been so happy she hadn't noticed that the car in front of her had moved up several yards, leaving enough space for another car to cut in if she didn't get into gear and pull up. "Oh, yay, the traffic jam is finally breaking up. Christ, it'll just be nice not to have to drive for a week."

"Thanks, Zee."

"For what?" She'd shifted gears-—oh, maybe they weren't moving after all. Oh yes, yes, they were, slowly but steadily.

"You know... everything."

"Hey, you'd do the same for me."

"You'd never get yourself into the shit I have."

She should have been silent for a few more seconds. If she'd just waited, let him continue... but she hadn't. She'd been so anxious to get moving again, to not hold up the traffic behind her, to make up for the time she'd lost. Fuck. She'd been more concerned about the damn driver behind her than about Jax. "Well, what's done is done. Okay? Listen, I've got to go, we're really moving now. I'll call you once I've got my ticket. I love you, Jax."

"Love you, Zee." Sometimes when she replayed those last words they sounded like his usual casual sign-off. Other times they seemed fuller somehow, weighted with meanings. Once or twice they carried with them a finality, as if he'd known that he'd never say them to her again. A few times she found herself thinking, I'll have to ask Jax what he meant when he said that. Actually formulated in her mind that exact phrase: I'll have to ask Jax what he meant when he said that.

That's when she came closest to finally crying, in the seconds after having that thought, when she was dowsed by the realization that she'd never be able to.

So, in a way, knowing that Jax was dead, confirmed by the police after Jax's dental records had been emailed over (the body had been not just decomposed but also partially eaten by animals, and no, she was not going to think about that at all; it was enough that she saw the torn-apart limbs, the flaps of skin, the exposed tendons in her dreams, vividly enough that she'd woken up on Richard's sofa choking on vomit, and she'd just made it to his bathroom, though not to the toilet—no, she'd replay her last conversation with him again, focus on his words, his inflections, Love you, Zee)... So in a way, knowing that Jax was dead didn't bring an end to her walking in circles in a sludgy fog.

Jax was dead, but there was no finality. Not even the finality that time had given to their father. One day he was gone, and that was it. Maybe he was still alive, maybe not. Those first days, weeks, maybe months, she'd expected to see him again, hear his voice on the other end of the phone; if nothing else, to see his handwriting in a letter. At night she'd curl herself into a ball beside Jax in the bed they shared and ask him, whispering so their mum didn't hear, when he thought Dad would be back. Then if he thought Dad would be back.

Till one night Jax had asked if she missed him. Hugging her knees, she rocked back and forth as she pondered. "Not really," she concluded. "Me either," Jax replied, rolling over so that his back was toward her, which was his signal for her to stop talking and get to sleep. And her father became a once-plush, now-threadbare teddy that you used to sleep with till it went missing, and after a few nights of frantic scrabbling under the bed yet again and futile scouring of the drawers and cupboards, you realized you could sleep just as well without it as with it, and then you didn't much think about it anymore. The finality of obsolescence.

But she still needed Jax. Despite all the times he'd lied and relapsed and let her down, it had always in the end been just the two of them. Like when they were kids and their parents were having one of their knock-down drag-outs. Funny how vividly she remembered them now, after years and years of not thinking of them at all. It was more than remembering; she could again taste the lump of phlegm rising in her throat as Jax locked their bedroom door and they scarpered to the narrow scrap of floor between their bed and the wall, feel her knees pressing hard against her chest as she wrapped her arms around them. Jump with each slamming of a fist against a wall or crashing of a plate onto the floor or slapping of a palm against—what? furniture? flesh? And feel, as much as hear, Jax's whisper as he retold a story his class had read earlier that day or made up a story of his own. There was one of his in particular that she used to ask for, The Back-School Girl. It was about a girl Jax's age who, because she refused to do her homework or pay attention in school, kept getting sent back to a lower class, until by the end of the story she was sixteen and attending reception, the sides of her bum hanging over the edges of her toddler-size chair. And if their parents were still fighting even after Jax had finished the story, or if the fighting was over but their mum was crying as she slammed the cupboard doors and cleaned up the mess, Suzanne would crawl under their bed, and Jax would shimmy beside her, and sometimes they even fell asleep under there, or at least she did.

If only she could cry. Cry it all out, so that she could stop hearing and seeing and feeling Jax while knowing that he was dead. She kept locking herself in Richard's loo to force out a sob, but the more she tried, the more her emotions shrank away from her.

So she scrubbed Richard's oven. She emptied his fridge and scoured the shelves with vinegar. She let him make her cups of tea that she never drank. She wondered when the gaping wound that was the loss of Jax would begin to close, if it would, and how deep a scar it would leave.

CHAPTER 14

"Are you sure you'll be all right?" Richard stood between Suzanne and the door. "You can stay as long as you want..."

Suzanne laughed, a faint copy of her usual laugh, like a photo of a photo of an original drawing. "I'll be fine. I'm hardly the first person in the world whose brother died."

"I can cancel tonight with Pam—" He meant it. Suzanne looked so... hollow. And lost. He remembered his first weeks out of hospital, how when he was emerging from a hiccup of time he'd find himself touching whatever was to hand—the kitchen counter, the rim of the tub, the door handle—as if to anchor himself to his present. With her gaze unable to settle on any fixed point, her shoulders hunched, she looked as he had felt.

"No, you're not canceling—"

"Or you can join us—"

She laughed again, a bit heartier this time. "I'm not going to join you." She puffed out her lips as she sighed, working a cigarette and her lighter out from the pocket of her gilet. "The only difference between now and last week is that now I know he's dead. He's been dead all these months without it making a difference, so why should it make a difference now?" She stopped to pull a long drag.

"Because now you know," he said.

She exhaled a thick steam of smoke between them. "And now I know, and now I'll get on with things." She forced a faint grin. "And so will you, tonight. I'll call you in the morning—not too early," she added, wagging her brows, "to see how everything went." She reached past him for the doorknob. "Have fun," she said as Richard stepped aside so she could pass. The undertone of wistfulness in her voice urged him to reach out to hug her. But as he debated whether it was the right thing to do, she left, closing the door behind her.

* * *

The flat was cleaner than it had ever been, even when Pam had lived here. Richard found himself perching on the edge of the couch rather than leaning back, so as not to dent the cushions, and rinsing off the bar of hand soap after using it. He tried to start work on Suzanne's website, which was simple enough, but he couldn't sit still to write more than a line of code at a time. He considered taking a walk but was afraid he'd have a memory lapse and forget to return to the flat in time.

He picked through his CD collection, trying to find the perfect disc to be playing when Pam arrived. *Laid* was a safe bet; James had been her excuse for coming over to talk with him that first time. Then again, so much of the album was about obsessive love. No, not safe at all. Besides, Pam preferred poppier stuff—Girls Aloud, Sugababes, Justin Timberlake—and she'd taken all her discs with her when she moved out. Maybe he'd just put on Lantern FM; one less thing to worry about.

Should he wear a tie? Christ, he didn't even know where his two ties were. His wardrobe was one of the few parts of the flat that Suzanne had not seen her way to sorting out and scouring. Besides, a tie would be trying too hard. He should have asked Suzanne's advice before she left. No, that would have been too bizarre. This entire situation was bizarre enough, thank you very much.

He had made the sauce for the spag bol last night, from scratch rather than just emptying a jar into a pan.

He sat in front of the computer again. Wrote a bit more code, found himself making stupid mistakes because he couldn't focus. Enough. He rolled a cigarette and called up one of his computer games. Demolishing aliens was as good a way as any of killing time. And he smiled, at the thought of having time to kill. For months he'd been losing hours, days of time, unaccountable, never to be retrieved. And now he was, for the moment at least, in control of his time, and he didn't know what to do with it.

Suzanne shut her book. She'd been staring at the same page of *A Clockwork Orange* for who knows how long. She reached over for the mobile on the cushion beside her. Nope, no missed calls or texts.

Christ, she needed to get back home, get back to work, get back to her life. Her lawyer said the police would prefer if she stuck around at least a few more days while they finished dotting the i's and crossing the t's. Those had been his exact words, and she hadn't cared enough to ask what exactly that entailed.

Maybe she should try again to take a nap.

Richard was brushing his teeth again when the door buzzed. Right. He ran his palms against the thighs of his jeans. Good. He knew who he was, where he was, what he was about to do. Which was open the door to Pam.

She looked... *gorgeous* was such a weak word, but she was. The way she bit her lower lip so that you glimpsed just a glint of her front teeth. The way her eyes seemed to swell when she looked at you, as if she were focused solely on you. Her smell, slightly citrusy, almost astringent, but sugary too.

She handed him a bottle of wine. "You still like merlot, right?"

As he took it from her, his fingers grazed against the back of her hand and he jumped, as if from an electric shock. But instead of jerking away, he jolted closer toward her. And in one of those noiseless, timeless moments that he'd seen in films but had doubted really occurred, he and Pam both leaned into each other, their heads tilting. Their lips met, then their tongues.

"Why didn't you ever bother keeping the flat this clean when I lived here?" Pam teased, rubbing her shoulder against his as they sat side by side, toying with the remaining strands of spaghetti on their plates because they didn't want to leave the table, leave each other, for something as mundane as clearing the plates.

"I didn't do much of this," Richard admitted. "Suzanne did."

Pam reared her head back and stiffened, just enough for him to notice. "Why?"

He told her just about everything: how they'd met when he was unable to remember where he lived, how she'd come here looking for her brother, how she was really Soozie Northrup ("Oh my God! When I had her in my chair I told her she looked like her but prettier. Am I a numpty or what?"), how she'd found out on Saturday that her brother was dead. He did not tell Pam that they had slept together.

Pam was shaking her head. "This is so unbelievable. I mean, this could be a movie in itself."

He didn't know what to say, so he said nothing. He could do that with Pam.

She laid her hand on top of his. "That was nice of you to let her stay."

He shrugged. "What could I do? She's all alone here in Billicombe... I feel like I should ring her now, make sure she's okay."

"You can if you want to." Pam didn't remove her hand. "I don't mind."

But what could he say to Suzanne that he hadn't already? She probably needed some time alone. Some time so that she could stop pretending she was fine and cry in peace. He lifted Pam's hand to his lips.

After laying on her back and staring up at the ceiling, listening to the gulls, counting backward from 100 in English and then in French, Suzanne sat up. She would do what she did when faced with an unactable scene: She would act out loud an imaginary scene that led up to it. She'd go into the bathroom, shut the door, run the shower, and talk to Jax. She'd pretend she'd caught him about to shoot up that last time.

Jesus, she must be crazy.

Well, this was no crazier than some of the stuff her old therapist used to make her do. The first time Jax had gone into rehab, her mother had sent her to a shrink. "To help you handle everything," she said. "I don't want Jax's problems affecting you." At the time Suzanne had suspected she meant "affecting your ability to keep working," but since then she'd given her mother the benefit of the doubt. Jax's first rehab had coincided with her shooting a cable miniseries, and one evening, while driving her home, her mother said, "You know, if it all gets to be too much, I'll see if I can negotiate a lighter schedule for you." She'd spoken stiffly, eyes trained on the road ahead, hands tight on the steering wheel at the ten o'clock and two o'clock positions. "I know it must be a lot at once, and the last thing I want is for you to feel that you're under so much pressure that you, well, end up like your brother." Even then, it seemed to Suzanne now, her mother was writing Jax off. Just as she'd written off their father.

At any rate, Suzanne had said no, she was fine with the schedule. Though she didn't tell her mother this, it was being home, just the two of them, that was the most difficult part. Having to assume the role of her mum's only child and sole focus was more demanding than pretending in front of the cameras that her father was off fighting in World War II while her mother struggled to save the family farm.

So she dutifully saw a therapist every Tuesday morning at eight. Janice, she was meant to call her, though in her mind Suzanne addressed her by her surname, Wakeman. Wakeman gave her all sorts of exercises to draw her out.

She had her write a letter to Jax in which she told him how his addiction made her feel. She made her draw pictures of her family. ("I see you always draw your brother in the center and make him so much taller than you and your mother." "Well, he is a lot taller than me and my mother.") Wakeman was a big proponent of dream interpretation. Suzanne didn't remember many of her dreams, and those few she did recall—driving a car whose brakes failed as it neared a brick wall, being told at the last minute that instead of riding a horse in a scene she had to steer a camel—she wasn't about to share with Wakeman.

More than anything else, Wakeman liked to have Suzanne act out what-if scenarios. What if your brother came by when you were out with your friends and he was high? What if he stormed into your bedroom while you slept and demanded money? What if he had refused to go to rehab, what would you have said to him? The playacting was the least painful part of the sessions, because she didn't invest herself in the scenes; she just said and did whatever she thought would be the most fun to depict. So she burst into tears at the imaginary Jax's demand for money; she folded her arms and turned away when the imaginary Jax said no to entering a facility. None of it helped her any, but it didn't hurt either.

This time, though, she was going to do it right.

She brought her cigarettes and ashtray and Diet Coke into the bathroom, resting them on the narrow sink basin. She ran the shower on full blast, cold water so that the mirror above the sink didn't fog. She lit a cigarette.

"Jax," she said softly, just in case someone walked by outside and the water didn't quite cover her voice, "what the hell are you doing?"

She waited. Nothing was coming to her. She smoked, eyes closed, imagining the stone shelter, the dampness, the smell of mold and dried dung and the burnt metal of the spoon in which he'd cooked his fix.

"Jax, what the hell are you doing?"

Zee, what are you doing here?

"I've been looking all over for you. What the hell are you doing?"

What's it look like? He was trying for irony but was too shaky to succeed.

"But why? I mean, you were doing so well..."

No, I wasn't.

"What do you mean? Come on, put that down—" In the mirror she saw herself reaching forward for the spike pointing up between his thighs, for the belt he had strapped around his upper arm, but then she halted, afraid that if she reached any closer, he would go right ahead and jab himself before she could stop him.

Just leave me to it, okay?

"No, it's not okay."

Zee, remember when I told you to start caring a little less? This is why.

"I can't."

You have to. Because I can't stop.

"Come on, you did. You were clean for months. What happened?"

He shook his head. His hair hung lank, hiding his face from her. *Nothing happened. That's just it.*

She crouched beside him, softened her voice. "What do you mean?"

I mean, nothing happened. One day became another. I didn't drink. I didn't use. And I didn't do much of anything else. He paused. She waited.

And it wasn't as if she were waiting for her imagination to come up with a response. She was waiting for Jax to respond.

Everything I tried to do—go to school, get a job, just be normal—I failed at. And maybe it's because I don't really want to do them.

"Why don't you try rehab again, a different type?"

I can't keep doing that to you. Taking your money...

"I don't care—"

Giving you hope only to disappoint you again.

She saw him, sucking on a strand of hair. Heard him flicking the syringe with his forefinger, a few droplets spritzing from the tip of the spike. "So what, then? You're just going to keep killing yourself with this shit?"

No. I'm going to do it right, once and for all.

"What? Jax, you can't do this to me. Don't I mean enough to you to keep you from leaving me?" Her voice startled her with its shrillness. She lit a fresh cigarette from her old one, ashes scattering about the floor. "Jax, don't do this. I love you. I need you."

You shouldn't.

"But I do."

But you shouldn't. Because I will always let you down.

"You won't."

Come off it. That's all I do.

"And by... by offing yourself, you won't be disappointing me?"

He tossed back his hair and turned to her. His eyes were clear and bright, but beneath them were the dark circles and creased bags of a man twice, three times his age. *I'll be disappointing you just this one last time. Think of it as saving you from a lifetime of disappointment.* He shifted himself so that his back was toward her. He put the end of the belt between his teeth and jerked his head to the side as he picked up his works...

She was crying now. Thick, fast rolling sobs. She bent over on all fours and gasped between the sobs, struggled to catch her breath so that she could cry some more.

When her cigarette burnt low enough to scotch her fingers she sat up, wiping her nose with the back of her hand, and leaned over enough to toss the butt into the toilet bowl. She forced herself to control her breathing, to subdue her sobs into hiccupping bleats. The muscles beneath her breasts ached, and her cheeks stung. She didn't think she had enough strength to stand up and turn off the shower, let alone grope her way toward the bed.

But other than being sore and exhausted, she didn't feel any different. Any better. Any worse. Anything other than sore and exhausted, really.

To think he used to take this for granted: moving alongside and inside Pam as if the two of them were on a glider sailing higher and higher into a pristine sky, smooth, certain, trembling but not with nerves, because no matter how high they reached, how far forward or backward they swung, they couldn't fall.

And afterward, Pam's head nestled beneath his chin, their sweat melting into each other's pores so that her scent and his were no longer distinguishable. Stroking the scant down of her forearms. Her toes pressing against the arches of his feet. The little murmur deep in her throat—mmm— as she drifted off to sleep.

CHAPTER 15

Her one bag, a generic black wheeled suitcase, stood by the front door. The car to take her to the Bristol airport would be coming in a few minutes. Standing beside the bag, she lit a cigarette, not because she wanted another one, but because she didn't know what else to do.

Richard rattled the doorknob back and forth. "I'm going to miss you." He looked over her head, toward the kitchen, as he spoke.

"You're going to keep the flat clean, right?" Suzanne chuckled, to show that she was kidding, sort of.

He laughed awkwardly in return. "At least until Pam moves back in." He and Pam had decided, without verbalizing it, to ease back into living together. The second morning she'd stayed over, two days after their first night together again, he'd been startled to find her beside him when he woke in the early hours to use the loo. He had time-shifted again, he thought, even as he gingerly, so as not to disturb her, ran his forefinger along the top of her shoulder. She squirmed and, still sleeping, scratched her shoulder where he had just touched her. He'd stumbled to his feet, his lungs tightening on him. Forced himself through the litany: His name was Richard Sommers. He lived in Billicombe. He was twenty-six or twenty-seven. He'd been in a car accident on the twenty-first of October. He used to live in the flat with his girlfriend, Pam... and yes, that really was her asleep in what had been their bed. Today, months after the accident, not before. And thank God she'd stayed asleep throughout this momentary panic of his.

He didn't mention any of this to Pam when she woke up several hours later. He didn't want to give her any cause to doubt getting back together with him.

But if he was still unsure of how she'd react, if he couldn't trust her to stick with him, was he right in wanting her back? The question had nagged at him the rest of the day. Not until that night, when he was back in bed, alone this time, the sheets stiff and cold without the warmth of her, did he realize that right or wrong didn't matter. He wanted her, and if that meant not being able to completely relax in the knowledge that she'd stick with him, it was still better having her for whatever scrap of time he could than not having her at all.

Suzanne patted her hair at the mention of Pam. Pam had insisted on giving her a free cut, though Suzanne had refused her offer of stripping the color back to its natural dark blonde. She liked the anonymity of being a brunette. Pam had wanted to crop her hair above her shoulders, give her a deep side part. "You have such gorgeous eyes! You shouldn't hide them." But Suzanne said her agent would have a fit if she cut her hair before reading for the period role she was up for. It wasn't true, but she didn't want to look too different. Enough had changed for the moment.

She had let Pam and the rest of the staff pose with her for a few pictures, and she said that, once she left town, if they wanted to post the photos in the salon or even send a press release to the local paper stating that a former cast member of *Lakeview Drive* had enjoyed a cut at Options, that was fine. "I'll even have Richard put something up on the website he's building," she said.

Pam had taken her out for drinks that evening, after the haircut. "It's the least I can do," she said, waving away Suzanne's money. "I mean, if it weren't for you, Richard and I..." She'd trailed off.

Yes, if it hadn't been for her forcing Jax to go to rehab in England, he would never have wound up running out into the middle of the A361 outside Billicombe, causing the accident that had driven Pam and Richard apart. Suzanne knew better than to blame herself; it wasn't as if she could have predicted any of it. All the same, she squirmed. She stared out the pub window behind Pam, watching a woman struggle with her umbrella against the wind before folding it shut and forging ahead, bent forward, head down.

"The frames for the website will be waiting in your inbox by the time you get home," Richard was saying.

"No rush," she said, walking over to the table to stub out her cigarette in the ashtray, even though it was only half-smoked. "I'm going to wait outside."

"I'll come with you."

She shook her head. "Don't. I'm crap at goodbyes." She seized the handle of her suitcase. "But I meant what I said about visiting. Whenever you want to, say the word. The airfare will be my payment for the website, since you won't take cash."

He opened the door for her, then reached out and drew her against him, wrapping his arms tight around her. "Thank you so much. And I'm sorry," he murmured.

She flashed back to Jax's last moments in California. How she squeezed herself against him, trying to still his trembling. How difficult it had been to let him go. How easily he'd slid away from her. How abandoned she felt afterward, even though she'd been the one ordering him away. She stared at the fibers of Richard's navy-blue jumper until the tears that had been threatening to spill over receded.

"Thanks," she said as she stepped backward to break open his embrace. She took hold of her bag and left without looking back, as Jax had done. Once she was outside the building, she blinked. A few tears tumbled loose. This must have been how Jax must have felt. If she had known, she would never have let him go.

CHAPTER 16

The London premiere of *By the By* was tomorrow night, but Suzanne and one of her costars, Patrick Donahue, had flown in a few days prior, to make the rounds of the chat shows and do a photo shoot for one of the Sunday supplements—the shoot had been this morning, but already she'd forgotten which paper it was for.

She was relieved to be spending the time with Patrick rather than Davis; Patrick didn't take any of it too seriously, and because his boyfriend was originally from London, he knew some great out-of-the-way restaurants and pubs. Patrick's boyfriend hadn't been able to take off work to join him, and even if he had, Patrick's agent would have dissuaded him from coming.

Suzanne's boyfriend hadn't been able to take off time from work either. Eliot was a tax attorney, and April was part of his busy season. She was glad, in a way. Life was so much easier when you kept the present separate from the past.

But tonight she was having dinner with Richard and Pam, and Richard was accompanying her tomorrow to the premiere. If she'd pushed hard enough, she probably could have wangled a ticket for Pam as well. But she hadn't pushed, and if that made her selfish, she could live with that.

Richard was surprised to see Suzanne smoking a cigarette outside the restaurant. A month or so ago she'd said she'd all but quit. But that was definitely her, pacing in front of Benito's, not bothering to push her hair off her face as the wind blew it forward.

He'd been nervous about seeing her again, though they talked periodically, and emailed, and he maintained her website, posting any articles he came across about her. Lately there'd been quite a number of them. *By the By* had opened in the States two months ago, doing better-than-expected

business and garnering her a lot of attention. "Northrup has fun spitting out
the insults and putting a sly spin on dialogue that is at times barely
serviceable. But she also reveals a despondency and a conscience to her
character that wasn't on the page." "In her hands, the character of Cathy is no
mere Austen pastiche but a fully rounded, fully human girl negotiating the
transition to womanhood." "In the role of Cathy, Northrup catapults herself
into the ranks of Oscar contenders." When he'd mentioned that last review
to her, she'd snorted, "Everyone who's ever been in a film is labeled an Oscar
contender eventually. That and fifty cents will get you a cup of coffee."

As he and Pam approached the restaurant, squeezing against each other
to let pass a woman in a hajib and her children, one holding each hand,
Richard tried to remember how he and Suzanne had first met, but couldn't.
He could see her hoovering his flat, could even hear the asthmatic whirr of
his old machine above the distant wail of a siren and the indistinct babble of
passersby darting across Earls Court Road. He could recall sitting alongside
her on the couch, their sock-clad feet on the coffee table as they watched one
of the soaps, and he felt the same minute electric jolt he'd experienced when
his right foot had accidently skimmed against her left one. But he couldn't
remember how or where they'd met. It was as if he'd always known her, or
didn't really know her at all.

Pam rushed ahead to embrace Suzanne. "It's so good to see you again!"
Suzanne curved her arms around Pam in return, patting her back awkwardly
for a few seconds before stepping away. If they'd both been strangers to him,
Richard would have pegged Pam as the film star, not Suzanne. Pam with her
expansive, easy smile, her bright glossy lips, standing tall, her skirt caressing
her bum. Beside her Suzanne seemed hunched, almost furtive, fingers cupped
around her cigarette as she took a final drag before tossing it toward the curb.

"It's strange to see you wearing a jacket other than that pink gilet,"
Richard said, nodding at her black coat, which stopped just a few inches
short of her ankles.

"Yeah, well, this time I allowed myself a bit more luggage." She cocked
her head as she looked up at him. "It's strange to see you without little tufts of
hair sticking up all over your head."

He smoothed his palm over his crown. "One of the benefits of having a
live-in stylist," he said. She laughed, the right corner of her mouth higher
than the left. And then he remembered how they'd met, that evening on the
Promenade, but it no longer mattered.

* * *

"You look great," Pam said once they were seated. "I wouldn't have thought auburn hair would suit you, but it does."

Suzanne wrinkled her nose. "The film I start in two weeks, the character is supposed to seem mousy at first but then you realize that she actually has a huge mean streak. So of course that means red hair." She grinned. "Anyway, what's up with you guys?"

"You sound so American," Richard said.

"Really?" She pulled at her lower lip. "I think being in England brings out the American in me. When I'm back in L.A. I still sometimes get, 'I just love your English accent.'" She reached into her handbag (not the canvas Marimekko tote she'd carried last year in Billicombe but a trimmer black leather bag with a gleaming silver buckle) and pulled out her cigarettes.

Pam looked at Richard before speaking. "Would you mind not smoking at the table? It's just that—"

Suzanne cocked her head. "You're pregnant, aren't you?"

"How did you—"

"I knew it!" Suzanne slapped her palms together. "When I saw you putting your hand on your stomach as you were walking to the restaurant, I thought you were, but you aren't showing yet at all, so I wasn't going to say anything." Pam began to speak, but Suzanne rushed on. "I was in a bookstore once with my boyfriend's sister, who's a bit round, and she had her hand on her stomach and was playing peekaboo with the daughter of the woman in front of us. And the woman said, 'So, when are you due?' and my boyfriend's sister gave her this look—" Suzanne lifted her chin and narrowed her eyes "—and said, 'I'm just fat, thank you.' I don't know who felt worse, her or the woman. But anyway—" now Suzanne was waving her hands in front of her face, as if to clear away her aside "—congratulations! When are you due? Do you know if it's a boy or a girl?"

"We're not going to find out the gender," Richard said.

"But we were wondering if you'd be a godmother," Pam interjected.

Suzanne glanced from Pam to Richard, then quickly back to Pam. "Really?"

Pam reached over the table for Suzanne's hands. "Is that a yes?"

Suzanne's face seemed to freeze. She was still smiling, showing all her teeth, her cheeks stretching up to her eyes. But her eyes themselves grew more liquid. Just for a moment—and if Richard, puzzled by Suzanne's excessive animation, hadn't been studying her, he probably wouldn't have noticed. But he did, just as he noticed, a few seconds later, when Suzanne replied, "Of course! I can't believe it!", that her voice had become a shade more throaty.

She and Pam chattered for another moment about due dates and morning sickness before Suzanne excused herself. "I really have to use the loo. If the waiter comes while I'm gone, can you order me a glass of red? Thanks." She scraped back her chair and headed to the rear of the restaurant.

Pam turned to him, beaming. "I told you she'd say yes." She leaned over and pecked his cheek, ruffling his hair as she did, then expertly fluffing it back into shape.

Suzanne managed to make it into a stall before her face crumpled and tears dribbled, though she bit on her forefinger to keep from making any noise. There was absolutely no reason for her to cry. Except that this was the closest she'd get to becoming an aunt. And that the only reason these people were a part of her life was because of Jax. And because even though it was eighteen months since she'd last spoken with him, since he'd left her on her own, she still missed him. And because at the oddest moments, like now, it would hit her once more that she'd never get to see or hear or feel him again, and each time the blow was just as sudden and winding and sharp as every previous time.

Richard was waiting outside the restroom door. "Are you all right?"

She planted a bright smile on her face and nodded. "Sure. A bit of—" She couldn't finish.

He held out his arms just as she leaned toward him to bury her face against his scratchy jumper. Squeezing her eyes shut, she concentrated on keeping her breathing steady. She was not going to spoil this for him.

"It's okay," he said, softly.

"It's just... when I see you, I can't help but think of Jax. I guess because of how we met. It's like the two of you are intertwined in my mind." She took a shaky breath. "That doesn't sound right."

He rested his chin on top of her head. Those first weeks after Pam had moved back in, she'd be talking about the flat she'd just moved out of, and he'd almost blurt out, "Why do you keep saying 'Boutport'? We were in London, remember?", confusing now with the first time they'd moved in together. Or she'd be getting ready for work and he'd panic about missing the deadline for the pet shop he'd been designing a website for before the accident. Or over dinner he'd begin to tell her about the website he was building for Suzanne and he'd stop and think, How would she know about Suzanne? Today's Pam was enmeshed with yesterday's Pam, so deeply that he lost track of the present more in their first few weeks together again than he had in the weeks prior.

"Would it be easier if we left?" he asked.

Suzanne pulled away and looked up. "No. Don't go." Her nose shined red beneath the fresh powder she'd put on in the loo. She shook her hair onto her face. "It's just... and this is going to sound silly... but you're the closest thing I have to a brother now." She looked away.

"When I was a kid I used to want a little brother." He hoped he was hitting the right note. "But I guess a little sister will have to do."

She laughed, somewhat convincingly. "We'd better get back."

Suzanne had offered to put Richard and Pam up at Claridge's, where she was staying. But he'd refused.

"Come on, it's the least I can do," she'd said. "Especially as you refuse to let me pay you for my website."

"Your website is nothing. You never even send me any content to update it." If he hadn't taken it upon himself to set up Google Alerts so that he was sent news articles about her, the site would have been unchanged from the day it had gone live. Besides, that site had gotten him at least a half-dozen other clients: actor friends of Suzanne, then a local cinema chain. And the actors paid not only for developing the sites but also for maintaining them, and they kept him busy, their management continually sending new photos, press releases, news items.

So he and Pam were staying just a few blocks from the restaurant. And when Suzanne had offered to send a car to pick him up and bring him to the Claridge prior to the premiere, he'd refused that too. "I'd feel a right poser stepping out from the Premier Inn and into a limo," he said as they stood outside Benito's after dinner.

"I didn't say I'd send a limo," Suzanne hooted. "Someone's getting ideas above his station, methinks."

"Oh, is that some fancy dialogue from your movie. 'Methinks'?" He laughed, that sharp barklike laugh of his. Then, aware that Pam was standing off a bit, smiling gamely as if she too thought the conversation amusing, he reached out and pulled her against him, his arm draping over her shoulder.

Suzanne had asked Richard to come around an hour or so before they had to leave for the cinema, so that they could catch up over a drink or two. But now, her hair already straightened and glossed, her makeup set except for the last-minute powder and lipstick, pacing about her room barefoot in her gray strapless dress, trying to stop herself from pulling the top up over her scrap of cleavage, she dreaded having to spend an hour alone with him. This was how she'd felt the first time she visited Jax in his first rehab. For the initial twenty-eight days he wasn't allowed any visitors or phone calls. Suzanne had insisted that their mother drive her to the center on day twenty-nine. It was out near Victorville, on the edge of the Mojave, two hours away, but Suzanne had flat-out refused to go to the callback for a TV film she was up for unless she saw Jax first.

She and Jax took a walk around the grounds. She didn't remember where their mother was or why she hadn't come with them. The grounds were typical desert garden: red rocks, red dirt, cacti arranged too precisely to look natural. On the car ride up her mind had overflowed with questions to ask him, anecdotes to tell him. Now that he was walking beside her, though, her thoughts were as dry as her mouth, as arid as the dusty beige plane that stretched beyond the facility's iron fence. They trod in silence, save for Jax's sharp intakes of breath as he pulled on his cigarette.

He spoke first. "Well, this is awkward, isn't it?" She'd forgotten how strong his English accent remained. It sounded especially out of place here, amid the stark sunshine and the heat that, rising from the ground and bearing down from the sky, threatened to compress them into two-dimensional paper dolls.

"Sorry," she mumbled.

She thought she heard him sigh. "Why should you be sorry? I'm the one who fucked up." He stopped and, shading his eyes, looked out beyond the fence. "Mum's still pissed off. But you're not, are you?"

It hadn't occurred to her to be angry, not yet. "Of course not."

"Good. I think." He turned his gaze to her. His nose was peeling with sunburn. "Though maybe you should be." He paused, chewing on his hair. "That's the thing about this place: It fucks with your mind so that you don't know anything anymore. Other than that you definitely don't want to end up back here again." He looked away quickly, as if afraid of divulging anything else.

She jumped as the phone rang. Reception telling her a Mr. Sommers was here. She told them to send him up.

"Blimey, look at you," he said as she opened the door to him.

"I didn't know people still said 'blimey.'" She gestured toward the armchairs.

He sat in the one farthest from the door, still staring.

"What's wrong? Is my dress falling down?" She tugged the bodice up.

"No. It's just... I've never seen you all done up before."

She folded her arms over her chest. "I try to think of it as just another costume." And before he could continue, she added, "You clean up nice yourself." Beneath his black suit he wore a gray vest that revealed a splash of a dark red tie against a crisp white shirt. "I'm going to go out on a limb and say that Pam picked out your ensemble."

"Hey, I resent that." He tried to sound hurt but spoiled the effect by laughing.

She strode over to the minibar. "Want a beer?"

"Sure."

She grabbed one for him and one for herself. They cracked them open almost simultaneously, the pop of the cans for a moment managing to overcome the ticking of her travel alarm clock.

"So. This is how the other half lives, is it?" Richard said, taking in the brocade drapes puddling on the floor, the mahogany table off to the corner whose surface gleamed like a mirror, the crisp lilies in their round vase atop one of the bedside tables, the silver ice bucket on the floor beside the fridge.

Suzanne sat at the foot of the bed, busying herself lighting a cigarette. "By the way, I'm sorry about last night. Getting all soppy on you."

He reddened. "Forget it." Watching her exhale, he said, "Can I cadge one off you?"

She leaned forward to hand him the pack. "I thought you quit."

He shrugged. "I allow myself a few whenever I have to attend film premieres."

She laughed. But then the silence stiffened around them, like a pair of brand-new, slightly too large jeans. They smoked, carefully avoiding looking at each other.

"Pam looks good," she said.

"She's so chuffed that you've agreed to be a godmother." He looked around for an ashtray. Suzanne got up and fetched the clean one from the bathroom. As she exited he couldn't help but notice how the dress hugged the curves of her arse. It seemed to have rounded in a womanly manner since last year. Womanly: He wasn't used to thinking of Suzanne in that way. Even those few times they'd been together, it had been like he was in secondary school or college again, a teenager romping about with another teenager. Not two full-fledged adults.

"So how's Eliot?" he asked after Suzanne handed him the heavy glass ashtray and retreated to the edge of the bed.

"Good. Busy, but good."

"You must miss him."

She shrugged. "Not really. I like being on my own."

"So you're saying he's not the one?"

She grinned. No, there was nothing womanly about that grin. "My shrink says I have intimacy issues stemming from a fear of abandonment. For that I shell out a thousand dollars a month." She laughed. "Geez, I sound like such a cliché. Next I'll be complaining about my Mexican maid and my Honduran gardener."

It was all so artificial. Sitting here in this overly decorated room with someone who was really little more than a casual acquaintance, albeit a casual acquaintance with whom she'd ended up sharing the most difficult event of her life. How would Matthew rework this scene? she wondered. He wouldn't. He'd delete it from his computer and start again.

"Doesn't it seem weird," she blurted. "I mean, we'd never have met if—"

"If my memory hadn't been shot. I know."

She stopped short. She was going to say, "if I hadn't been looking for Jax." But as far as Richard was concerned, their meeting had more to do with his memory and less to do with her brother, who of course had already been dead for months by then. Granted, he didn't know that Jax had caused the accident, and if she hadn't sent him to England—but no, she wasn't going to trudge down that path again. She took a final drag, then crushed out her cigarette. In the proverbial million years she never would have finished the sentence as Richard had.

"So I guess the accident was good for something, eh?" he continued.

"You really mean that?"

He ground out his fag. "Well, it's easy to say now that I'm a fully functioning human being again and back with Pam and such like. But, yeah."

He looked up. The line that formed between his brows when he was puzzled emerged. "Sorry. I know those weeks in Billicombe were different for you."

Shit, she was beginning to tear up. First last night, then this. And her makeup would run, and she'd have to reapply it, and it never looked good when you were putting new on top of old. No.

She had a flash of another premiere, a more low-key one, when she was thirteen or fourteen. Her mother wanted to do her makeup, but Suzanne wouldn't let her. Her mother was of the school that green eyeshadow was the best complement to brown eyes and that contouring the cheeks with two shades of blusher really did work. They had a row, and Suzanne locked herself in her room. A few minutes after her mother finally stopped shrieking, a soft knock. "Can I come in?" Jax asked.

She let him in, and he picked through the makeup strewn across her bed. Selecting a taupe eyeshadow, he walked around to Suzanne, seated on the other side of the bed. He motioned for her to close her eyes, and he stroked some powder on her lids. He lightly brushed some mascara onto her lashes as well, and asked if she had any petroleum jelly. She directed him to the top of her bureau. He brought it over and handed it to her, pointing at her lips. Then he told her to look in the mirror. She looked like herself, only more defined. When she started thanking him, profusely, he shrugged. "Have a great time, Zee. Don't let anything get in the way, yeah?"

She was okay now. She took a deep breath. She was not going to let this be about Jax. He wouldn't want it to be anyway.

Richard was looking around the room, his hands dangling between his knees. She didn't know what to say, but it didn't matter, somehow. Then he caught her watching him, and they both smiled, shyly, each quickly turning away.

"I don't know why this feels so weird," she said, bending down to retrieve her beer from the floor.

"Maybe because we're all dressed up in this fancy room?"

She jumped to her feet. "Take off your jacket," she commanded, dashing into the bathroom. He shrugged himself out of it, and she returned a moment later swamped in a huge white robe. "Is this better?" She giggled.

He laughed, then kicked off his shoes. "Yeah."

"Now tell me about this baby. Were you trying?"

He pretended to scowl. "You're not supposed to ask that."

She grinned, plopping herself on the bed, crossing her legs. "So it was an accident, then? Hey, my mum used to say that me and Jax were each bottle babies—if it hadn't been for the bottle of booze they'd been drinking the night they conceived us, we wouldn't be around."

He raised his brows. "That seems like a rotten thing to say to a kid."

"Really?" She cocked her head, genuinely surprised.

He nodded.

"Oh, well, now I have something else to talk to the shrink about. I was afraid I was boring him." She grinned again, so that, even with the full makeup and the straightened hair, she looked about twelve.

"I don't think you have to worry about that."

"Because I'm so fucked up?"

"Because you're so not boring." He drained his beer. "I miss having you around, even though it was only for such a short time."

She stopped, can midway to her mouth. "That's the nicest thing anyone's ever said to me. Honest." She took a long swig. "Do you even miss me nagging you about keeping your flat tidy?"

"I don't miss that. Christ, it's a good thing you haven't seen it lately."

She laughed. The phone rang. She bounced up to the head of the bed and reached over to a side table to answer it. "Yes, I'm made up. Yes, I'm dressed. Yes, I'll be waiting in the lobby." Hanging up, she turned to him. "Okay, one last cigarette, I'll put my dress back on, and we're off. By the way, the flashbulbs and the lights on the red carpet are more intense than you'd expect. And the noise. And the people shoving you out of the way so they can get a picture." She swung her feet over the side of the bed. "I hope you don't mind."

"It'll be an experience," he said, reaching out for the cigarette pack she offered him.

"That's what Eliot said. Before he went with me to the L.A. premiere. He really got pissed off about the photographers shooing him away so he wasn't in any shots, and the reporters ignoring him except to ask if he was my boyfriend. He kept pursing his lips and making this *tsking* sound. Well, I think he was making the sound, I couldn't really hear him. But I know his face when he makes it, and he was definitely making that face." She imitated him, eyes rolling upward, mouth narrowed, shoulders hunched. Richard laughed.

"I won't make that face. Promise," he said.

"Jax came with me to this one event—" She pressed her lips together.

"Does it bother you if I talk about Jax?"

"Why would it?"

She exhaled a cloud of smoke. "Do you think I talk about him too much?"

"He was your brother. So it makes sense you'd think about him during special occasions, doesn't it?"

She gave the barest of nods. "Anyway, I forget what I was going to say." She hadn't really, but it was as good an excuse as any to change the subject.

"You were saying about the time you took Jax to one of these events."

Richard didn't have to prompt her. He could have just let it drop. But he didn't. Almost as if he had known Jax too, and didn't mind remembering, at least the good things. She leapt over to him and hugged him. He squirmed, but not too much. "Since when did you become so touchy-feely?"

She laughed as she released him. "Shit, I better get dressed!" She strode off to the bathroom. "Before we go, you've got to check it out in here," she called through the door. "It's bigger than the trailer at Caldicott Cross. Hell, the tub is bigger than that bed!"

She hadn't been exaggerating about the brightness of the lights, the noise, the incessant flashing, the shouts for her to come closer, to turn this way, to look over here. On the opposite side of one of the ropes separating the red carpet from the pavement, teen girls and a few boys pressed forward, waving their cameras and mobiles and autograph books around the burly figures of the security guards, hoping to get a picture or a signature. Suzanne walked over and obliged them, smiling, chatting a bit, occasionally looking down the line at Patrick, who more than once had to disentangle himself from a fan girl's embrace. Everything seemed to be in soft focus and slow motion compared with her. She pulsated. Watching her, you couldn't help but smile and feel your own pulse quicken. She belonged here, more so than in the stuffy hotel room, more so than in Billicombe those few weeks. In fact, Richard found it almost impossible to remember her as she had been there: in that pink gilet and the faded jeans, pale under the frizzy dark waves. In his mind's eye the Suzanne of Billicombe was as wan and gray as the cloud-congealed Billicombe sky.

Richard felt himself getting lost amid the glittering gold and shiny fabrics of the celebrities and supposed celebrities, the TV crews and the reporters, the PRs and the runners with their walkie-talkies. The overlapping waves of clashing perfumes. The shouting of names, none of them his. He found himself reciting his litany to moor himself. My name is Richard Sommers. I'm almost thirty. I live in Billicombe with my girlfriend, Pam. We're going to have a baby. I'm at a film premiere with my friend Suzanne.

Suzanne took his hand. "We have to head in," she said, jerking her head toward the cinema lobby. "You okay?"

He squeezed her hand. "Of course."

A reporter shoved a microphone in front of Suzanne, motioning to the cameraman behind him. "Great to see you." He sped through the sentence as if terrified he wouldn't get a chance to finish. "So who's this with you, Soozie?"

Suzanne looked up at Richard, hesitating, but only for a second. Then, once again turning on her smile, she said, "This is my unofficial brother."

ABOUT THE AUTHOR

Sherry Chiger lived for three years in North Devon, the area of England where *Beyond Billicombe* takes place. A writer and editor, she's worked for and had articles published in magazines on both sides of the Atlantic. She's also the author of two nonfiction children's books. Born in Philadelphia, she lives in Litchfield County, CT, with her husband, their daughter, and their dog.

sherry-chiger.blogspot.com

15447401R00101

Made in the USA
Charleston, SC
03 November 2012